NICE PLACE FOR A MURDER

BRUCE JAY BLOOM

Blazer Books

CHAPTER 1

Whenever Roger Teague succeeded in contacting me, I knew that at the very least he'd ruin my day, and at most, the rest of my life. So I did what I could to stay beyond his reach.

I didn't return his answering machine messages at my home phone, and I refused to give him my cell phone number. But whatever I did to keep him away, it was never enough. He'd use messengers and e-mail, and once he actually drove the hundred miles from New York to the North Fork of Long Island so he could ambush me at my house. When it came to tracking me down, Teague had no equal.

If I'd ever thought selling Empire Security to him would get me out of the investigation business, I didn't any more. Teague figured he owned me.

So I was dismayed but not surprised that he'd phoned the marina where I kept my boat and persuaded the boss there, my pal Wally Prager, to call me on the radio. Teague had surmised, correctly, that on this brilliant afternoon I'd be out somewhere on the Elysium, chasing big October bluefish. Now, with Wally relaying Teague's message to me via radio, he'd tagged me again, even though I was out on the water at the very tip of Long Island, without another living soul to be seen.

Wally's voice crackled though the radio speaker, telling me

Teague's news of a death on Shelter Island, the drowning of an Empire client. "Teague says you should go there now. Insists that you go, actually, if I'm reading him right."

I squeezed the talk switch on the radio microphone. "Tell him no chance I'm leaving here," I said. "There's a blitz on and I'm the only boat in the Gut." I looked over the bow north across the waters of Plum Gut toward Long Island Sound. From the lighthouse on the west to Plum Island on the east, two hundred yards of water were churning with slammer bluefish, ravaging schools of squid and baitfish they'd herded together for a long, violent meal. Swarms of seabirds above wheeled and screamed, diving to the water's surface to snatch up the scraps of the carnage. One drift through the Gut with just a single-hook diamond jig lure on my line, and I'd already put two ten pounders into Elysium's fishbox. It was one of those extraordinary fall afternoons fishermen wait for, where you get even for a whole summer of so-so fishing.

"Seems to me it doesn't matter if you go or not. The guy is cold and dead. Finito." Pieces of Wally's words were dropping out through the radio static.

"Cops there on Shelter?"

"Been and gone," Wally said.

"Nothing for me to do there, right? Waste of time."

"Far's I care," Wally Prager said, "But it's not me, you understand. Your associate on the phone here's the one's getting all red-faced and bug-eyed."

"If he's on the phone, how do you know he's red-faced and bug-eyed?"

"I can tell. Es mucho agitado." Wally spent a week in Mexico City once, and learned maybe twenty-five words of Spanish. He liked to pitch them in, right or wrong, as the spirit moved him. Real Mexicans laughed at him.

"Tell him this is not my affair."

"It distresses me, really, but Teague insists." In my mind's eye, I could see Wally tilted back in his swivel chair holding the microphone in one hand and the telephone in the other, those impossibly skinny bow-legs of his crossed on his battered desk, the smoke from his black Napoli cigar poisoning the air in the marina's back office.

"I'm not going anyplace," I said. "Tell him."

There was an extended pause, as I drifted north on the slow tide, past the underwater blitz, from the bay out into Long Island Sound.

Finally, Wally was back. "Teague says stop dicking around killing fish nobody wants anyway and go to Shelter Island directly. Particular stress on directly. The drowned guy's name is Nellis. No, Newalis. Something like that. One of Julian Communications' suits."

"This happened where? Ingo Julian's place?"

"He the big dog at Julian Communications?"

"Yes."

"Then that's the place," he said.

"What do they need me for? Tell Teague to deal with Julian himself."

"He says some wheel named Alzarez specifically requests that you handle this," Wally said over the radio. "Only you, Ben Seidenberg, because you're so smart and fearless. Alzarez is on the Long Island Expressway now, but it'll take awhile before he gets there, with the ferry to Shelter and all."

I watched the birds plunge into the water after the bits of baitfish, heads mostly, because the blues like to bite the tail ends off. "So Alzarez is almost here. What does he need me for?"

"How about this, then, muchacho?" Wally said. "Your pal told me remind you the Julian Communications retainer has a lot to do with your payout, and does this approach hold any appeal for you?"

I held my fishing rod up against the cloudless sky, watching the shiny jig dangle at the end of the leader. I wanted Teague to leave me alone, stop calling me, vexing me, drawing me in, keeping me close. But why should I expect him to let me go, ever?

But what I couldn't escape, even in my anger, was that Teague was right about the Julian Communications retainer, the half million a year they paid for providing security services to their three divisions, plus background checks on anybody the brass wanted to hire, sell to, buy from, or destroy utterly. Trouble with the Julian account would suck the dollars out of my pocket, because the money Teague was paying me for the company I'd founded was based on Empire's profits year by year. Big profit, big payment. Small profit, small payment. No Julian Communications, likely no payment at all.

"Come to a conclusion," Wally said. "I got to go feed the chickens."

"What chickens?"

"I'm getting some. Talk to me."

I stuck my pole into a rod-holder on the Elysium's gunwale. "Tell him he has engaged my attention, and reaffirmed his reputation as a world-class prick."

"That mean you're going?" Wally said.

"Shit."

"Well, in general that is a sensible decision. Didn't know you had one in you. What you going to do with a box full of blues, anyway? They're fish, for chrissakes. Now, if you could pull some rib-roasts out of the water, then you'd have something." Wally left the mike open so I could hear him talk on the phone to Teague. "Ben says he's on his way."

"I told you tell him he's a prick," I said.

"Hung up now. Anyway, you need help with the way you express yourself. You want me to show you where the Julian place is?"

"I know where it is."

"You want me to meet you there?"

"Thanks. Don't bother," I told him.

"You might need backup."

"Not necessary."

"You might wish you had me along."

"Go feed the chickens" I turned off the radio, wishing I'd never left it on in the first place.

Now Elysium rocked in the swells of the Sound, the cries of the sea-birds growing faint as the tide drew the boat farther from the frenzy of fish. With a phone call Roger Teague forced me back into the wearisome pursuits I'd schemed so hard to escape. But it was Hector Alzarez who'd asked for me, and I found it difficult not to feel flattered. Alzarez was general counsel for Julian Communications. He'd opened the doors of his company to Empire, when Empire was just a runt in the business, and his company on our client list moved us up fast. I owed Alzarez, and I liked him, too.

I fired up the twin 200-horse Yamaha outboards and turned the Elysium back through the fish and the birds, then around the Plum Gut lighthouse, toward Shelter Island and Ingo Julian's place.

I saw it from a mile away. Julian's island retreat was one of those showplaces you point out to guests on your boat as you motor by. It was a distinctive architectural statement, a modernist's delight, all angles and glass, perched on the rocks high above the narrow beach. Julian had himself a wraparound view of the world, with a protected harbor on one side and the Greenport waterfront across the bay on Long Island's North Fork.

A single boat was in the bay, a smallish, grime-stained commercial fisherman a hundred yards out from the Julian dock. Strange, because a commercial boat wouldn't normally work these waters. The professionals liked a deeper bottom, and a more appealing catch than the porgies that lived here. I turned the Elysium and stopped, put the engines into idle, moved back to the stern and raised my binoculars for a better look.

Even with the lowering sun painting painful yellow circles

inside the binoculars, I saw the rifle barrel seeking me out. Across the water on the commercial boat, the gunman was steadying himself against the back of the wheelhouse, taking his aim. A lanky, shirtless guy with the broadest chest I'd ever seen, both arms and both shoulders covered with tattoos. I lurched toward the throttles on Elysium's console, trying to thrust the outboards into gear and put distance between me and the man with the gun. I felt the binoculars swinging hard against my belly from the strap around my neck.

I was still a giant step away from the throttle levers when I heard the crack of the rifle across the water. A hole appeared in the Elysium's vinyl side-curtain, and the windshield glass shattered as the bullet exited.

I dropped down on all fours, with the Elysium's gunwale shielding me from the shooter. Crouching there, my binoculars bumping against the deck, I couldn't help but wonder whether the Grady-White boat company had built enough fiberglass into this hull to stop a bullet. It was a fishing boat, after all, not an invasion craft.

Another shot, then another, the noise crisp across the quiet bay. I could hear the gunman working the rifle's bolt, thrusting a new round into the chamber as each shot echoed away. Then the fisherman's engine starting, flatulent diesel sounds, belching and growling. The gunman had ducked into the wheelhouse to start up.

I poked my nose over the gunwale, hoping to find I had enough time to get to the console and power out of there. But the gunman was already back outside the wheelhouse, lining up another shot. Dropping down again, I heard the bullet thump the Elysium's stern. Instantly, the starboard engine shuddered and died.

Now the fisherman's engine revving, smoothing out and rising in pitch. The gunman had to be back inside the wheelhouse, busy piloting the boat, giving it plenty of throttle. But I heard the diesel growing louder, more insistent. He's bearing down on me, I thought. He's not giving up.

Can't run for it now, I told myself. No way to win a race with one engine gone, even against a clumsy commercial fishing craft that might make eighteen, twenty knots, tops.

Protected by the gunwale, I crawled to the hatch, swung my legs around and slid down the two stairs into the cabin, reaching into the aft bunk to pull out my lever action Remington 30/30 by the stock. I'd had it aboard since Wally and I battled a seven-foot mako shark to a standstill in the ocean off Montauk a year ago last July, then lost it when we tried lash it to the stern. I'd vowed never to go shark hunting again without some firepower to finish the job. Thus the rifle.

As I sat on the bunk shoving cartridges into the Remington, I felt my angina kicking in, as it always stood ready to do when I gave my 56-year-old heart too much to handle. I tried not to acknowledge the familiar tightening across my chest, but it was too strong, too insistent. Get past it it, I told myself, because there's this guy who's coming right now to wipe you out.

The sound of the diesel grew louder. I cranked the lever to cock the Remington and moved up onto the deck. The other boat was maybe a hundred feet off, heading right down my throat. I raised my gun to my shoulder, and as soon as I did, the boat veered away hard, leaning over precipitously in the water. The shooter didn't want a fight, not if I had a gun, too. He was running away, heading around the island and back to Plum Gut. I squeezed off a shot at him, but couldn't tell where — or if — it hit

I was wheezing now, and feeling the thump of my heart as it struggled to keep up with me. Ignore it, I thought, and maybe it won't kill you right this minute.

The fisherman was at the bend of the island. No way to miss letters over a foot high on the stern. They proclaimed that the boat's name was Lulu.

With a weapon in my hands, I was bent on some ass kicking of my own. I'd been surprised and puzzled by the attack, but right now I was more wrathful than mystified. Shot at with grave intent, one of Elysium's big outboards out of commission, the boat's right windshield a spider's web of cracks with a three-inch hole in the middle. All accomplished in less than two minutes by an unknown shooter from a boat called Lulu.

Elysium's port outboard was still alive and idling. I pushed the throttle forward and the bow moved up as the boat responded. I spun the wheel and turned to follow the fisherman around the bend of the island. The bow leveled as the boat struggled up on one engine and began to plane. I had the throttle full forward now, but the engine peaked at 3800 revs, far less than the 5000 it could crank out if the starboard engine had been helping. The heavy boat was creating backpressure that overwhelmed the single Yamaha still firing. Elysium could fly on two engines. On one, she was limping.

Lulu had maybe seventy yards lead. Her wheelhouse was open toward the stern, and I could see Mr. Hit-And-Run, holding the wheel with both hands, looking over his shoulder at me against the glare of the sun.

The Elysium was running down the middle of Lulu's wake. I punched the barrel of the Remington at the cracked glass of the windshield to enlarge the bullet hole, then leaned forward with my elbows on the console to fire through the opening, once, and then again. No hits that I could see. The marauder stood at Lulu's wheel, urging the boat ahead, looking over his shoulder every few seconds.

The distance between the two boats grew. I fired off two more rounds while I still had a prayer of hitting the shooter, but my prayer went unanswered. Lulu outrunning me, putting two hundred yards between us, then three hundred. The fisherman heading toward Orient Point, tip of the North Fork. In fifteen minutes she could be around the Point, north through Plum Gut and out into the Sound. From there she could make anywhere on the north shore of Long Island, or head across to Connecticut.

The gunman was gone. I eased the throttle back and stopped dead in the water, watching Lulu's wake roll away in the glassy calm.

It was quiet now, only the patient idle of Elysium's good engine breaking the stillness. My heart continued to work overtime, stepped up by the chase. Adventures weren't good for a man my age, with a rusty circulation system. Yet, in a willful way, I liked to remind myself I could still get the juices pumping when I had to.

Thinking, well I'm into it, whatever it is. Somebody owes me answers. I turned the boat and headed back toward the Julian dock.

CHAPTER 2

There was a boat in one of the four slips. Thirty feet of red and white Cigarette, fundamentally an outsize engine with a cockpit on top, designed for speed and not incidentally, noise. That's what Cigarette owners crave, the thunder as much as the speed, maybe more. It resonates in the chest, then heads downward and makes the masculine hormones surge. Piloting a Cigarette flat out requires a sure hand and a contempt for danger. The boat was Ingo Julian's toy, evidently.

I pulled the Elysium into an empty slip and began tying up.

From behind me a woman's voice said, "The body is gone. They took him away." I made the stern line fast and turned to look at her. Her blue eyes were set remarkably wide apart, and the nose was slightly flattened like a prizefighter's, but the face, taken all in all, was constructed from a classic plan, more elegant than mannish. She had close-cropped red hair, muscular but shapely legs that disappeared under her silky peach beach jacket.

"Away where?" I said.

"Heaven, I suppose. To see if they'll let him in."

"Who exactly are we talking about here?"

"You don't know?"

"Not to a certainty."

"Kenny. Kenneth Newalis. Vice president, advertising and public relations, Julian Communications. Thirty-five years old, more or less. Brilliant, in his way, but insecure."

"So you think Kenny might not make it past the Pearly Gates?" I said. "Why is that?"

"Who's certain to get into heaven? Are you, Seidenberg?" She sat on Elysium's gunwale, making the boat rock in the water.

"I'm lucky if they let me into a decent restaurant."

"Why is it I think modesty doesn't tally with your profile?" she said. "I hear you're smart and tough. But I thought you'd be younger."

"I am younger. I just look old."

"Smart and tough, though?"

"Don't have to be tough any more. I've weathered with such refinement, people are embarrassed to pick a fight with me."

"And so you get what you want?"

"Don't want much. I keep my life simple," I told her. "That's why I'm wondering how I got involved in this particular complication. Now I'm here, what am I supposed to do? And by the way, now that I've shared my inner life with you, who are you?" I tried to catch her looking at the bullet hole in my boat's windshield, but she gave no indication of being aware of the damage.

"I'm not sure what you're supposed to do. Safeguard the prestige and best interests of Julian Communications, probably. I'm Lisa Harper. Ingo sent me, asked me, to meet you." She threw a glance upward, toward the Julian house that commanded the precipice thirty feet up. I took the gesture as quiet confirmation that the real authority resided above us.

"And what is it you do here?"

"Around here I mostly run along the shore, and then I drink orange juice. Back in New York I head up marketing for Julian Communications. For Ingo. He asked me and Kenny to spend the weekend here, brainstorm next year's promotions."

"Bad move for Kenny."

"As it turned out," Lisa Harper said. She pushed her nicely sculptured ass against the Elysium and made the boat bump against the slip.

"So what happened?"

"He drowned."

"Oh, yes? Where? In the bathtub?"

She held up a forefinger, staring at me, making me wait, amusing me with her studied arrogance. Finally, "Patience, Seidenberg. All will be revealed. He drowned swimming in the bay."

"Swimming in October? Water's pretty cold."

"People do it. Ingo swims into November."

"Really."

"Cold doesn't bother him. Nothing does. Phenomenal endurance. He's a fitness freak, like me."

"You into fitness?"

"My passion."

"Thus the running and the orange juice."

"Kenny swam out thirty yards and did laps in front of the house. We watched him from up there." She pointed to the deck well above us, a cantilevered affair that seemed almost to float in space, barely touching the main structure of the house. "Suddenly he was in trouble. He stopped swimming and started flailing around in the water. Almost immediately he went under, disappeared."

"Then what?"

"We ran down, Ingo and I, and went in after him. Hard to locate him. The water's been so murky since the storm. It took us awhile, too long, but Ingo found him under water and we towed him back to shore. He gave him mouth-to-mouth and I ran up to call for help, the local ambulance corps. They got here right away, but it didn't make any difference. They worked on him with a resuscitator for forty minutes, right there on that rock. But he was gone."

"I'm surprised anybody could find the guy below the surface. You think he'd drift with the tide, maybe end up a mile away."

"That's what Ingo thought, too." said Lisa Harper. "But it was slack tide, we found out. The water wasn't moving."

"How deep is it out there, where he was swimming?"

"Maybe twelve, fifteen feet. Why?"

"Just that I wonder why he was out so far if he was swimming laps. For exercise, right? He could have done that in four feet of water."

"The bottom drops off sharply here," she said.

I shrugged. "So what was it, a cramp did him in, you think?"

"I suppose, yes."

"No reason to look for any other explanation, then?" I said. I folded my arms across my chest, resting them on my stomach, which I made no longer made any effort to suck in. Three years ago, when my weight had stabilized at 225 pounds, putting me beyond the far side of what was appropriate and healthy for a man of a certain age standing five-eleven, I had decided there was no more room in my life for vanity.

"What else could it be? He just suddenly went under."

"Try heart attack. Try food poisoning. And there's always that old favorite, foul play."

"Oh, please. He was all alone out there when it happened. And anyway, who would want to do harm to Kenny? I mean, Kenny, after all."

"I take that to mean you think he was an innocuous soul who couldn't have had enemies."

"Your words, not mine. He was a competent, effective executive. Ingo doesn't hand out vice presidencies to morons."

"A good guy, then? You liked him?"

She stood and walked to the end of the dock, looking across to the Greenport waterfront. A film of clouds, tinted orange by the lowering sun, had gathered on the horizon to the west. "I liked him well enough. But now you're thinking why am I so stoic about it, why aren't my eyes red from the sorrow of it all. After all, I helped pull his body out of the water. Looked into his cold, dead face."

"Yes, you did," I said.

"Never saw the sense of crying about anything. It's unproductive. Whatever happens, deal with it and move on." She almost smiled. "Write that down, if you want."

"You're tougher than I was when I was still tough."

"I'm the Iron Woman, Seidenberg."

"That what they call you?"

She turned to face me and undid the belt that held her beach jacket around her, then with a languorous realignment of her shoulders, let the jacket slip free and fall to the dock. The sharp angle of the fading autumn light traced the highlights of her form, shoulders broad and round, breasts full without being rude, narrow hips radiating a sense of power, sculptured thighs. Lisa Harper was an athlete, filled with muscular possibilities. She was dynamics at rest, ready to leap in an instant. The whole package was bound up by a bathing bra and thong bottom, both white against her tanned skin.

I caught myself gaping at her. "Aren't you cold?"

"Not really," she said. "Point is, my wavelength is the physical world. That's the only reality. Sorrow and regret and frustration, they just waste you."

"Is that what makes you the Iron Woman?"

"Every year I compete in the Iron Woman Triathlon. Train four months to get into shape. The competition is fifty miles that brings me to the limits of what this body can achieve. The experience is as close as one can get to absolute rapture. First bicycle, then swimming, then running. That's the reason they call me the Iron Woman."

"Only reason?" I said.

"Let's get back on track. I told you I liked Kenny. It was a hideous accident. We couldn't save him. We did all anyone could possibly do."

"I'm sure you did."

Ingo Julian's voice was a rasp that came from above. "Come up, Lisa. Bring him."

I had met Ingo Julian only once before, two years after the crash of his private plane that disfigured the man, and taken the life of his brother Felix. The sight of him now came as no surprise, but still, his appearance was so disquieting I had to force myself not to look away. There wasn't a trace of hair anywhere on Ingo Julian's head. Even his eyebrows were gone, sacrificed to the surgery that had repaired him after the fire and trauma of the crash. His head was a pattern of scars, the most prominent running from the top of his head, down his forehead and cheek, to just below his right ear. Another began at his left temple, then forked into two lines as it made its way behind his neck. The restructured appearance of his skin was accentuated by the sun, which had left him bronzed in some places while leaving mottled patches of white, outlined by his scars, in others. It was as though a membrane of some sort, damaged and mended, had been stretched over his head and neck.

"Thank you for coming," he said, his voice, as I remembered it, raw and labored. "Ben, isn't it? Yes?"

"Flattered you remember," I said.

"You've put on a few pounds. Living the good life on the North Fork."

"My lady friend likes hefty men. She insists I eat well." I was taken by the sheer size of the great-room in which we stood, the cathedral ceiling with its huge exposed beams, the expanse of polished oak floor.

"I'm not sure what you can do here. Might be a waste of your time," Julian said. "Hector thought it would be a good idea. Lawyers are so circumspect. Well, they keep us from doing foolhardy things. If we let them, they also keep us from doing productive things, isn't that so?"

Lisa Harper lingered in the room's entrance archway, beach

jacket draped over her shoulders. "You don't need me anymore, do you, Ingo? I'm longing to take a run."

"Run," said Julian, motioning toward the beach.

"I can be found if you need me, Seidenberg," she said. I felt her focus linger on me for an instant before she turned and disappeared.

"You left Empire, didn't you?" said Julian. "You cashed out. The fact is, old Teague made it worth your while. Yes?"

"It was time to move on," I said.

"Yet the fact is, here you are."

"Old loyalties."

Julian lowered himself into a black leather chair near the tiled fireplace, and pointed to a matching chair facing it. I sat. "Not all loyalty comes from the heart, does it?" Julian said. "The best of it is bought and paid for. I suspect the Julian Communications retainer fee has something of an impact on your payout from Empire. Three more years. A strong basis for your loyalty. Yes?"

"Absolutely," I said. "How is it you know everything about me and Teague and Empire?"

"We pay you a great deal, as fees for your sort of services go. I'm compulsive about looking into the people we do business with. You would know that, certainly."

"You investigate the investigators, then?"

"Of course." Julian said. "So I know Teague is a malicious, single-minded fellow you'd rather not deal with. Sleazy looking, too. Not someone you'd take to dinner, but then again, perhaps a good man to have on your side in a fight." He dismissed the subject with a wave of his hand, and leaned back into his chair. "About the accident today, I believe it's more of a public relations project now than an investigative matter."

"Do you?"

"Kenny Newalis was an officer of a good-sized company. His loss will be felt throughout the organization, and beyond. The industry will want to know how we're going to deal with that loss.

The financial markets, too."

"Why should the financial boys care? You own the company. There are no other stockholders."

"There are, actually. A few shares here and there, to valuable people. But you're out of touch, Ben Seidenberg. If you were still in New York instead of out here on the North Fork, you'd know there's talk about Julian Communications going public."

"Is it true?"

"There's always that chance." Julian shrugged his brawny shoulders. I watched his oversize biceps move beneath his blue T-shirt. "Many rumors of that kind end up being true. Yes?"

"Are you telling me the death of Newalis comes at a particularly bad time?"

"Why would you think that's what I meant?" Julian said, shaking his head.

"Reading between the lines. It's a talent investigators are supposed to cultivate. If there's a public offering, the loss of a key executive could be embarrassing. Or at least, it could muddy the waters for you."

"Accidents happen. People understand that."

"Sometimes." I stood. The sliding glass doors that defined an entire wall of the great-room were open, and the vista drew me through them onto the cantilevered deck that extended high above the beach and the dock. It was like floating over the bay.

"The man drowned," Julian said.

"By accident?"

Ingo Julian rose and followed me onto the deck, digging his hands into his pockets and striding deliberately. "We saw him go under with our own eyes. Right from where you and I are standing. He was out there all by himself. Those are facts. Why would you think it wasn't an accident?"

"I didn't say what I thought. I asked what you thought." The sun was sinking now, the horizon blazing red-orange.

Julian's hand on my shoulder. "I respect your pursuing what you believe to be Empire's responsibilities here. I recognize this and I appreciate it. But the facts in this matter are unambiguous. Inventing far-fetched scenarios for what happened would be counterproductive, and possibly contrary to the best interests of Julian Communications. You can acknowledge my point of view. Yes?"

"It makes sense as far as it goes."

"You think I don't go far enough?"

"That's right. But don't mistake my motives, Mr. Julian. Your concerns are my concerns."

"Ingo. Call me Ingo."

"Interesting. I call you Ingo but you call me Seidenberg."

"Yes, it is interesting, isn't it?" Julian ran a hand over his hairless head.

"When you were watching Newalis swim, and when you ran down after he got into trouble, did you see a boat here, a commercial fisherman?" I stepped to the railing and pointed toward the water offshore. All at once the height and a sudden illusion of no support beneath disoriented me. For an instant I felt I might actually topple over the railing, and a sudden swell of anxiety prompted me to step back.

Julian was watching me. "Others have had that reaction. Something about the design of this deck, the way it extends out into the void. It scares people. For me, it's the best feature of the house." He leaned far out over the railing. "Being here excites me. It's like soaring above the earth."

"About the boat," I said.

"The boat?"

The subject was making him uneasy. I kept silent and waited for him to continue.

"Yes, a boat." Ingo said, finally. "I believe there was a boat."

"At anchor?"

"Perhaps. I'm not sure."

"Did you call to the boat for help when you saw Newalis go under?"

"It occurred to me, but it was far away, and I couldn't see anyone on it, anyway. He must have been on the other side, facing Greenport. Fishing, I suppose. We didn't have time to worry about the boat, Lisa and I. We were racing to reach poor Kenny."

"Yes, poor Kenny. Did you see the boat after you found Newalis and pulled him ashore?"

"I have no idea. I had no reason to be concerned with the boat. We were trying to save Kenny's life. I'm beginning to sense you're cross-examining me, Seidenberg. Yes?"

"You pay us to dig out facts for you," I said. "That's what I'm doing. You don't have the whole picture."

"And you do?"

"Let's say I have a different perspective." I paced across the deck and back again, processing my thoughts, as Ingo waited silently. "Think about this. Why should a commercial craft be anchored here? There are nothing but porgies in this part of the bay, and commercial boats don't bother with them. It was slack tide, anyway. The fishing slows up when the tide stops running. He wasn't after fish."

"Maybe he had engine problems. Maybe he was cleaning his catch. Maybe he stopped to urinate."

"None of the above," I said. "Look down there. There's my boat in the slip on the right. See the windshield? A bullet did that. The guy on the boat was still here when I motored up, and he started shooting at me. I chased him east toward the Sound, but he outran me. He knocked out one of my engines, and I was no match for him with just the other one." A narrowing sliver of sun remained above the horizon, and now I felt the October chill distinctly. "So, are my concerns far-fetched?"

"I don't know who shot at you, but it wasn't anyone in the boat out there during the accident."

"How do you know that?"

"Because I remember seeing that boat leave when we pulled Kenny ashore. It went off to the west, toward Southold."

"Are you sure? Did you catch the name of the boat?"

"I was occupied trying to start a man's breathing. I wasn't looking for something painted on the side of a boat."

"On the stern, actually. You did say you saw the boat leave."

"You're cross-examining me again, Seidenberg."

"Was it Lulu? Because that's the name of the boat I tangled with."

"Asked and answered," Julian said brusquely. "I can't confirm what I don't know for a fact."

Client or no, Ingo Julian was being more difficult than he had a right to be. It was clear he'd rather I went away, but that wasn't an option now, not for me. "Somebody shot at me," I said. "I find that irritating. I also think it's not much of a leap from my skirmish on the bay to some kind of connection to the drowning. So I think maybe we ought to take a long look into the circumstances of just how poor Kenny expired. That's what I think. What do you think, Ingo?"

Again, Julian sidestepped. "I regret the damage to your boat. Have it fixed and I'll pay for it," he said. "It's getting dark. Let's go in. Yes?" He moved back into the great-room, waiting for me to follow before sliding the glass doors shut.

Ingo was stonewalling me, and I felt my disposition heating up. Any more of this exchange, and I'd be saying things to the chief executive officer of Julian Communications that could put my financial future into jeopardy. Thus I was not at all unhappy to recognize the voice of Hector Alzarez as he strode through the archway into the room. "You honor us, Ben."

His attire was, as always, flawless. His dark gray pin-stripes from Paul Stuart on Madison Avenue were miraculously wrinkle-free, despite Hector's two-and-a-half hour ride from

Manhattan on the Long Island Expressway. Inevitably he looked too good to be real, but he was real, all right. Better than real. He was incisive and shrewd and more than a little canny. If he felt there was a need for me, I knew he had reasons.

CHAPTER 3

I come when you call," I said to Hector. "Now tell me why you called."

"I think you're a skilled man in a crisis. You have a way of dealing with situations before they become unpleasant. You make people feel secure," he said. "I thought you'd be flattered. Did I disturb your retirement?" He started to slip out of his suit jacket, then stopped and looked to Ingo, as if to ask permission. Ingo replied silently as well, with a strained smile and a scarcely perceptible why-should-I-care shrug. Hector slid the jacket off, gracefully, slowly, folded it meticulously and laid it across the back of a chair.

I said, "Yes, I was flattered. And yes, you did disturb my retirement."

"I'm trying to be gracious," Hector said. "Teague told me you were in your boat fishing when he got to you on this case."

There was an edge to Ingo's voice. "Please don't refer to this incident as a case, Hector. It's not a case and not a crisis. This is — was — an accident, yes?" He moved about the room, switching on lamps against the approaching sunset. "I was there. I saw it happen."

"Does anyone think it wasn't an accident?" Hector said.

"Only Seidenberg has mentioned that possibility," Ingo said. "Not the ambulance people, not the police. Certainly not me, and I don't think Lisa, either. Go ask her."

"Were you swimming with Kenny when it happened?" Hector said.

"I didn't go in till we ran down to go after Kenny," Ingo said. "I'd planned to swim, but I was too busy today."

"There's something you should know," I said

Ingo jumped in quickly. The look on his face betrayed his impatience at an account of events other than his own. "Seidenberg had an unpleasant incident on his way here. But there's no reason to think —"

"A guy in a boat just offshore here shot at me," I said, "He got away."

Ingo frowned. "And what did that have to do with Kenny?"

"I'll find out."

"Don't do it on my account," Ingo said. "You understand my position on this, yes?" He took Hector by the elbow and turned him away from me, as though that would somehow assure their privacy. "I don't think there's a need for Seidenberg. We've had a tragedy, but there's nothing more to be done, is there? Let's move on." He glared at Hector with an intensity that said this was more than a suggestion.

But Hector was far too confident to be unsettled, even by the high voltage of Ingo Julian. He moved close to the man, radiating his best I've-got-this-under-control manner. "I understand your concern. Give me a few minutes to square this away with Ben."

There was a clumsy silence. "I'll be in the library," Ingo said, finally, and turned to walk through the archway. Watching him from the back, I noticed for the first time he had an odd, rolling gait that pitched him forward slightly each time he stepped out on his right leg. Old damage from the crash, I thought. He halted and turned. "Thank you, Seidenberg. I appreciate your coming. Hector, be sure to thank Teague for sending him." And he was gone.

"Do that, Hector," I said. "By all means, thank Teague for sending me."

Hector knew Ingo's mention of Roger was an irritation. He touched my shoulder and gave me a knowing smile. He was so adept at this, smoothing matters over, stroking you, making you forget you were angry. "You know how Ingo is, Ben."

"No, how is he?"

"He's stubborn and autocratic and inconsiderate to the point of rudeness. He's also a clear minded leader who makes every decision based entirely upon what's best for Julian Communications."

"Whether it's right or not, I suppose."

Hector moved to a chair and settled into it. "Right? Come on, Ben, only politicians and clergymen talk about what's right, and even they don't mean it. In the end, when they say something's the right thing to do, you can bet they mean it's consistent with their own agendas."

"You shock me, Hector. Don't you believe in the rule of law?"

"Law, yes. I'm all for law. Took an oath. What does that have to do with right? Come and sit down. Ingo told me his version of everything on the phone. Now you talk to me."

I didn't feel like sitting, so I paced in front of him. "I'm saddened to learn how the world of Julian Communications really works."

He grinned and shook his head. "How did you get so righteous, Ben Seidenberg, tapper of phones, intimidator of enemies, hoodwinker of lawmen, professional hard-ass."

"Retired professional hard-ass," I said. "I'm not making judgments, Hector. The morality of Julian Communications is none of my business. Empire Security will do anything you tell us. Almost anything. But there's been a death I think is suspicious, and I've been shot at with serious intent, on the water just out there. You're too smart to believe in coincidences. But now your big guy is trying to blow it all off. I won't just let it go. There are bullet holes in my boat, pal."

"I'm waiting," he said. "Tell me."

I walked and talked, detailing it all, starting from Teague's summons at Plum Gut. I told him what I saw, what I thought, what Ingo said, what Lisa Harper said. Every time I crossed in front of the chair in which Hector sat, I could sense the barest trace of his cologne hanging in the air. The good stuff, rich and complex, a hundred and fifty bucks a bottle. But of course, this was Hector Alzarez.

He listened, perfectly still, following me with his eyes, while I laid it all out for him. "So what do you think about that, counselor?" I asked him when I'd finished. My weary legs told me this would be the right moment to sit down, so I did.

Hector shifted in his chair a bit this way and that as he sorted out what I'd said. Then finally, "Of course you're right, Ben. I think Ingo doesn't want to admit there may be something wrong here. Or maybe he just refuses to find out what it is."

"Doesn't sound like the reaction of a clear-minded leader to me," I said. "This is life and death stuff. Why would he stick his head in the sand?"

"There's talk of Julian Communications going public. Did he tell you that?"

"He mentioned it. Is it going to happen?"

"Let's say I'd be terribly surprised if the announcement of an initial public offering didn't show up in The Wall Street Journal within the next ninety days. Barring some disaster, the IPO is a done deal. So Ingo doesn't want anything to get out that might make the market nervous. Check the arithmetic." Hector began making his points by tapping the fingertips of one hand with the forefinger of the other. "If the issue is thirty million shares, and the price goes off at twenty dollars, we're talking about $800 million.

Most of that goes into Ingo's pocket. And he still owns half the company, by the way. But if the market gets shaky over a mysterious death at Julian Communications, he might decide to postpone the issue, possibly even cancel it. And even if he does go ahead, every dollar the market knocks off the price costs Ingo big money, right away. Does that clarify the picture for you?"

"Beautifully." I said. "Who else has a stake in this? Ingo told me there were other shares out there right now."

"The company's top executives."

"You?"

"Don't I look like a top executive?"

"All right, who beside you?"

"Most of them. I think." Hector ran both his hands through his thick, black hair. "Ingo's kept that to himself. He'll have to make all the holdings public when the issue goes to market, but at this point, even I don't know, and I'm the corporate counsel, for God's sake. I'm fairly certain all of us have equity. That's why everyone's so steadfast and dedicated, and why we're all holding our breaths waiting for the offering. But who's got how many shares? That I can only guess."

"Are you telling me we're talking about large amounts of bucks here?"

"Yes, if you consider two million a large amount of bucks," he said. "I doubt that anyone's shares will be worth less than that when the stock hits the market. Some a lot more, maybe. Arthur Brody, the president, he might be in for twenty, twenty-five million. I don't know. But we can't sell our shares for two years, and we have to remain with the company. That's to keep us from cashing out right away and leaving. And to make sure we keep the stock price up, by toiling every hour of every day. Including Saturdays, Sundays and holy days of obligation."

"So you'll be a big-time millionaire yourself when all this happens. Don't you share Ingo's fear that — "

Hector held up his hand to stop me. "Listen to me, Ben.

You have to accept this. Ingo doesn't fear anything. It's a strength of his. And sometimes, I think, a perverse kind of weakness. Ingo has concerns, of course. He's much too smart not to recognize a problem. But afraid? No, I've never seen him afraid."

"All right, then. Don't you share Ingo's concern that what went on here today will shake up the market? About the stock, I mean?

It was almost dark outside now. Inside the great room, the lamps cast a warm, flattering glow on Hector Alzarez. Handsome bastard. Did I ever look as good as he does, I thought? No, sorry.

"Sure I'm concerned," he said. "And my concern goes beyond what happened today." He leaned forward with his hands on his knees. Lowering his voice, "It might be part of something else. Just between us, I get the sense that all is not right at Julian Communications. Lately, that is."

"Like what?" I said.

"Something to do with a sudden strain between Ingo and Brody, after the two of them have been so close for years. They barely acknowledge each other."

"Do you know why?" I said

"No. Neither one will talk about it," Hector said. "I just thought you should be aware. As you look into this for me."

"Look into what? You know I'm not in the investigation business any more," I said.

"I'm expecting you won't refuse me."

"You're forcing me to do this, then? Is that it?"

"You always did understand me perfectly," he said. "Stay on this for me. Just you. Quietly. Find out who shot at you, who was out there in that boat. See if Kenny's death could have been — well, make certain it was really an accident."

I said, "But Ingo wants me out."

"I'll talk to him, tell him we have to look into this or it could bite us on the ass. He has to go along with me."

"If you say."

"I say. And talk only to me, personally. I want to know everything as soon as you know it. Get to me at the office, at home, anyplace. Whatever's wrong here, we have to deal with it." He pulled his tie and unbuttoned his collar, uncharacteristic moves for Hector Alzarez. Maybe Ingo feared nothing, but I thought Hector looked a touch worried. "I'm staying tonight. Ingo, Lisa and I will go back to New York in the morning, early. Check in with me in the afternoon." We both stood, and he shook my hand. "I'm glad you came," he said.

"Just one thing," I said. "I'm curious. You asked Ingo if he was out there swimming with Newalis. Any particular reason?"

"Only that he hadn't mentioned it to me on the phone. I thought he might have been nearby when Kenny went under, seen something. Ingo swims every afternoon when he's out here. A ritual with him."

"Except for today."

"So it seems," Hector said.

It was chilly now back on the dock, and a night breeze was kicking up from the northeast. I pulled my jacket out of Elysium's cabin, put it on and zippered it. The bay was beginning to churn up. I could make out a few whitecaps against the lights of Greenport on the mainland.

I was about to start the single good engine I had left to me, when I heard the soft approach of footsteps moving on the beach toward the dock. In the near-darkness I could see Lisa, back from her run, still ignoring the October weather in her abbreviated bathing suit.

"Had enough running, Iron Woman?" I said

"Not nearly. But it's getting too dark. There are rocks and chunks of driftwood all over the beach. Don't want to put myself out of commission with a turned ankle." She approached and stood with her thighs against Elysium's gunwale, she on the dock, me in the boat. "Did you tell Ingo about the bullet holes in your boat?"

"You did notice, then."

"You thought I didn't?"

"I underestimated you."

"Always a mistake," she said.

"Tell me something, as long as we're being so candid. How come Newalis was swimming and Ingo wasn't? I heard Ingo goes swimming every afternoon when he's out here. And he swims right into November, you said."

"What are you suggesting?"

"I'm not suggesting anything. I'm trying to get a grip on what happened."

"Why are you bothering? I got the impression Ingo didn't think there was any need for you to get into this."

"That what he told you? Even before I showed up?"

She slid her hand around Elysium's radio antenna. "You were Hector's idea, not Ingo's."

"Why was Newalis in the water and Ingo not?"

"Ask Ingo," she said.

"I did. He said he was too busy to swim today. But if he was so busy, what was he doing up there on the balcony with you, watching Newalis do laps?"

"Yes, we were busy. We'd met all day long, starting at a six o'clock breakfast. Ingo holds marathon meetings."

"Come on, Iron Woman," I said, "the meeting was over. How come Ingo wasn't swimming, like always? And how come Newalis was out there? Was he impervious to cold, like you and Ingo?"

Lisa perched on the gunwale, swung her legs into the boat and moved into the captain's chair. "Kenny? Hardly."

"Oh? So Kenny was not an Iron Man?"

"Let's say he was more the cerebral type. Didn't care for athletics, physical pursuits. That trait amused Ingo. He'd rag Kenny about it, sometimes." She added quickly, "In a friendly way, of course."

"Of course. So what did he do, dare Kenny to swim in the cold water?"

"It wasn't like that," she said. "It was Kenny's idea."

"And you two muscular people stood up there watching the wimpy guy try to prove himself."

"Are you going out of your way to antagonize me, or are you always this rude?"

"Neither, I think. I'm just being direct, is all. I get touchy when people don't give me straight answers, especially when I'm trying to help. But I wouldn't antagonize you, Lisa Harper. A smart, gorgeous woman like you. Never."

"Oh, that's wonderful. I love cheap flattery. Say it again."

"You're smart and you're gorgeous."

"So you can utter something civil, after all." As if in slow motion, she took hold of my jacket and pulled me close, touched her lips to mine. Dry and gentle, nothing that would kindle a fire, but still, I thought, not a bad gift for an older man with a forty-two waist.

"Does this mean we're friends again?" I said.

"Were we before? Well, maybe now." She climbed out of the boat, made her way across the dock and disappeared into the darkness.

I started the single engine, untied and motored up the bay toward the lights of the marina. I was tired, but the day was far from over.

CHAPTER 4

I turned Elysium's spotlight on to search out the channel marker buoys, because there were clouds now, and the three-quarter moon kept disappearing. I crabbed the boat against the wind to maneuver into my slip at Wally's Marina. Most of the other spaces were empty now, the boats either stacked away inside Wally's big corrugated metal storage building until spring, or shrink-wrapped in white plastic to protect them from the approaching winter and placed on blocks outside, a less expensive option for their owners. At the end of each season I put Elysium inside, but only when there were no more fish left to catch in Long Island Sound. That didn't happen until November, or sometimes even into December.

Bare bulbs burned at each corner of the dock, but now, at seven o'clock, the marina was long deserted. Wally sent his crew home early when the season slowed and only the die-hards like me took their boats out to fish.

Mine was the only car parked against the building that was Wally's office and service shop. I started it up and drove past rows of shrink-wrapped boats, ethereal in the beams of my headlights, to turn onto the Main Road toward Southold, heading gladly to the warmth and comfort of Alicia Bianchi.

Her neat, cedar-shingled ranch house was at the end of a winding gravel drive which led from the roadway past two other houses, then kept on to a grove of immense elm trees. Alicia's home was tucked there, two hundred feet from her nearest neighbor. For all her sociability, the woman valued her privacy.

Alicia had seen my car approach, and was waiting for me just inside the door. She kissed me decisively, holding my face in her hands. "You got fish?" she said.

"I had two blues, but they spoiled. I had to dump them."

"Good," she said. I followed her into the kitchen. The table was already set for dinner. "Enough of bluefish. Enough of all fish. I give my love to a fisherman, I got to eat fish all week long. We make pasta, instead, OK?" Before I could answer, she was into the refrigerator, pulling out raw materials and putting them on the kitchen island's butcher-block top. "Ritchie at the market made that good sausage today. Look how nice. And I got broccoli rabe. Bright green. Good. We make a sauce to go with fettuccini. You know, with garlic and wine and broth and the sausage, with the greens. You like that one? Anyway, that's what I want. I got a taste for it all day, you know?"

"Sounds fine," I said. Alicia is a complex person with so many facets to her, it's hard to pick and choose among them. Quick, clever, unerringly accurate in sizing up people. Open, yet mysterious. Black eyes and flawless olive skin from the Mediterranean. All that. The whole package of her astonishes me every day. But most of all I delight in listening to her talk. That husky voice, the delicious accent, the funny stories about her family back in Calabria, that way she has of saying things that make me believe I'll live forever.

"More enthusiasm about the fettuccini would be good," she said. She undid two big bunches of broccoli rabe, stripped away the coarse stems and put the leafy parts in the sink, which she began filling with water. "Full of grit sometimes, the greens. Best to soak them completely." She stood barefoot on the rough brown tile of the kitchen floor. Alicia was always barefoot at home, even in winter. She claimed that what she most looked forward to at night after retuning from her art gallery in Southampton was kicking her shoes into a corner. "Look, you want fresh pasta, the real thing? Instead of dried from the box? Much better for this dish," she said. "Takes a few minutes only. But you make it. By the time I finish the sauce, you can have it all done."

"I'm your man," I said.

Campy and seductive, "I know that." She took her shiny pasta machine from a drawer in the island and clamped it to the butcher block.

"I mean, yes, I'll make the fettuccini," I said. "In a minute. I have to talk to Wally Prager."

Using the wall phone in the kitchen, I dialed Wally at home. "I don't mind you calling in the middle of my dinner," he said. "Just choking down some dried-out pot roast I made last Tuesday, is all."

"Only take a minute," I said. "Do you know of a beat-up old commercial fishing boat around here, maybe 28, 30 feet, called the Lulu?"

"No boat I know," Wally said.

"Could you ask around? It's important."

"I could. You want me to?"

"Please. And another thing. There's a hole in the port engine gas-line on my boat. And there's a hole in the windshield, too."

"What kind of holes?" Wally said

"Bullet holes," I told him.

As I spoke on the phone, I watched Alicia listening to my end of the conversation. With the mention of bullet holes she stopped washing the broccoli rabe, and stood there quietly, with her dark eyes boring into me.

"Well, now, muchacho," Wally said on the phone, "you really had yourself a happy old time on Shelter Island."

"I'll tell you about it when I see you. Have your guys fix up the boat, will you? Go eat the pot-roast." I replaced the phone on the wall.

Alicia turned back to the sink and stared at the water splashing on the greens. "Somebody shoots at you?" she said. "I thought you don't do such dangerous things any more."

"I thought so, too," I said. I took flour from a cupboard plus eggs from the refrigerator, and started the pasta dough in a big bowl. "Teague got to me today, actually reached me out in the boat, and the next thing I knew I was in the middle of a case."

"Again? This must not go on. You have a duty to tell Roger Teague to go to hell."

"Just as soon as he hands me the final dollar of my payout. And then I'll drive a stake through his black heart."

"Very nice, but you're no good to me if that man gets you killed. Run away from him. Or if you want, I have Uncle Tito come fly over next week and feed Teague to the fishes for you. You don't need Teague's money. I got money. You know that frenchy landscape painter I show now, that Pichou? I sell one today for seven thousand dollars. Thirty-five hundred profit, just like that. All the money you want," Alicia said.

"I don't want to be a kept man."

"Why not? Men wait their whole lives for such an offer."

"I have this stupid pride," I said. "The money I get isn't Teague's money. It belongs to me. All I want is what's mine." I filled the big pasta pot with water and put it on to boil.

She shrugged and sighed, rolling her eyes at the ceiling. The unspoken message was that I was stubborn and impossible, but she'd known that since the day we met. "Open some wine now. Merlot," she said. "Then you tell me how you got bullet holes."

I opened a bottle and we started on it. As I told Alicia the story, I kneaded the dough on the butcher block with my hands, rested it a few minutes, then cranked it through the pasta machine to form long strands of fettuccini.

Alicia sauteed chopped garlic in olive oil, added the broccoli rabe to the big skillet and wilted it down. She took the vegetable out and browned bite-size pieces of Italian sausage in the oil. The aroma was already irresistible.

"So this Ingo, he makes fun of Kenny, and Kenny is so humiliated he swims in the cold water to prove how brave he is?" she said.

"Something like that." I said. "Then he goes under and drowns. Maybe a cramp. Who knows? But maybe somebody pulled him under, somebody from the boat. It would've been hard to see because the water was murky. And just maybe, Ingo knew what was waiting in the water, and sent Kenny out there to die. What I know is, Ingo was too anxious for me to go away. He doesn't want me digging into this."

"OK, maybe." She took an open bottle of pinot grigio from the refrigerator, poured wine into the skillet and turned up the fire. It quickly bubbled up and began to boil. "But you tell me Ingo mostly goes swimming himself in the afternoons. You think maybe somebody is out there waiting for him, kills Kenny by mistake? I think this story is better."

"Why?"

"I don't believe such a rich man like Ingo kills people. Why should he make such a risk? Too much to lose." She added chicken broth to the skillet, some chopped fresh marjoram and basil, salt and several grinds of pepper. The sauce boiled down fiercely in the skillet. She salted the water in the pasta pot, and put in the fettuccini. "Five minutes," she said. "Get the bowls."

In four minutes exactly, she drained the pasta and finished cooking it in the skillet, where the sauce was now thickened just slightly. She added the broccoli rabe, turned the food over and over with tongs, then filled our oversize pasta bowls, spooning a bit of the sauce over each portion.

The dinner was better than mortals have a right to expect, rich and garlicky, covered with the Parmigiano-Reggiano cheese which Alicia grated, just so, into our bowls. We ate it all and finished the merlot, talking about the shooting and Ingo and Kenny and Hector.

And Lisa.

"So," Alicia said, mopping up the last few drops of sauce in her bowl with semolina bread, "this Lisa, what do you think about her?"

"I'm not sure. She seems too anxious to make Ingo's case for him."

"But you kiss her, anyway, yes?" she said, without meeting my eyes.

"No. She kissed me. But you knew."

"I am a sorceress. I know such things. I tasted it on your lips when you came in."

"It was a joke," I said. "I talked tough to her, and when I finally said something nice, she felt she had to respond. Couldn't stop her."

"Hey, it's OK. What can I do? You drive women crazy."

"You know how passionate I am for you." I said. " Only you, on this entire planet."

"Say more."

"As long as you can make pasta like this."

She tossed her head back and laughed. "Who else is going to put up with you? Not some iron lady from New York. Look, you want to stay and make love to me?"

"You want me to?"

"Not if you're going to fall asleep. You look tired."

"Been a demanding day."

"Go home then," she said. "Tomorrow you make up for no love tonight. Don't forget."

I didn't meet another car on the five dark miles of road from Southold to Greenport. North Fork highways that are busy on summer nights are desolate by October. It's as though someone turns a switch and closes down the whole area at nine o'clock. When I turned onto my street I could see the lights of the ferry terminal four blocks away, and the far-away reflection of illumination on Shelter Island in the water.

I parked the car in the driveway and mounted the steps to the front porch of my house, a two-bedroom bungalow, built in 1922, renovated in 1964, and not touched since. I was eager to fall into my bed. But a voice from the dark corner of the porch stopped me before I could put the key in the door.

"There are matters we should discuss, Seidenberg," said Lisa Harper.

CHAPTER 5

She was sitting on the wicker love-seat, her feet up on the cushion, clasping her knees with her arms. I could make out her face in the faint beam from the streetlight outside that spilled through a hole in the overgrown bushes against the porch. Had she deliberately placed herself in that dim spotlight, or was it just one of those cosmic coincidences?

"I'd just about given up on you," Lisa said. "Out to dinner?"

"You could say that," I said.

"With a friend?"

"That, too."

"Ah. A romantic attachment. Am I right? A strong relationship."

"I'm pleased with it."

"And of course she is, too," she said

"Oh? Why do you think that?"

"I think you're reliable. I think you're levelheaded and realistic. I think you're probably a thoughtful lover."

"All that after having met me just this afternoon? I never realized how quickly people find me out," I said. "You come on the ferry?"

"Only two cars and me. Seemed a shame for the boat to make the trip just for us." She swung her legs off of the love-seat and stood to face me. "It's chilly out here. You going to invite me inside?"

I unlocked the front door and we stepped into the living room. I turned on the lights with the switch just inside the door. "To think that just a few hours ago you resented my questions. And you took such pleasure giving me a rough time. You get off on irritating people?"

"How can you say that, Seidenberg? I did kiss you, didn't I?"

"My lady friend knew it, too."

"How?"

"She's a sorceress. But she wasn't angry about it. I told her it was a joke."

"You think I was just having some entertainment with you?" She settled herself on the sofa.

"Let's say I don't think you were expressing a truly profound emotion."

"What do I have to do, Seidenberg," she said, "take off my clothes?"

"One, it's too chilly in here to play. Two, though I hate to admit it, I'm too tired to do a really first-rate job. Three, and most significant, my lady friend would know about it, and that would disturb me a lot." I reached to the coffee table and took the top off a glass candy bowl, the single hospitality item in my largely unadorned living room. "Have a hard candy. I think the orange ones are best."

"I'm not much on sweets. I'm more of a meat-and-potatoes person. Though you wouldn't think so, would you?" she said, pointedly stroking her sleek forearms, then her thighs.

"You carry it well," I told her. I took an orange candy for myself, and lowered my overstuffed body into an overstuffed armchair, trying not to embarrass myself by wheezing as I sank into it. "And now, you didn't really come to seduce me, did you? You said there were things we ought to discuss. Wasn't that it?"

"I came here because Hector thinks your suspicions could be right. He trusts you completely. If he's that high on your judgment, then I'll go along, too. At least until you screw up."

"I can't tell you how moved I am by your confidence in me," I told her. "And to think you came over on the ferry to tell me." I crunched my hard candy and chewed up the pieces. "And why else did you make the trip?"

"You think there's more?" she said.

"Isn't there always? "

She offered the barest hint of a smile, and nodded her head just once. "Yes, all right," she said. "After you left, Hector told Ingo we couldn't just pretend there hadn't been a drowning and a shooting, and that he'd asked you check into it. Ingo finally agreed we had to do it, but he wasn't happy about it. All through dinner he worried about word getting out and screwing up the stock deal. He wouldn't let go of it. Over and over, he said there was so much at stake, and could we be sure of Seidenberg."

"So Hector said not to worry about me, that I was discreet, and that I was a fair hand with touchy situations."

"Something like that," Lisa Harper said. She stood up for an instant, tucked one leg under her on the sofa and sat down again. How do women do that? "But Ingo was still on edge, so he — "

"All right, let me guess the rest," I said. "Ingo said get to me and make sure I understand how critical it is to keep this quiet. As if I didn't know already."

"Yes. To calm Ingo down, Hector said he'd phone you. But I said I'd take care of it, face to face."

"Why you?"

"I wanted to. I told Ingo you and I have a rapport." Again that barely perceptible smile. "Did I overstate it, Seidenberg?"

"Certainly not," I said. "We're communicating beautifully, I think."

"I'm so pleased."

"Now that we understand each other so well," I said, "maybe you can clear up something that's puzzling me." I didn't wait for her to respond. "Why aren't Ingo and Arthur Brody getting along these days?"

"You know about that?"

"Hector said it was no secret. Why don't they talk to each other?"

"I don't know. But I feel, whatever it is, it's coming out of Brody's office. It's tough to read Ingo sometimes, you know that. But I think he's upset about the present state of affairs, distressed by it. He'd depended on Brody, consulted with him about everything, when he got out of rehab and returned to the company after the crash, still using a walker, Arthur Brody was with him constantly, helping him, advising him. From then on, Ingo didn't make a decision without running it past Brody."

"Tell me about the plane crash."

"You know about that," she said. "You were at Empire then, weren't you?"

"Tell me anyway. I never knew the details."

She said, "Ingo was into flying then. Always searching out new thrills. Still is. He'd got his license and right away he bought a light plane. He was flying up to Quebec with his brother Felix to go skiing. The plane went down in the Adirondacks, and there was a fire. Somehow Ingo dragged himself out. But Felix was burned up in the plane. A helicopter took Ingo to a hospital in Utica. He was horribly burned, with broken bones everywhere. It was grim. There were operations, plastic surgery. They literally pieced him back together. We thought he'd never be able to return to the company. But he refused to give up. He rehabilitated himself with a vengeance, month after month. He made himself strong again. Look at him now."

"Yes, look at him." I said. "So Brody actually took charge right after the crash?"

"He did. As soon as he got the word about the crash, he

chartered a plane to Utica. He was at Ingo's bedside that night, and through the whole ordeal. In the hospitals and during the rehab, and ever since. That is, until now. Brody ran the company for Ingo until the day Ingo returned to the thirty-sixth floor. Loyalty to Ingo was how Brody got his own corner office. He'd been exec vp, but Ingo was so grateful, he made him president, and moved himself up to chairman."

"So you're telling me about Brody because — why?" I said.

"Because you asked me,"

"I mean, you think the problem between Brody and Ingo is Brody's doing. Isn't that what you said? "

She got up from the sofa and came to my chair. "I think it's Brody because I don't think it's Ingo. Here's how it sorts out for me, Seidenberg, Hector feels you're some kind of hero and that we should trust you. I'm telling you what I know because it just might tie in somehow, I'm not sure. I'm here to do what's best for Julian Communications. Surely you don't think I made the trip to get your fat ass into bed."

"My lady friend tells me I drive women crazy," I said. "But I'm taken."

Lisa Harper was choosing from among the clever things she might reply when we heard the gunshot and the sound of shattering glass. Looking toward the noise, I saw shards fall from the front window. Someone had shot into the living room from the street directly in front of the house.

I pulled Lisa down, in a clumsy move that tripped her against my feet and brought her crashing against my stomach. "Get flat on the floor," I told her, as I pulled myself from beneath her and started on all fours toward the light switch. I could hear the slap-click of a rifle bolt working on the street outside, the same lethal sound I'd heard across the water in this afternoon's encounter. Same rifle, I thought. Same shooter.

"Stay down, hug the floor," I called to Lisa. I reached up

and snapped off the lights, throwing the room into blackness. I thought that would end it. No light, no targets. But the shooter wasn't quitting just yet. I stole a quick look through the shattered window, and saw the silhouette of a figure against the streetlight outside, moving fitfully from one side of the front yard to the other, then back again. The impulsive type, erratic and unpredictable. Would he storm into the house?

I pulled Lisa to her feet. "You told me to hug the floor," she said.

"New rules. Our friend may be coming in after us." Half pushing, half dragging, I got her onto the stairway to the second floor.

"Don't you have a gun or something?" she said, stumbling to the top. "I thought investigators had guns."

I felt the angina starting to creep up my chest as I scrambled after her. "I do. It's in my bureau drawer,"

"Great place for it," she said.

"You think I carry a gun, go around shooting people?" I led her down the black hallway into my bedroom and closed the door behind us.

"This might be a good time to start," she said.

The angina was going quickly from grating to painful. This was not an insignificant episode. A nitroglycerine pill under my tongue would dilate my arteries and get me the blood flow for which my body was begging. But the pills were in my pocket or the medicine cabinet or someplace. Never had them when I needed them. Even in my condition, I knew that right now getting my hands on my .38 Police Special was the higher priority.

Straining for breath, I pulled open a bureau drawer and ran my hands under my shirts, searching for the weapon I hadn't touched in years, It wasn't there.

"I hear something downstairs." There was an uncharacteristic desperation in Lisa's voice. "The gun, Seidenberg. Where's that gun of yours?"

"I'm getting it," I said, hoping I wasn't lying. I tried to suck in the air to make the tightness across my chest go away. No help. I opened my sock drawer. No gun. This was not going well.

"I heard the door," Lisa said. "He's in the house."

Now my ears started to ring. I pulled open another drawer and stuck my hand in. At last I felt the cold metal of the pistol. "Yes," I said. "Under my shorts."

"Of course. Where else would you keep a gun?"

"Next time I'll look there first," I said. "Stay here." I cocked the hammer of the .38, opened the bedroom door cautiously, and edged my way down the hall to the stairway. Peering over the top rail from a few steps back, I made out the form of a man framed in the open doorway to the porch below. Before I could decide what move would win me the upper hand without getting me killed, he reached to the wall and snapped on the lights.

Suddenly we were staring at each other, both squinting in the light. It was him, I was certain, gangly and remarkably broad from shoulder to shoulder, the shooter from the Lulu. Only now I was close enough to see his flat, homely face, close-set eyes, strings of yellow hair. And the tattoos, thick green and red snakes coiling their way down both his arms. He was some beauty.

He started to raise the rifle, but saw he was already squarely in the sights of my .38. In an instant he ducked out the door and took all four porch stairs in one leap. I could hear him running up the street, but I didn't have the energy to chase him. It was all I could do to make my way down to the living room and out onto the porch.

From down by the water came the sound of a car starting. The shooter was gone into the night. Again he was beyond my reach.

Now I heard my neighbor calling to me from his front porch. He was in his pajamas. "Ben, you all right? Was that a shot I heard?"

"I heard it, too. Firecracker, I think. I can still smell it in the air. There were kids out here. Ran away." I could only hope he'd buy into it. If he got antsy and called the cops, the episode could end up in the newspapers, and nobody wanted that right now — not Hector or Ingo or me. "Seems quiet now," I said, trying to sound unconcerned.

"Damn kids around here are a pain in the ass," my neighbor said. "'Night." I heard his front door shut.

Lisa was sitting on the bottom stair inside the house. I barely noticed her as I fell back into the easy chair and closed my eyes, the pistol still in my hand. In my head I conjured up the image of my own circulatory system, churning away fitfully inside my body. Mentally, I willed the functions to return to normal. I read somewhere once that if you focus, you can do that with your body, think it and make it happen. It seemed to work. Or maybe just sitting there quietly had something to do with it.

"I'm a believer." Lisa finally broke the silence. "Something bad is going on."

"Bad doesn't begin to cover it," I said.

"Was he trying to shoot me, do you think? Or was he after you? Or both of us?"

"Can't tell yet. He was the same guy who shot at me out on the water today. Maybe he felt like finishing the job. Or maybe he's somebody with a grudge against Julian Communications and wants to knock off the top people. Of which you happen to be one." My head was still back, my eyes closed. "Of course, you were alone on my porch before I got here. For how long?"

"Maybe forty-five minutes," she said.

"He could have come after you then, easy. Maybe he followed you here to find where I live, then waited for me to show up."

"Why follow me? You're right there in the phonebook, easy to find."

"Right. If he knew my name, somehow," I said. Then, "I

got a good look at the guy tonight. I have no idea who he is."

"He's still out there," she said.

"You bet he is. And he may want me. He may want you. Or Ingo or Hector. Or all of us. No way to know yet. This is a dangerous guy. I saw him pacing around in the front yard after he shot out the window. A wild man. You should have protection."

"And you?"

I held up the gun. "I've got this."

"In your bureau drawer, under your shorts."

"No, it's in my hand now, and I intend to keep it close." I pulled myself out of the chair and walked unsteadily to where she sat. "Any reasonable person would bring the cops in. But if I do, Ingo will blame Empire Security for letting bad news get out and screwing up the IPO. He'll fire us, and I'll spend the rest of my life in poverty and desperation"

"What are you talking about, Seidenberg?"

"Just the ramblings of a man who's been shot at twice in one day. Look, I can't simply do nothing about all this. It's my ass getting shot at, too — my fat ass, as you put it so delicately."

"A figure of speech," she said. "Nothing personal. Your ass isn't that fat."

"Whatever." I offered her my hand. She took it and got to her feet. "Ingo doesn't want to listen to me because he's afraid I'll rock his corporate boat," I said. "Go tell Hector what happened to you tonight. Tell him I want to put some Empire people on the scene, here, and in New York, too. People who carry guns. We'll do it discreetly, tell him, and Ingo won't know they're around. Will you do that?"

"I'll tell him."

I checked my watch. "The ferry is going to stop running for the night. You'd better not go back to Shelter by yourself, and walking alone is out of the question. So I and my revolver are going to drive you onto the ferry and deliver you directly to Ingo's door."

She put her hands on my shoulders. "Are you as good as Hector says you are? Smart and strong? What do you think?"

"Look, Iron Lady, I'd be flattered to have you kiss me again, but it complicates the hell out of my established relationship. Nothing personal. So you can adore me if you must, but mostly from afar."

"In that case, I take back what I said about you."

"What?"

"That your ass isn't that fat. Let's be honest. It really is."

CHAPTER 6

The autumn fog that hung across the bay was so heavy I could barely make out the contour of Shelter Island from Wally's Marina, a distance of three quarters of a mile. If I were going out fishing, I'd play it cautious, keep the Elysium safe in the slip and drink coffee for an hour, until I was sure the morning sun was well on its way to burning off the mist. The sun's supposed to do that, but sometimes it refuses. I don't like fog, anyway, not since it unexpectedly descended on me in Plum Gut one afternoon, and the New London ferry coming across Long Island Sound passed Elysium's stern with fifteen feet to spare.

But the fog was no threat today because the Elysium wasn't going fishing, or anywhere. When I arrived at the slip, a mechanic was busy cementing a new piece of glass into the windshield frame, and hadn't yet started on the broken gas line.

Wally stood next to me looking into the boat, his thumbs hooked into his belt. "He's got another hour, maybe two."

"At seventy-five bucks an hour," I said.

"Eighty-five. Plus parts." He pointed to the stern. "You know the bullet tore out a plug of fiberglass? Not all the way through, though. Way above the waterline. No big deal. We'll patch it when we put her away for the winter." Wally turned and walked up the ramp to the yard. I followed. "Listen, amigo, I asked everybody here if they knew a commercial boat named Lulu.

Nothing Then I called marina guys I know in Sag Harbor, Orient, Shinnecock, Mattituck, Jamesport. More nothing. Now, there's a lot more marinas than that around here, but I don't know all those guys." He took a box of black Napoli cigars out of his shirt pocket, shook one out and lit it, cupping his hands around the flame of the match. He took a big drag and let the pungent smoke out, making me regret I was standing near him in the still air. "One thing, though."

"And that is?"

"There is a Lulu. But this Lulu isn't the boat you're looking for, it's an actual live woman, Lulu Lumpkin."

"Really? Lulu Lumpkin? Unfortunate name."

"She's been around for years. Everybody knows about her. Owns a bar on the South Fork, in Shinnecock. Runs the place herself. Kind of a shit-hole where the commercial salts hang out for their shots and beers. I stopped in for a drink with a guy one time, asked for a martini. She made it for me, said it was the first martini'd been ordered there in nine years. Gives you an idea. Es muy colorful, I suppose, but you have to be pretty desperate for some sauce to belly up to Lulu's bar. Anyhow, she's not a boat, is she?"

"Maybe somebody likes her enough to name a boat after her," I said.

"I already talked to Bill Evans at the Shinnecock marina. If there's a commercial boat called Lulu anyplace around there, he'd know. I'm not so sure Lulu Lumpkin's the kind of woman somebody'd name their boat after. She's not a great beauty, and no kid, either. Tough old broad."

"Could be you're right," I said. "But Lulu's such a curious name these days. Kind of old-time stuff, right? I mean, did you ever know anybody else actually named Lulu?"

"No. So?"

"Such an offbeat name. I know it's a stretch, but what the hell. It's a place to start. Only one I have," I said. "What time does she open, you think?"

"First thing in the morning. Her customers, some of 'em, their breakfast is a cup of coffee and a shot of Seagrams Seven." He looked at his watch, raising up his cigar hand and giving me another whiff that distinctive Napoli aroma. "She's been serving for a couple hours already."

"You know where her place is, right? Come along and show me."

"Got work."

"It's October, Prager. The season is over. Whatever's left to do, your people are doing. Not only don't you, personally, have anything to do, you won't until March."

"Just shows what you know about running a business. Now I understand why that Teague guy in New York has you by the balls."

"I'll buy your lunch," I said. "Hell of an offer, I think."

"A McDonald's Value Meal in Riverhead, you mean? Not likely. I do this, I want to come back on the North Road and get a lobster roll and a slice of that chocolate mud pie. Cost you twenty-five bucks, with the tip, mi compadre. More, if you eat, too. But what the hell, it's not your money, right? You're going to put in for it, anyway."

"We leave in fifteen minutes," I said.

"Why not right now?"

"Because it'll take you that long to smoke up that hideous cigar. You're not getting into my car with that thing."

It hardly mattered that Wally'd finished his smoke and disposed of the butt in the approved GI fashion, pulling it apart and scattering the tobacco. The smell of cigar smoke still clung faintly to him as he sat next to me in the car. "I still smell that cigar," I told him.

"Tough shit." His quick reflex answer. "It goes away. Two hours, tops."

I swung onto Route 27 and headed west toward Shinnecock. There was barely any fog now, because we were away from the water. I said, "What can you tell me about this Lulu?"

Wally thought for a moment, staring ahead at the road. "Every bayman, dock hand and rummy out here seems to know her. Story is, she just showed up one day and bought herself a saloon. It used to belong to John Argyris, an old Greek who figured it was time to pack it in and go back to Athens to die. Along comes Lulu with a handbag stuffed with hundred dollar bills, and the next thing you know, Lulu's behind the bar, and Argyris is on an airplane. That was, like, a dozen years ago."

"Where'd she come from?"

"All kinds of stories. One is she was a madam from Pennsylvania someplace. Another, she was on the lam, embezzled the money from a tire factory in Ohio. And get this. Somebody even said she was the bastard daughter of Lyndon Johnson, and that the bar was paid for with hush money from the Democratic National Committee. All bullshit dreamed up by drunks. The truth is, nobody knows, really. And she's never said. Hey, you want to find out, I think you should ask her."

We drove on until the highway crossed the Shinnecock Canal, a man-made waterway that connects two of Long Island's big bays. Boats can go from the Atlantic Ocean on the south up into Shinnecock Bay, then through the canal, with its lock, into Great Peconic Bay. It's a practical route for boats of all kinds, and Shinnecock is ringed with docks and marinas.

"Turn off here," Wally said. "Then take the third left, and another left. Over there. See it?"

I saw it. An exhausted old building covered in asbestos tile that hadn't been painted in so long it was hard to tell what color it used to be. The sign on the roof still said John Argyris Tavern, no apostrophe, in faded green and blue letters. I had to look hard to decipher it. The car rocked as I drove it across deep ruts in the graveled lot. I parked.

"How do you like it so far?" Wally said.

Though the morning sun was out full, once the tavern door closed behind us, it was late afternoon inside, dismal and totally drained of color. Two grizzled old-timers sat murmuring to each other near the door, as they filled the air with cigarette smoke. There were empty coffee mugs and shot glasses on the pitted wooden table in front of them. The only other customer was an obese woman in a ghastly green housedress who sat at the bar drinking Coors from a long-neck bottle. Her hair looked as though she hadn't combed it since Elvis Presley died.

"That's not her," Wally said, quietly.

"I hope not," I said.

The centerpiece above the bar was an ornate advertising clock, framed in red and purple neon, that said Hale's Pale Ale. I remembered the Hale brand, an extinct regional brew that quenched its last thirst sometime in the late 1970s, I think it was.

A door behind the bar opened and it was the fabled Lulu Lumpkin who appeared, as I could tell by Wally's smile and nod to me. She carried a full pot of coffee. I had to agree with Wally's assessment of her looks. With an ample nose and chin that gave her face the coarse appearance of someone right at home pulling draft beers and breaking up fights, she was not a beauty queen contender. Still, she had a remarkable figure for a woman of what? sixty, maybe more, and an unmistakable come-hither presence. She wore a denim workshirt with sleeves rolled to the elbows, and jeans.

Lulu Lumpkin came from behind the bar and filled the mugs of the two old guys with coffee. "And what can I get for you gents?" she said to us.

"Two coffees," Wally said.

"Got any donuts?" I said.

"You must be lost," she said. "Dunkin Donuts is the one with the big orange sign over in Hampton Bays. This here, where you are, is a tavern, and everything we serve is a liquid of one sort or another. Coffee we can do, though mostly it's a chaser for something stronger."

"Just the coffee, then," I said. "Two black. Little early for stronger."

"Something only a sissy would say, you know that?" She went behind the bar, brought up two mugs, thumped them down and filled them with coffee. She looked at Wally and said, "Him I don't know, but I seen you before, didn't I?"

"Been in a couple of times. You made me a martini once," he said.

"Oh, yeah, right. I remember because it was a real event. Only guy ever ordered one. None before or since." She reached onto the back-bar and pulled out a bottle of dry vermouth. "Same bottle came with the place when I took over. No telling how long it was here before that."

"Could last forever," said Wally.

"It'll last longer than I will, anyway," said Lulu Lumpkin, replacing it. "So how come you two swells wandered in here this hour? I generally get just the hopeless boozers in the morning."

"I wanted to meet you," I told her.

"That's a thrill for me," she said. "Any special reason, or is it just my famous charm and beauty?"

"Because your name is Lulu," Wally said.

Lulu Lumpkin leaned far over the bar and peered into my face. "What is it, you got a thing about my name? A Lulu freak, is that it?"

I'd barely opened my mouth, and already Lulu had me on the ropes. She clearly could be more than the equal of any tough drunk. So feisty you just had to like her. "Lulu's a fine name, a hell of a name," I said. "There's a commercial fishing boat somewhere around here called Lulu, too. I'm trying to find it."

"What, you're trying to find a boat?" she said.

"That's right," I said.

"Look around," she said. "You see any boats in here?"

"I thought you might know. Thought maybe somebody named a boat after you. An admirer."

"I discourage admirers," she said. "I wouldn't let some fool name a boat after me even if he wanted to. Just what I need, a smelly fish boat with my name on it."

"I think you're saying you don't know of any boat named the Lulu," I said.

"I think that's what I'm saying, sport."

Wally sipped on his coffee and grinned at me. "Well, like you told me going in, muchacho, it was a long shot. But I want you to know how much I'm looking forward to that lunch."

Wally may have been ready to give up on Lulu Lumpkin, but I wasn't. Maybe she knew more than she was giving me. I suspected she was a woman who liked to keep her own counsel, as they say. And anyway, bartenders know things. Secrets. "Are you interested in learning why I'm looking for the boat?" I said to her.

"No. Don't tell me."

"Because the guy who owns it has important information I have to find out," I said, shading the truth in case Lulu felt protective. "Maybe you know him."

"What's his name?"

"See, that's my problem. I didn't get his name when I met him. I only know what he looks like. Gangly guy. Big, broad shoulders, way out to here." I saw the expression on Lulu's face start to change. "Kind of a flat, pushed-in mug." There was a glint of recognition that was unmistakable, so I kept on. "Eyes close together. Long yellow hair, kind of ratty. Big snake tattoos on both arms." That did it.

She leaned in close again. "What do you want with him?"

"I told you. He has some information I need. You know him?"

"Information, bullshit, " she said. "The only reason anybody'd want that guy is to beat the bastard to death."

"So you do know him," I said. "No, I don't want to kill him."

"Too bad. Somebody ought to." Lulu poured a mug of coffee for herself, then came out to sit on a barstool next to us. "You're no cop. You're too old for a cop."

"I'm investigating for a big company, a client," I said. I got the feeling she wanted to tell what she knew, so I kept talking. "I think this guy was involved in a death on Shelter Island. Looked like an accident, but I don't think it was. He also tried to kill me. Twice. Tell me about this guy? Who is he?"

"I don't tell anything about anybody. A customer comes in here, even if he's the filthiest wharf rat on Long Island, whatever he does or says, I never repeat it." She stopped, drank from her mug, shook her head. "But I don't do that for Hick Sosenko. Not him. And the guy you described has got to be him. There's nobody else on this earth looks like that."

"What's his name?" Wally said. "Hick — ?"

"Sosenko, " she said. "Absolutely insane son-of-a-bitch. The most unpredictable, most vicious human being I ever met. And we get some rough ones here. He started coming in maybe a year ago. Bad trouble right away. Fierce temper. Start fights for no reason at all. Nearly choked a guy to death once, right on top of this bar, because he didn't like his shirt. And my luck, he was crazy mad for me. Night after night, wouldn't leave me alone. He'd sit there at the bar and sing to me, a song he made up. You know how it went? 'Lulu, I love your titties,' over and over. I told him get out and don't come here no more. But he kept showing up. One night last month he walks in here with a knife on his belt, you know, from fishing. He gets drunk and starts coming after people with the knife. I take my gun from behind the bar and I say get out or I'll shoot you. He just laughs and keeps flashing the knife around. So I shoot him."

"You actually shot him?" Wally said.

"Are you paying attention? I actually did. Just once, grazed his leg. And he walks out under his own steam. You know what? He's back again, bandaged up, limping in here the next night, singing to me. I get out the gun and point it right between those ugly eyes of his. I tell him I'll kill him dead, he doesn't stop bothering me. So he leaves. But he says he'll be back, just loves me so much he can't stay away from me. Right now I'm worried he'll walk back in here one of these days. So I wouldn't be unhappy to have him far away, behind bars, maybe. Or dead."

"Why don't you call the cops, tell them about him?" Wally said.

"Yeah, sure," Lulu said. "That's all my customers got to hear, that I'm talking to cops. Goodbye, Lulu."

"Maybe we can help you, get him out of circulation for you," I said. "Where can we find him?"

She sighed, long and deep. "If I knew, I'd tell you."

"You don't know?" said Wally

"Jesus, you are slow," she said to him. "But what can you expect, somebody who orders fancy drinks."

"So we still don't have a fix on him," Wally said to me.

"I do." It came from the fat lady with the Coors. "I know where Hick Sosenko lives. And I'll tell you."

I turned to face her. "How do you know him?"

She slipped off her barstool and made her way down the bar, her huge stomach leading the way. "Well, he fucks me about once a week or so. Rapes is the right word, I guess, because I don't really want to do it with him. I live up the road from him. He pulls me in when I go past his place. I read in a magazine fucking is fun, but this sure isn't. I'd kind of like it to stop. You might take him out late at night and drop him in the bay. That would be a good way."

"Tell us where he lives," I said.

She did.

Wally and I were about to get back into the car when the door to Lulu's Lumpkin's gin mill opened and she appeared. "Be goddam careful," she called to us. "Hick Sosenko is one dangerous piece of shit."

CHAPTER 7

Grim as Lulu's saloon was, it couldn't begin to reach the depths of dilapidation we found at Hick Sosenko's place.

It was easily the most run-down of the half dozen shacks that lined an unpaved lane, a street that made you feel discontented just to look at it, filled with tall grasses and overgrown shrubs, and dotted with piles of broken furniture, old TV sets and kitchen appliances, and black plastic bags stuffed with things I didn't dare to imagine. To the side of Sosenko's place stood the remains of what I suspected was once a 1969 Ford Fairlane sedan, tires gone now, resting on the rims of its wheels, all the windows broken.

The shack itself was all of fifteen by twenty feet, blackened wood that had never seen paint, with a rusted metal roof. The stairs to a tiny front porch lay in pieces on the ground. A small stool stood in their place, evidently to provide the needed step up or down.

"This sure is a tour through the low-rent district today," Wally said. "I wouldn't want to go in there even if there wasn't some crazy son-of-a-bitch with a gun and a knife inside."

I lifted my jacket up so he could see the .38 in the holster on my hip. "Stay in the car." I got out.

"Don't tell me stay in the car," he said, getting out, too. "Makes me feel like a wimp. However, I'm going to let you lead this operation because of all your professional experience."

We made our way slowly toward the shack. I didn't take my eyes off of the two windows that faced us. I could see no movement inside. "I'm going up. Stay here," I said softly. I saw he was about to argue, so I added, "You're not a wimp. I never said you were a wimp." I took my gun out of its holster and held it down at my side as I stepped on the stool, then onto the porch. Up close now, I could see the door to the shack was barely ajar, maybe half an inch. I stood to the side and rapped on the doorframe. "Sosenko? Hick Sosenko? Time for us to talk."

There wasn't a sound, not from the house, not from anywhere. I reached around from the side and put my toe against the bottom of the door, pushing it open slowly. Raising my .38, I stepped cautiously into the doorway and looked inside.

It was all one room. A filthy mattress on a bedframe, single chair with the upholstery in tatters, TV set with rabbit ears perched on top of two milk crates, half-size refrigerator, two-burner hot-plate, ancient cast-iron sink, small shower unit tucked into a corner, and, right out in the open, a toilet, unflushed since its last use.

There's no place like home.

But Sosenko wasn't there. I holstered my gun. "Nobody home," I said to Wally, but when I turned to face him through the open door, he'd disappeared from the front. I heard his voice calling me. "Come around back. I found Lulu."

When I got off the porch and around the shack, he was holding up a sizeable piece of quarter inch plywood, painted white, on which was lettered the name Lulu. There were pencil mark outlines for the letters, obviously made with the aid of a ruler, filled in with black paint, and nails protruding around the edges of the sign. It was Hick Sosenko's maritime disguise, a sign he'd made to nail onto the stern of another boat, probably his own, to give it a false identity while he was out on the water ending the life of Kenneth Newalis.

"Found it face down in the weeds over there," Wally said.

"He really does have a thing for Lulu, doesn't he? What a guy."

We both sensed a barely audible approach through the high grass. Someone was moving toward us from around the far corner of the shack. I pulled my gun out of its holster and raised it, looking over the barrel as I waited. The noise continued, an uneven rustling, as if someone were deliberately kicking at the undergrowth. But no one came. Wally glanced at me, shrugging. What to do? I put out my free hand, palm down. Wait.

Finally our visitor appeared, turning the corner, then stopping dead still, as he saw my gun pointed at him. "You going to shoot me, give me a minute to get ready," he said, after a reflective pause.

He was on crutches, a pot-bellied old man with a wild growth of mottled gray beard on his chin, and no hair at all on his head. He wore cheap rubber sandals, faded brown pants and a shirt that displayed the residue of a week's meals. He looked skyward, as though for inspiration, then put his hands together in an attitude of prayer. He glanced over at us to make sure we were paying attention. "Dear Lord, if you're going to take me now, I sure would appreciate having a ready supply of Old Crow bourbon waiting for me in my heavenly home. And it would be nice if I could have a friendly old lady who's got some good fucks left in her. Amen."

Once again I put my gun in its holster.

"Good thing he's not going to send you to your reward right now, amigo," Wally told him. "Looks to me like you couldn't handle that old lady if you got her."

"Hard to tell, because I don't receive that many offers. But I could try," he said. He approached us at an incredibly slow pace, pushing the grasses away with his crutches as he came. "Looking for Hick?"

"That's right," I said.

"With a gun," he said.

"We have to talk to him, but they say he can get nasty," I said. "You live here?"

"Over there. I'm Hick's neighbor." He pointed at a shack only marginally less hideous than the one we stood behind. "Talk to him? That mean you're not here to shoot him?"

"Not unless I have to," I said.

"That's a disappointment," he said. "But," he paused for effect, "life is a compromise."

"We thought he was home," Wally said. "Door unlocked, and all."

"Door's never locked. There is no lock." He looked at me. "You went inside. See anything anybody'd be desperate enough to steal?"

"You know where Sosenko went?" I said.

"He doesn't tell me where he goes. Matter of fact, he doesn't say boo to me. A lot of the time he's at his boat, the Tiderunner, just there at the dock." He pointed down the lane with one of his crutches. "But he's not there now."

"How do you know?" I said.

"Saw him drive off in his pickup, first thing."

"But his boat, it would be at the dock now?" I said. I gave Wally a look that told him I'd like to check it out.

"Bound to be," the old man said. "Look, if you catch up with Hick, don't let him know I talked to you. Unless you're set to kill the bastard. Then I'd appreciate it if you'd tell him it was me just before you do him in. Long as he can never come looking for me, I'd kind of like him to know it was me put you onto him." He turned and began his slow motion journey back to his own shack. "Watch yourselves," he said as he moved along.

Tiderunner was Lulu, all right. We could see the marks where the phony name had been nailed to the stern of the shabby wooden boat, then pried off later. We boarded to take a better look inside, but found the door to the wheelhouse secured with a padlock. Seemed Hick Sosenko worried more about his boat than he did his home.

"No problemo," Wally said. "I'll get a screwdriver or something from the car, pop the hasp."

"Don't bother," I said. "I see what I need to see. Look on the deck inside."

Wally pressed his forehead against a wheelhouse window, using his hands to keep reflections on the glass from obscuring his vision. "Scuba tank and regulator. And flippers."

"He changed the name of the boat, in case anybody might see it," I said. "He anchored near the Julian place, and when Newalis went into the water, he did, too, with scuba and flippers, on the Greenport side of the boat where nobody could see him. He pulled the poor bastard under and drowned him. Then he got back on the boat and took off. It was all planned out."

"Adds up," Wally said.

"But why did he do it, anyway?" I said. "And why did he return? He was back there hours later, when I arrived. Doesn't make sense."

CHAPTER 8

Time was you could get a lobster roll for four bucks, complete with the little paper cup of cole slaw. Now the menu begged the subject of money entirely with the announcement "market price," which was supposed to mean the price of a lobster roll changed with what the restaurant had to pay for the lobster that went into it. What it really meant was that a lobster roll cost more every time you ordered one. Today it was fourteen ninety-five.

Which didn't stop Wally Prager from relishing his, his long fingers covered with the mayonnaise that leaked out of the roll, his mouth stuffed with lobster salad. "I never get tired of these," he said, "especially when you're buying." He wiped his hands on a paper napkin and extracted slaw from its cup with a fork. "So? Que pasa? Now you know who he is and where he lives, you could just wait till he shows up and grab him, shoot him, whatever."

I finished the remains of the clam chowder that was my lunch, tilting the bowl to get the last spoonful. "Maybe. Or maybe he won't show up there anymore."

"The guy is a bayman. All he has in his miserable life is his shack and his boat. Can't believe he'd just walk away from all he owns," Wally said.

"He has a truck, too, don't forget. Guy like that, he could go anyplace, live anyplace. Live in his truck, if he had to. He knows I'm looking for him. And that I have a gun."

"Yeah, but he doesn't know Lulu Lumpkin fingered him. And he still thinks you're looking for a boat called Lulu." Wally dispatched the last of his lobster roll, then raised his hand to summon our waitress away from the handsome bus boy she had cornered nearby. "A slice of that chocolate mud pie, and another iced tea," he told her. Then to me, "You want dessert?"

"No, but it's thoughtful of you to ask," I said. The waitress departed for the kitchen. "Look, Sosenko is plugged in out here. He could find out what we've learned. Don't forget, Lulu knows, the fat lady at the bar knows. And the guy with the crutches, he knows, too."

"You think Sosenko's smart enough to get the picture? People seem to detest him so much, they might not volunteer to tell him anything." Wally said. "He could go back home figuring he's OK there."

"But you just know there's going to be a buzz about us poking around, asking questions. These low-lifes, they know each other, talk to each other," I said. "My guess is Sosenko knows how to make people talk, even if they'd rather not. Anyway, he may have a reason for what he's doing that's bigger than a shack and an old boat."

"Like what?"

"I don't know yet. Something." I took out my cell phone. "I have to call Hector Alzarez."

"The guy who asked for you to go to Shelter?"

I nodded. I dialed and waited. By the time I had Hector on the other end, Wally's dessert and iced tea appeared. I watched him eye the chocolate concoction for a moment, anticipating the lusciousness of it all. It was almost with a sense of reverence, eyes closed, that he finally took a bite. It was worth paying for the pie just to watch him eat it.

"Lisa Harper tell you about last night, about the shooting?" I said into the phone.

"She told me. Awful story. You were right. Something

major is going on," Hector said. "Lisa told me you weren't sure whether the shooter was after her or you,"

"I still don't know. But I found out who he is. And I'm sure he's the same one killed Newalis." Hector listened in silence as I gave him the whole story. "So I know the who, and the how, but not the why. Could be there's a connection of some kind with Julian Communications. Let's give it a shot. Run the name Sosenko through your computer, all your databases. Customers, employees, suppliers, wherever there are lists of names. He's called Hick, but I can't believe that's a real name. Just try Sosenko."

"I'll have that done right now," Hector said. There was a pause that told me he was about to get into something awkward. "Look, I hate to ask you to do this." Another pause.

"But you're not going to let that stand in your way," I said.

"I need you to come to New York. I know you're trying to put the city behind you, but Arthur Brody wants to talk to you. In person, not over the phone," Hector said. "I tried to keep him out of it. I'm not comfortable dealing with Ingo on one hand and Brody on the other. Not the way things are between them. But the news about Newalis is all over the company, and I felt I had to tell Brody about the shooting last night. He's the president, right? And he asked for you. Come in tomorrow morning." His tone told me it was more than a suggestion.

"What does he want me for?" I said

"It's best you hear that directly from him."

"You know, of course, that I don't want to do this. Come to New York, talk to Brady, dig myself in deeper."

"Yes, I know. But we need you. I need you."

"The truth is, you need more than me. This is a dangerous situation, and if I had to bet, I'd say it'll get worse. There should be cops on this case. Or more protection from Empire."

"Ingo won't do that. Neither will Brody. Not yet. Not with $800 million at stake. Ben, please."

"All right," I said, hating to hear myself agree. "I'll be there at 11."

"Come in and see me first. I'll tell Brody you'll be in his office at 11:30. If we find anything about this Sosenko, I'll have the information when you get here. And my friend — thank you."

Wally had nearly done away with his pie by the time I was finished with Hector. "Trip to New York? What, tomorrow?" he said.

"They're pulling me in tighter and they won't let me go. First Teague and now Hector. And it's all on me because they won't bring in the cops, or even more people from Empire. It's an invitation to a disaster, and it'll be my fault. Goddamn, I hate this."

Wally scraped the last trace of chocolate off his plate, then licked his fork. "That's what happens when you make yourself indispensable. You're the one they ask for, and your ass is on the line all the time. You should do what I do. Pretend you're incompetent." He leaned back in his chair and laced his fingers across his stomach. "I'll say this one last time. I wouldn't be so quick to walk away from that Sosenko guy's shack. Or Lulu's saloon, for that matter. Where else is he going to go? He'll show up. Take that wise advice in payment for a swell lunch." He smiled. "I'd have another piece of pie, compadre, but I don't want to ruin my dinner."

I thought Wally just might be right, so I spent the evening in Shinnecock, checking Lulu's place three different times, with quiet looks inside, and watching the shack from my car the rest of the time. I stayed at it until midnight, but there was no sign of Sosenko or a rusty Dodge pickup. Wally was wrong on this one, and I was wrong for thinking he might be right. And for this, amigo, I gave up an evening with Alicia.

It was one in the morning by the time I climbed into bed, and I knew there was no way I was climbing out again at four-thirty to make the only morning train from Greenport at five-twenty. Driving the hundred miles to New York was another unappetizing option. Early morning traffic was wicked on the Long Island Expressway, and once you managed to get into Manhattan, impossible. Which only left driving an hour to Ronkonkoma, halfway to the city, and taking a train from there, where they run to Penn Station every half hour. Not my most enthusiastic choice, either, but at least I'd get to sleep till seven.

I was about to leave the house in the morning when I saw the light flashing on my answering machine, something I'd overlooked in my hurry to get to bed the night before. I knew it had to be a message from Roger Teague, and it was. A bad-tempered communication delivered in his customary snotty tone. What did I find when I got to Shelter Island? What was I doing? Why hadn't I reported to him? And had I forgotten how important Julian Communications was to all of us?

Much as I wanted never to speak another word to Teague, I knew I'd better steel myself against his incivility and fill him in. I suspected I was likely to need his help before this business was over. And beside, a call to him on my cell phone would sharpen my wits for the rest of the day's confrontations. Something challenging to pass the time once I got on the train.

I knew he'd be at his desk. He was always conspicuously in place by eight AM, so he could cast a superior look at each staff member who arrived to begin the day's work. If you walked through the door before nine, it still didn't earn you any points from Teague. In his mind, the only thing that really mattered was: he was there before you were. He used to give me that look when I came in, too. And I was the boss back then.

Everyone called him Teague. I'd been as close to him as anyone, and I never called him Roger. He wasn't a first name guy. That would have implied some kind of cordiality, and it simply wasn't there. From the first, he was cold, vulgar, egotistical and unfailingly severe. But he was smart as hell. Nobody could outwit him. And he was one of those rare people clients trust precisely because they're so blunt. Five minutes with him, and you knew he wouldn't take crap from anyone, and your company was safe with him. That's why I'd hired him, then made him a partner four years later.

Nevertheless, these days I thought he was a prick. The day we signed my buyout deal he started treating me not as a former colleague, but an indentured servant: Do what I tell you, or you don't get your money. Hardly what an aging retiree with sluggish arteries likes to hear.

I got on the train at the Ronkonkoma station and stood in the vestibule of my car to get what little privacy can be found on the Long Island Railroad. When we were well under way I took out my cell phone and called Teague.

"Why didn't you wait a few days longer to get back to me? After all, it's only our biggest fucking client you're playing around with," he told me on the phone.

"Is that what I'm doing, playing around? You're right, Teague. It's a kind of game with me. I really enjoy going on errands for you, getting the run-around from Ingo Julian, chasing after some evil son-of-a-bitch who keeps trying to shoot me. It's comforting to know I can still be useful, even though I'm retired. Fills up my day for me. I get involved like this, I wonder where the time goes, sometimes."

"Where are you?"

"I'm on a train just passing Jericho. On my way in to Julian Communications for a command performance. I've been summoned by Arthur Brody."

"Brody? Why?"

"I won't know till I get there," I said.

"I'll meet you. Go in with you."

"You can't."

"Why not?"

I turned toward the window in the door and watched the Long Island countryside speeding past. "Because," I said, in my most sincere, most measured tone, "everyone at Julian has made it very clear that right now they want only me. Maybe it's because they share my view that you are a loathsome prick. I'm terribly sorry for you, Teague. It must be hard to accept that kind of rejection at your high level. But you did get me into this, so you'll just have to let me handle it. I'll call you if I need you." There, I thought, that should push his buttons for him. And it did.

"Don't you fuck this up, you hear." He was shouting now. "I want to know everything that's happened, everything that's going on. You come over here as soon as you've finished with Brody."

"Can't do that," I said. "I don't work there, and don't start thinking I do. You want to see me, you'll have to come uptown. You know what? You could buy me a nice lunch. And we could talk. Say one o'clock?"

"I don't eat lunch. You know that."

"But I do."

I could hear him mumbling to himself. Then, "Meet me in front of the big library, by the lion on the right. I'll buy you a hot dog."

"And a soda?" I said. But he was gone.

CHAPTER 9

When you come to New York City every day, it doesn't seem to change. It's like looking into the mirror each morning, and thinking you look exactly as you did the day before. But if somehow you looked in the mirror only once every six months, you'd know you'd changed.

As I walked from Penn Station to the Julian Communications offices at Forty-Eighth Street and Park Avenue, it was like that. I hadn't been in New York in six months, and all those little changes to the midtown area had added up. There was a new Korean greengrocer on Avenue of the Americas, with boxes of perfect fruits and vegetables displayed outside on the sidewalk. An old building on Madison Avenue had had an all-glass face-lift, and looked brand new. A busy lunchroom that had been on Forty-Seventh Street forever was now a jewelry store. The midtown that had always been so familiar to me was alien and unfriendly this morning. I couldn't help but think I'd rather be fishing.

I started out briskly at Penn Station, feeling confident that my coronary system was prepared for some walking. Mistake. By the time I reached Fifth Avenue I had slowed to a stroll, and when I finally got to Park and Forty-Eighth, I was experiencing what I knew as moderate distress — including the strong desire to sit down on the curb. But I remained upright, leaning on the handrail that led up the stairs into the building, trying to look as though I was in control, while I considered whether to take a nitroglycerin pill or not. I decided not, because I could feel myself beginning to stabilize. After five minutes of quiet standing, I made my way, shaky but resolute, up the stairs, through the lobby and into an elevator. I stepped out onto the thirty-sixth floor ten minutes late. Couldn't be helped. Sorry.

This was the topmost of the four complete floors Julian Communications occupied in this building. While there were units of Julian elsewhere in New York, and in a half dozen other cities across the country, it was from here that the Julian brass administered the complex of companies. Here on the thirty-sixth floor was where the big wheels turned, where Ingo and Brody and their staffs sent directives to the floors below, and from there out into the world. Here at the top it was all deep carpets and teak and marble and rich, muted colors.

And intrigue. Which I was sure was about to swallow me whole.

Hector came around his desk and closed his office door behind me as soon as I came in. "You look drained," he said, motioning me into an armchair. "Something happen to you?"

"Yeah. My father had a bum circulatory system, and he passed it on to me."

"What?"

"Nothing. I'm dealing with it," I said. "Did you get a computer hit on Hick Sosenko?"

"Yes." He pulled an armchair next to mine and sat. That was Hector's style, to sit next to you rather than behind his desk. Put himself on your side right away, instead of putting a barrier between the two of you. "He used to work for us, at one of our companies." He reached over to the desk and picked up a file folder, then handed it to me. "It's all in here, but I can tell you the whole story in two minutes. Sosenko — his name is

Herman Sosenko, by the way — worked as a warehouse grunt at Rainbow Graphics, a big printing shop on Long Island. We acquired Rainbow eight years ago to print our women's magazines. Sosenko's employee evaluation sheet says he was a horror story from the day he showed up. He fought about everything, threatened people, scared the hell out of every woman came near him. Finally his supervisor said no more of this, and told Sosenko he was fired. Sosenko went nuts, threw the supervisor off the loading dock, jumped down after him and beat on him with a hammer. Broke his collar bone and two ribs."

"That's our boy. Fits with everything else I've heard about him," I said.

"There's more," Hector said. "At first the company didn't want to make a big thing out of it. You know, don't shake up the troops, just let it blow away. Even the supervisor finally agreed that the important thing was that the guy was out of the company."

Hector paused to take a breath, so I took the opportunity to say "But?" There's always a *but* in stories like this.

"But then Ingo heard about it," Hector continued. "He was furious. He called in the police and insisted that Sosenko be prosecuted. Sosenko wouldn't have had a prayer at a trial, and the public defender pled him guilty to assault with a deadly weapon. Bottom line, Sosenko got one to three. And he was such a bad-ass in prison that he served every last day of the three years."

"So? You telling me Sosenko is getting even now for the time he spent in prison?"

"Looks like it."

"And this all happened when?" I said.

"The assault?" He took the file folder back from me and thumbed through the papers inside. "It'll be six years ago in

January. That would make it just a month before I joined the company."

"So Sosenko's been out of the slammer for nearly three years, now, right?" I said. "You have to wonder why he's waited all this time to make his move."

Hector shrugged. "Maybe it's been on his mind, preyed on him, finally pushed him over the edge."

"He had three years in prison to think about it. Why start killing people now, just like that? Something must have happened." I got up and walked to the window. Hector's office had a fabulous vista of the west side cityscape, to the Hudson River and beyond, into New Jersey. "There's something else that mystifies me. Sosenko is an appalling excuse for a human being. He's threatened people, beaten people, caused big trouble wherever he's gone. But he hadn't actually killed anybody that we know of, not till now."

"Matter of time," Hector said. "It's not as though he just suddenly turned vicious. Seems like he was born vicious. He was a killer waiting to happen."

"Maybe." I looked down onto Madison Avenue, the faraway people and trucks and taxis. Up here you couldn't hear a sound. Julian Communications was above all that street hustle. "How old is he? Do we know?"

Hector searched through the folder again. "Six years ago he was thirty-five. He's forty-one."

"On the old side to do a first killing. Guys like him, animals, mostly they're younger," I said. "Anyway, now we're assuming he's after Ingo, looking for revenge. That means when he drowned Newalis, it was by mistake. Thought it was Ingo out there for his usual afternoon swim. He must have been watching Ingo for a while, to know about that. But me, I'm a problem for him, because I got a look at him out there. That's why he wants to make me go away, too, finish what he tried to do out on the water. And if I'm right, then he wasn't after Lisa.

It was me he wanted to shoot. He probably followed her to my door."

Hector got up and came to stand at my side. "Sounds right," he said, putting his hand on my shoulder as we looked out at the skyline together. "But it's wrong."

"Me wrong, really?" I said. "Hard to believe."

"Sosenko was stalking Arthur Brody. That's what Brody's going to tell you about, why he asked you to come in today. It's not just Ingo that this guy wants to kill. He has a hard-on for the whole company. It seems we're in a war. Us against Sosenko."

"You believe that?" I said.

"I think I do."

"If you're right, we need help. I can't protect everybody."

He gave me back the folder, and steered me toward the door. "Talk to Brody. I'll take you to his office."

The huge corner office was a poem to minimalism. An endless expanse of carpet with only a pair of sofas in the way as I crossed the room. Unadorned windows looking on the west with the same view Hector had, and on the north all the way to the George Washington Bridge uptown. A massive desk, bare except for a pad of lined paper and a chrome cup filled with freshly sharpened wooden pencils, all exactly the same length. Evidently Mr. Brody did not have pencils re-sharpened. Used just once, then given to the needy.

One look at the man and I understood the office. Nothing about him that might be considered adornment. Dark blue suit, white, medium-collar shirt, modest striped tie, and the plainest of black shoes, buffed to a shine that rivaled patent leather. In fact, the whole package looked so austere and perfectly turned out, put a coffin behind him and you'd take him for a funeral director.

Which he wasn't. He *was* the number two guy in a decent-size communications conglomerate, a player in publishing, broadcasting, telecommunications and God-knows-what else.

He stood in front of his desk with his hand out to shake mine, drawing me toward him. When I finally got there, his grip was resolute and dry, firm without being overbearing. Presidential. My reaction in about a second and a half. "You're good to come in. I know you don't like to travel to the city," he said.

I didn't protest, because it was true and we both knew it. Better to forget the niceties and get to the essential stuff. "Tell me why you wanted to see me."

He went behind his big desk and sat, and I took one of the three chairs facing him. I must have been ten feet away, looking across at him. "I know about Sosenko and the Newalis drowning and the shooting at your house. This man Sosenko has a vendetta against Julian Communications for the time he spent in prison. And I'm on his list — what do they say? his hit list. He's been after me."

"Tell me," I said. "Where and when did you see him? And how do you know it was Sosenko?"

"I noticed him yesterday in the lobby downstairs. He seemed to take a great interest in me when I came out of the elevator. I didn't know it was Sosenko, but I thought he was out of place around here. Dirty clothes and hair, unshaven, tattoos. A frightening look about the man. You don't see that in this building." Brody plucked a pencil from the cup on his desk and began writing on the pad as he spoke.

"So why do you think it was Sosenko?"

He set his pencil down and pointed to the folder in my lap. "That's the file Hector put together for you? Look inside. There's an employee identification photo of the man."

I did, and there was. Younger than he looked now, but

no prettier.

Brody started writing again. "Once Hector showed me the photo, I thought to myself it was the same person I'd seen in the lobby."

"Did you tell Hector?"

"No. At that point I wasn't certain. I didn't see the picture until later." Still writing, which was beginning to annoy me.

"Forgive me, but I just have to ask this," I said. "How are you able to talk and write at the same time."

He looked up and smiled, the first flicker of warmth I'd seen from him. Then he went back to his writing. "It's something I've always been able to do, listen and talk with half my brain, and write with the other half. Everything important, I make notes as I go. Helps me to focus. And to remember. People I work with have learned to indulge me this practice. Right now I'm setting down the key points of our discussion. Does it bother you?"

"It does, actually," I told him, but he didn't stop. "So, after you saw this photo, you thought the man in the lobby was the same guy. Were you sure?'

"Absolutely sure? I suppose not. Reasonably certain? Yes. But then I saw him again, twice. Then I was sure it was him, and he was following me. He was outside on Park Avenue at six-thirty last night when the limo picked me up to drive me to my apartment. He walked right up to the car while I was getting in."

"Did he say anything? Threaten you?"

"No. He just stood there, closer than you are now, and he watched me till the car drove off." He set his pencil to the side of the desk and took a fresh one.

"You saw him twice, you said."

"Last night, again. My sister in New Jersey invited me for a late dinner. I took my own car out of my building's parking garage and headed for the Lincoln Tunnel. I only went a few blocks when I had to stop for a red light. I saw him pull up right next to me. He was driving some old, beat-up truck. I thought I saw a gun, a rifle, in his hands. I didn't wait to find out. I ran the light. So did he. I could see him in the mirror. I went through the tunnel, and he was maybe six or seven cars behind me. In the end, I finally lost him on the Garden State Parkway. It was quite an adventure."

"Adventure? Mr. Brody, you have to put down the pencil and look at me," I said. He did. "We know how dangerous Sosenko is. We can't play games with this situation, or more people are going to get killed. And you seem to be right up there at the top of the list. We have to call the police and they have to catch this guy."

"No, Mr. Seidenberg," he said "You have to catch this guy. Quietly. I know you understand why."

"I can't believe your attitude toward this situation, you and Ingo Julian and Hector. There's a brutal son-of-a-bitch with a gun who's out to kill everybody, and all you can think about is your stock offering."

"Eight hundred million dollars, Mr. Seidenberg. Many people have risked their lives for a lot less. In any case, Hector's told us how good you are. We think you can do it."

"Hector doesn't know how good I am. He knows how good I used to be," I said. "I've gone to fat, and I have a heart problem and I can't run very fast any more. Are you willing to bet your life that I can get your bad guy for you?"

Arthur Brody folded his hands on the desk in front of him. "Yes. You can and you will. I know you're only involved in this because Roger Teague has pressured you to do it. The best you'll get from Teague is that he pays up what he owes you. I think it's only fair that we, how do they say? sweeten the pot for you. You, personally, that is, not Empire Security." He opened a drawer in his desk, took out an envelope and pushed it across to me. "This is fifty thousand dollars. All cash. It's a partial payment on your fee of one hundred thousand dollars for special security consulting. You'll receive the fifty thousand balance when Sosenko is caught. Or killed, if that's the way it turns out."

"Killed? You expect me to kill Sosenko for you?"

"Of course not. But, as you say, he's a brutal son-of-a-bitch with a gun. And you are armed too, are you not?"

"And push could come to shove, is that it?"

"There's always that possibility."

"I don't think I want to do this," I said. "Got the feeling I'll end up in jail, or very cold on a gurney. Anyway, I'm an investigator — retired — not an assassin."

"You might want to think this through a bit more clearly, Mr. Seidenberg."

"Oh?"

"Just consider, if you abandon the case, Julian Communications fires Empire as its security agency, and then Teague writes you off. So you lose. But if you bring this case to a quiet conclusion, Empire stays, Teague pays you what he owes you, and we give you an extra hundred thousand that Teague knows nothing about. You win." He came around the desk and stood there in front of me, perfectly composed, every hair in place. "Take the envelope."

"Only if you understand I'm not going to hunt Sosenko down and kill him for you. My line is security, that's all."

"Understood." With the forefinger of one hand, he carefully pushed the envelope to the edge of the desk, closer to me. I took it and tucked it into my breast pocket.

I grew uneasy having Brody look down at me, so I stood to face him. "Does Ingo Julian know about this?"

"Why do you ask?" he said.

"Word is you two don't talk much anymore. If you have a problem with each other, I don't want to be in the middle of it."

"We have some serious differences of opinion. But not on this. We're agreed that this IPO has to happen. It will make Ingo very, very rich."

"And you?"

"It will only make me very rich." He held out his hand and I shook it. "Stay connected to Hector," he said. "Let him know everything."

I stepped into the corridor wondering whether to somehow start tracking Sosenko or to grab a taxi to JFK airport and get on a plane for Sri Lanka. In just a few days I'd gone from contented fisherman to the object of a no-way-out manipulation, squeezed first by Roger Teague and now by Arthur Brody. Teague was on his way to meet me at the library right now, to buy me a hot dog and pump me for information. Should I tell him about Brody?

I had very little time to ponder these issues. Because I spied Sosenko's dirty jeans as soon as I entered the waiting area. He was sitting near the elevators, the only person in an island of leather chairs and glass coffee tables. I couldn't see his face or upper body because he held a newspaper up in front of himself, but you couldn't miss the tattoos. Tilted against the chair in which he sat was a large black portfolio case.

Big enough to hold a rifle, I thought.

I approached him slowly, feeling under my jacket for the gun at my hip. He sensed me coming. He looked over the top of his paper, then threw it aside and rose in an instant. He grabbed the portfolio case, ran to the exit sign at the far end of the waiting area, opened the fire door and disappeared through it, all before I could free my gun from its holster.

CHAPTER 10

It took me only two labored flights of stairs to confirm that a fifty-six-year-old with angina didn't have a chance of catching a forty-one-year-old who was fit, determined and mean. There was no question who would win this sprint down to the ground floor. Already Sosenko's clattering on the stairs grew fainter as he pulled away from me. In another minute it would be a runaway for him.

What I needed most was help, somebody waiting in the lobby to grab him when he finally appeared. But there was no help. It was just me chasing Sosenko in a high building, as in a bad dream. With the instant clarity that comes with desperation, I saw that my only chance to nail him was to make it to the lobby before he did. If he got there first, he'd be out the door onto Park, or maybe Forty-Eighth.

That meant my taking the elevator, and trying to get to the bottom while he was still dashing down the stairs. I had no way of knowing whether he'd short circuit me by taking the elevator route, too, but he hadn't yet, because I continued to hear him in the stairwell below me.

OK, new game plan. A poor chance, but better than none. Not that I really had a choice any more. Every breath was a struggle, and continuing the chase on foot was no longer an option.

The sign on the stairwell door said I was at the thirty-second floor. I pulled the door open and stepped from the dim light into a multi-colored expanse of Tokyo that had somehow been transplanted into midtown Manhattan. There was neon everywhere, reflected in polished chrome panels. The largest spelled out Doi Electronics in blue and white. An adjacent wall was made up entirely of TV monitors, floor to ceiling, with images of electronic devices and abstract shapes shifting in changing patterns to music. This waiting area was beyond dazzling, but the men waiting in it couldn't have been drearier, all in their dark suits, with attaché cases close at hand, staring patiently ahead. All were Asian, Japanese, I thought. Two more Japanese men stood waiting for an elevator, scanning the floor indicators above the six sets of doors.

I suspected the gun in my hand might be misunderstood, so I tucked it away. I hurried toward the bank of elevators, while my heart continued to issue serious warnings, and joined the two men who were waiting. I saw that both the up and the down call buttons were lit, and said a silent prayer that the down elevator would come first.

Which it did. An elevator arrived and the down button went dark. All three of us stepped inside, making me wonder, if we were all going down, who had pushed the up button? Instantly one of my elevator companions, a short man with a narrow, doleful face, began hammering with his closed hand on the destination button for the forty-first floor. The door to our car closed, then opened, then closed again. And the car began to rise.

The short man's face wrinkled into an unattractive smile. The little shit was beaming because he'd outwitted the control system, and made a down elevator go up, instead. I felt a strong inclination to take out my gun and stick it in his nose, but I knew that while it would make me feel better, it wouldn't get me to the ground floor any faster. Instead, I made my angriest face and said, "I have to go down. Down, not up."

The man smiled again and said something in Japanese. The other man stepped in to translate. "He says thank you for being patient. He must get to important meeting."

"Tell him to go fuck himself."

The translator was horrified. "I cannot tell him that."

"Why not? You didn't want to go up, either, did you?" The frustration wasn't doing my arteries any good.

"That is not a reason to be impolite," he said. "One must have patience."

Yeah, right. Patience is my middle name. What floor was Sosenko passing now, I wondered as the door to our car opened on forty-one and the little shit got out, then turned and made a barely perceptible bow toward us.

"You see," the translator said, as the door closed and we began to descend, "he honors us for helping him."

"In that case, you did right by not telling him to go fuck himself," I said. I massaged my chest and took a deep breath, hoping I could somehow coax my circulatory system back to some shade of normal before we got to the ground floor. The process didn't seem to work.

We stopped at thirty-nine, thirty-one and twenty-seven. At each floor the doors opened but nobody was there, despite the fact that it was lunchtime, a period when elevators are normally in demand. There are people in this world who push buttons to make elevators stop, just for the sheer hell of it.

The rest of the ride was an express. When the doors finally opened in the building lobby, my friendly translator scurried away without looking back, obviously pleased to escape from me. How long had it taken, this ride with its unscheduled detour and false stops? Was Sosenko still on his way down, or already out one of the doors and now three blocks away? Was it possible he took the elevator route and had even more delays than I did? Maybe his elevator had to stop at every floor. Or maybe he's still in the stairwell. Many possibilities.

Ah-so.

I looked around me. Elevators were opening, and

passengers hurrying out. I thought if I stood where I was, in front of the elevators and within sight of the stairwell exit, Sosenko just might pass by on his way to the Park Avenue doors. Then I would — what? Slug him? Shoot him? I'd deal with that. Find him first.

Trouble was, these weren't the only elevators. This bank serviced just the top floors, twenty-three through forty-two. Those that went from the ground to twenty-two were across the lobby, on the other side of a marble partition. What if Sosenko had cut out of the stairwell and taken an elevator at a lower floor? Then he'd most likely leave through the Forty-Eighth Street exit. If I stood where I was, I'd never see him. There was no vantage point where I could watch it all at once. The lobby was simply too big.

I decided to play the odds and stay put. Watching the stairwell exit plus a bank of elevators was a better bet than watching a bank of elevators alone. Nice reasoning, but sorry, no payoff. Ten minutes and hundreds of people passed, but not one of them was Hick Sosenko.

It didn't look as though today was my day to grab a piece of Sosenko, or get to feel just a little bit worthy of the fifty thousand dollars in my pocket. But I glanced out toward Park Avenue and all that changed.

There he was, standing just outside the Park exit looking in, distorted through the curved glass of the revolving door enclosures. But it was Sosenko, no question. The brazen son-of-a-bitch stood there holding the big portfolio case, as if waiting for me to spot him, daring me to chase him.

I headed for the door. He waited till I was halfway there, as though he was giving me a handicap, before he walked off to the right, down Park toward the Helmsley Building. He wasn't running from me. He was taunting me, staying just ahead of me, defying me to follow him.

Which I did, willing myself to run the first few steps down Park until my constricting arteries screamed an order to stop, which I considered, then disobeyed. Instead, I made what I thought was a necessary compromise, and slowed to a walk. I couldn't go any faster, but I refused to stop. Best I could do.

Some chase. Sosenko dancing around up ahead, turning every ten seconds to make sure I was still there, and me dragging myself doggedly along after him, hoping this wouldn't end with giving him the satisfaction of watching me expire on a crowded New York sidewalk, without a shot being fired.

He crossed Forty-Sixth Street and entered one of the open pedestrian arcades that runs through the Helmsley Building. I followed, stiff-legged and wobbly, my arms swinging wide in an effort to maintain what little momentum I had, breathing heavily through my wide open mouth, perspiration pouring off my face. People were gaping at me. You don't see something every day as grotesque as I was.

By the time I emerged through the arcade onto Forty-Fifth, Sosenko was entering the Met Life Building across the street, holding a door open and waiting for me to get closer before he slipped inside and let the door shut behind him. Drawing me on, the bastard, hoping I'd cave in. Fat chance. I wouldn't give him the satisfaction.

But how did he know he could play this game with me? Did he take a look at me and figure I was too old and fat to give him any serious competition? Or did somebody who knew tip him off about my little cardiac problem? And why would he take the trouble to goad me, anyway? Maybe for the same reason malicious little boys pull the wings off of flies.

I crossed Forty-Fifth and stumbled into the packed Met Life lobby. The building was emptying out for lunch, and the foot traffic was against me. I thought I saw Sosenko bobbing up ahead as he bucked the traffic, too, but when I finally reached the back end of the lobby, and the crowd began to clear, I couldn't find him. Only one place he could be now, down one of the escalators into Grand Central Station. Yes, and there he was, already standing at the bottom, on the edge of Grand Central's cavernous main concourse, looking up, waiting for me. I stepped on an escalator filled with people, watching Sosenko as I descended. He actually grinned at me, pointing first one way, then another, then another. Which way should we go now? No way you can catch me, but keep on trying. Till you drop.

He was on the move again. By the time I stepped off the escalator, he was starting down a stairway that led to the lower concourse.

What now? A tour of Grand Central? Out onto Lexington Avenue? Uptown to the Museum of Modern Art? Was he betting the chase would do me in, or was he deliberately leading me to a convenient place to kill me himself?

Sosenko could keep up this craziness a lot longer than I could. And even if I did manage to catch up to him, what could I do? Pull my gun and make a citizen's arrest? He'd open that portfolio case, take out the rifle I knew was in it, and we'd have our own private war on the East Side of Manhattan.

I couldn't stay with him much longer. My legs weighed three hundred pounds. Each. My fingers tingled. My eyes hurt. And there was a sense of dread I'd never felt before. If I cashed in right here, right now, it wouldn't be for lack of my body's warnings.

I stopped. I told myself discretion was the better part of valor. I told myself I'd like to go back to Long Island and make love to Alicia. I told myself I'd get Sosenko soon, anyway. Let him go.

I turned and got on an up escalator, drained but relieved, feeling the knots inside me begin to ease, just a little. My watch told me it was 1:25. Which meant that Teague had been pacing in front of the library, watching for me, for nearly a half hour. By now he would be, as Wally Prager liked to say, red-faced and bug-eyed.

Tough.

Back through the Met Life lobby and out onto Forty-Fifth,

then west to Fifth Avenue. Walking slowly, breathing deeply.

He'd doubled back and followed me. I felt his hand on my shoulder when I stopped for a red light at Fifth and Forty-Third. "Hey, fat-ass, don't you want to play no more?" Sosenko said, his voice higher than a man who looked like that should have. "You're pitiful, you know that? Gonna put you outta your fuckin misery. Pretty soon, now." He didn't just look dirty, he smelled dirty.

"We know who you are," I said. "We know what you're doing. We're going to track you down and you just might make me kill you."

"Well, I'm standin next to you right now, old man. Your big fuckin chance. Why don't you take out your piece and blow me away?" Another surprise: his laugh was a kind of juvenile giggle, high-pitched and discordant. "Better lock your doors," he said. He made a face, and turned back up Fifth Avenue. I walked on, quite certain now that I didn't know half of this story yet.

I could see Teague standing in front of the library with his fists on his hips. "Forty-five minutes I've been standing here," he announced while I was just barely within shouting distance. "You really go out of your way to piss me off, Seidenberg."

Just what I needed.

CHAPTER 11

It's not easy to tell when Roger Teague is truly angry, because even when he isn't exploding, he looks as if he's going to. His face is florid all the time, and you can see the veins at his temples. It's as though everything inside him is under great pressure. You get the notion that blood could easily spurt from around his eyes, though I've never actually seen it happen. Being near him is like walking through a minefield. There's always the sense that something terrible is going to happen.

I suspected that right now he was truly angry, though. I think it was the way he beat the air with his closed fists to punctuate what he said. "Forty-five minutes marching back and forth in front of the New York Public Library while you, what? take your goddamn time strolling down Fifth Avenue. I saw you. Couldn't move your ass much slower, could you?"

"You saw me coming?" I said.

"Crawling along. Let Teague wait, right? What you thought?"

"You saw me talking to that grimy guy with the black portfolio case, then."

"Got time to talk to every bum while you keep me waiting. Yeah, I saw. So what?"

"So what? So what is, his name is Hick Sosenko," I told him. "He's the sweet guy who killed David Newalis. Pulled him under water and drowned him, right in front of Ingo Julian's house on Shelter Island. Since then he took a shot at Lisa Harper, one of Ingo's inner circle. Been stalking Arthur Brody. Oh, and incidentally, tried to take me out a couple of times. "

"What? And you were just standing there chatting with him?"

"I wouldn't say chatting, exactly. I was telling him I'd have to kill him."

"But you what? let him walk away?

"I know I should have shot him right there on the corner, Teague. But there were too many witnesses."

"The hell's the matter with you?" he said. God, he looked tacky. Gold all over him, big ring, chain bracelet, heavy necklace lying against the tufts of chest hair peeking out of his open white shirt. I never looked like that when I ran the company. Maybe I should have. Maybe that's how clients want an investigator to look.

"I'm hungry, that's my problem," I said.

"And I'm running late now. Don't have time to watch you eat. Just tell me what I need to know."

I stared at him. "For all I care, you don't need to know anything. You are not my concern. My concern is me. My body has been close to shutting down today, and the day is only half over. I need food, and if I don't get it right now, I'm not saying another word to you. Not one single, solitary, fucking word. You prick."

Time was, he'd go livid when I called him a prick. Now he was inured to it. I'd worn it out through overuse. I should really come up with something new.

Teague looked to the sky and shook his head. Finally he dug into his pocket for his wallet and walked to a hot dog pushcart. I followed.

"Two," I told the vendor, who had enough dirt under

his fingernails to plant potatoes in, as my sainted mother used to say. "Mustard and sauerkraut. And an orange soda." I looked at Teague. "Pay the man."

We found a spot to sit among the lunch crowd taking the October sun on the steps of the library, and while I put away my hot dogs and soda, I gave Teague a quick history of the past three days. Plus I told him why the big shots at Julian Communications insisted on keeping the Sosenko matter under wraps, and why they didn't want anyone but me on the case right now. I thought it best to leave out the part about Brody's deal to me, and the envelope filled with money in my pocket.

"I can't believe they're being such assholes about this," Teague said. "If you don't nail this Sosenko right away, he's going to kill somebody else. Maybe a lot of people. Tell them."

"Are you paying attention, Teague? Watch my lips. I have to play it their way, or they'll dump Empire." I wiped some mustard off my shirt. "The thing I can't get out of anybody is why the big chill between Ingo Julian and Arthur Brody," I said. "Any thoughts on that?"

"I don't know. New development. Big surprise to me. Ever since the plane crash, Ingo hasn't done a thing without running it past Brody. Brody's been the key guy in everything. Ingo wouldn't wipe his ass without Brody handing him the paper. Smart move on Ingo's part."

"Why smart?" I said.

"Because once he made Brody president, and started listening to him, the company took off. Before, they were just another mediocre communications group. Nothing happening. Along comes Brody, and they acquire what look like shaky companies — magazines, radio stations — at bargain basement prices. They fire everybody, put in new lean-and-mean managements, and turn losers into big-time winners. I mean, stand back. The word is, it was Brody saw the potential. Why do you think they're so anxious to go public now? They have a hot growth curve and a phenomenal bottom line. This is the time to cash in. But communications has big ups and downs. The good times might not what? might not last forever."

"Seems like Ingo and Brody ought to be tighter than ever now," I said.

"Seems like."

I finished the last of my soda. It had all the taste of a melted Popsicle, but I liked it because it made me feel like a kid again, slurping down that orangey sweetness. "What about Lisa Harper? I don't know how she fits into all this. But it's clear she's Ingo's person. Out there on Shelter Island for a strategy session. In her itsy-bitsy bathing suit."

"Think he's banging her?" Teague said. "So what? Just part of her game plan. She wouldn't be the first broad who what? slept her way to the top."

"That how she got this far?"

"She was a junior executive, a nobody. Then Felix, the brother, notices her, and right away they're an item. No secret, everybody talking. Next thing you know she's director of the department, leapfrogging Newalis, who was in line for the job, and who is now very pissed. He finally gets the promotion, but only when they move Harper up into a VP spot."

"How do you know all this?"

"I'm an investigator, remember? I make it a point." A smug look that stopped short of being a smile.

"So Newalis wasn't exactly crazy about Harper," I said.

"I don't know if they ever made peace, or what. Remember, Ingo is handing out stock, and there's heavy talk about going public. These people are hoping to get very rich. You can put up with a lot of shit for a million bucks."

"So now you think maybe because Felix is gone, she's for Ingo?"

"You said. Looks like, maybe. I don't know," he said.

"I thought you made it a point."

"Felix wasn't smart enough to keep his affair quiet. If Ingo's doing the nasty with Harper, he'd never make that mistake. So it's hard to tell." Teague stood up from the stair and dusted off his seat. "It would be a good idea for you to stop zinging me and give some serious thought how you're going to handle this Sosenko guy. Empire's ass is hanging out a mile here. You could lose big time."

"Before I forget, let me thank you for making me a part of this," I said, standing.

"Alzarez asked for you. You're into it," he said. "Want some advice?"

"Absolutely not."

"The only way we're going to come out looking good here is if you can persuade Sosenko to go away. You know what I mean?"

"You always did want everything nice and simple," I said. "But I don't think this is as simple as it looks."

"Get the job done, Ben. And do it quick. You stay in touch with me. I want to know everything. Every day." He started down the stairs.

"Let me leave you with this thought, Teague," I said to his back.

He stopped and turned. "What?"

I was going to call him a prick one last time, but I didn't have to say it. He knew what I meant.

CHAPTER 12

Every player in this affair had an ax to grind. Including Teague, who you'd think would be on my side, cheering me on instead of threatening me. Truth was, nobody was on my side. I'd been hauled into this thing against my will, and instantly become the lightning rod. Goes to show you.

If I were smart I'd have headed crosstown, to Penn Station, and caught the next train back to Long Island. But nobody said I was smart, so I headed back up Fifth Avenue, my overextended heart trying to ignore the competition between the demands of walking and the struggle to digest two all-fat hot dogs. Was it by any stretch possible that Hick Sosenko had chosen this particular time, with a̶ ̶s̶i̶x̶ *eight* hundred million dollar Julian Communications deal hanging in the balance, to act on a hatred of the company that had been stewing in that Neanderthal mind of his for six years? Could be. But it was a story only a ninny would buy, and I liked to think that wasn't me. Clarification, I believed, was likely to be found at the offices of Julian Communications, where my weary legs appeared to be taking me.

Ingo Julian was the biggest question mark, I thought. He had the most to win, by far, when the stock went to market, and, strangely, he was the only one openly eager to shut me up and make me go away. Too late now, Ingo. Arthur Brody, at least, was ready to admit there was a problem, and to put some money on the table to solve it. Paying a hundred thousand to me wasn't all that much, considering the payoff waiting for him and the others. But it would buy a lot of fish bait for me. If I kept it.

I found it hard to keep from watching the slender girl with the long black hair and shapely ass making her way up Fifth in front of me. I couldn't see her face, but I knew she had an attitude, just from the way she walked. Plus, there was that intriguing naked space between where her halter ended and her low-slung jeans began. I pondered what she might look like from the front, but she turned west onto Forty-Fifth, and my pondering was over.

I knew Hector Alzarez well enough to believe he'd been telling me what he knew, without holding back. Still, he stood to become a wealthy man himself. That kind of money could taint the truth so subtly you'd hardly notice. And anyway, I knew a client can't help but put his own spin on a story, trying to sell the scenario that makes him come out clean and righteous. Even Hector.

Lisa Harper was a mystery. There were so many angles to her, so many places she fit in, or might fit in, it was hard to know how to think about her. She watched Newalis go under the water and helped pull his body out of the bay. Showed up at my house before Sosenko started shooting. Had a history with Ingo's dead brother. Almost certainly having a go with Ingo right now. Never, ever feels remorse about anything, don't forget that one. She'd been around Julian Communications longer than Hector. She knew things I wanted to know.

At Forty-Sixth Street I crossed to Madison and stopped in front of Crouch & Fitzgerald's leather goods store, where the window was filled with attaché cases that started at four hundred dollars. I called Lisa's office on my cell phone, talked my way past a terribly British secretary, told Lisa I had to talk to her and I was almost to her office.

"Just leaving," she said. "It's my forty-five minutes at

the health club. After that, meetings."

"Take a pass on the treadmill this time," I said. "You won't turn to flab in one day."

"Impossible. My body cries out for this. I told you, Seidenberg, I'm a fanatic."

"This is life and death," I said.

"Really? Whose?"

"Yours. Mine, probably. People like us, among others. Our friend Mr. Sosenko is in town. Parted company with him on Fifth Avenue not twenty minutes ago."

"And who is Mr. Sosenko?"

"The guy with the gun who shot up my house." A old black man walking by heard me talking and stopped, intrigued, waiting to hear more. "You know," I said clearly into the phone, playing it now to him, "when you and I were so cozy up in my bedroom. You wouldn't forget that, would you? Anyway, he's roaming the streets, and though I haven't actually seen it, I think he's brought his gun with him. So we have to get together."

"All right," I heard her say. "Then meet me at the club. We can talk in the exercise room while I do my routine."

"Will I have to strip down to my shorts." I said. The black man grinned in a kindly way.

"Optional," she said, and told me how to find her health club in the Met Life building. I rang off.

"That's some story," the black man said.

I pointed at the phone. "Gorgeous woman," I said. "Crazy about me."

He looked me up and down, stopping at my waistline. "How bout that?" he said. "There's hope for everybody, then."

And thank you for that, I thought, as I headed for Met Life.

For all the sweaty people working out, the place didn't smell like a gym. At these prices, members expected the tang of their bodies to be whisked away before they or anybody else could get a good whiff. There were exercise machines in clusters along aisles that went on forever. Some of these contraptions, I could only guess how they worked or what they were supposed to do for, or to, a human body. There were big-screen TVs everywhere, tuned to the endless financial news on CNBC. The whole place was immaculate and upbeat and nicely carpeted. Health playground for the carriage trade.

Trotting along effortlessly on a treadmill, Lisa Harper stood out. Among the men and women attired in drab grays and blacks and faded workout clothes of vague colors, only she was dressed in gleaming white spandex, a one-piece exercise suit cut to expose all of her thighs, plus maybe three inches higher. It clung to her so tightly, it might have been sprayed on. Blond hair tied back in a pony tail, she looked like the club's resident goddess.

I stood on the treadmill next to hers, leaning against the side-bars trying to look nonchalant and hoping no one would start the damn thing up. I told her what I knew about Sosenko.

"So you think. He wants to kill me?" Lisa looked straight ahead, chin up, as she moved on the machine, timing her talking to the breath control she needed to run. "I thought we decided. It was you he was after. Otherwise he'd have. Shot me before you got there."

"Maybe," I said. "I don't advise betting your life on that theory."

"I think it's you he wants. But anyway, what. Can I do?" Speeding up the machine and running faster now. "Ingo won't let anything. Get in the way. Of the IPO. Why don't you just. Catch this Sosenko? Do that and you'll. Solve everything. Come on Seidenberg. Be a hero."

"What I've trained my whole life to be," I said. "But what do I do with Sosenko when I catch him? Give him a really good talking to? Put him in a cage? What?"

Sweat running down her face. "That's your business. Leave it up to you."

Another player in this game who was perfectly willing for me to put my ass on the line. Just go track down this Sosenko, and then — what? Well, they don't like to talk about these things. But they wouldn't be terribly upset if I sort of killed him, somehow. Shouldn't be too hard to arrange. Take care of it, Seidenberg. This was not a subject I cared to dwell on. "You're expecting a lot," I said. "How about you giving me something?"

"What. Do you want?"

"Reality. I get this annoying feeling I don't have the whole picture. I can't understand why our friend Sosenko decides to get even with the company all this long time later. Why Ingo and Brody aren't buddy-buddy any more. There are things you and your pals aren't telling me. You know what? I hate that."

Lisa reached forward and touched the controls of the treadmill. The machine slowed, then stopped. She stepped off, wiped her face with a towel, moved close to me. I could sense the warmth of her body. Was it just the exercise, or did she always glow like an ember from a bonfire when she got this near?

"I don't have any secrets," she said. "Ask me anything." She crossed to a StairMaster, and I followed. She got on and started climbing to nowhere. I stood to her side.

"I want you to tell me about Felix Julian."

"Felix? What does he have to do with this? He's been dead for years."

"You said ask you anything."

She stopped her climbing and stared at me for a moment. Then, "Felix was Ingo's younger brother. But you know that. Felix started a business of his own ."

"How much younger?" I interrupted.

"A year, I think. Yes, just a year. Why?"

"I'm trying to get the picture here. Go on."

"Felix had this idea for a new system to deliver flowers by mail. This was before I ever knew him. He used start-up money from the family and got the business going down in Orlando. But somebody else came up with essentially the same system at the same time, and did it better, as it turned out. Felix struggled from day one and had to shut down after a year and a half. Not only did the business fail, but his marriage went bad, too. He'd married some bimbo in Orlando, a nut-case, they say. It took some more Julian family money to make her go away. All this was no secret, Seidenberg. Felix told it to me himself."

"You were pretty close to him, then?"

"You know that, already. Everybody does." She started climbing again, slow and steady. "We met in the office one day. We liked each other."

"So Felix went to work for his brother at Julian Communications."

"Ingo had decided to start a licensing and merchandising division. Felix was available, so Ingo put him in charge."

"Is that the way it happened?" I said. "Or did Ingo feel sorry for Felix, and invent a job for him?"

"Ask Ingo," she said.

"What's licensing and merchandising, anyway?"

"It's selling the rights to use the names and likenesses of Julian properties on other products," she said. "You know the 'Clown Town' television series for children that we distribute? If you're a marketer who makes lunch boxes for kids, say, and you want to use a picture of Cashew the Nutty Clown on a box, we'll let you do that. For a price."

"Is this a big business?"

"It can be. Depends on the economy, on what you have to sell. We sold our kid stuff. And the logos of our women's magazines — for use on cosmetics, cookbooks, vitamins."

"Sold? You saying you don't do it any more?"

"The division just shrank and disappeared when Felix was killed."

"So Ingo really did dream it all up to make work for his brother." I saw Lisa was about to put me down, so I held up my hand and said, "I know. Ask Ingo." I waited a moment, processing what she'd told me so far. It wasn't much, and none of it came together for me. "And so you were in love with Felix, is that it? A company romance?"

"Where is this going, exactly?" she said. "You're getting very close to things that are nobody's business but mine. I suppose next you'll want to know if I prefer the missionary position."

I moved to stand directly in front of the StairMaster so she'd have to look at me. "You want to talk about your sex practices, save it for another time. Dangerous situation we're all facing. Not as simple as everyone seems to think. And it didn't just suddenly happen. Reasons for it go back a long time. Whether you're aware of it or not, you could be deeply involved. I don't know yet, but I'll find out. So answer my questions, please, and I'll do my best to keep Hick Sosenko from shooting you."

For a moment I heard only the whirr and clank of the climbing machine as Lisa continued her routine, and the modulated sounds of CNBC drifting over from the TV set nearby. Finally she said, "Felix and I were serious about each other. He was a sweet guy, easy to like. It was a great loss when he died."

"To you?"

"To me. The Ingo. To the company."

"Yes, to the company," I said. "Was he like his brother? Smart, tough, a good businessman?"

"No, none of those things." she said. "He wanted to be

like Ingo, but he never was. Ingo's a killer shark. Felix couldn't bring himself to think that way. He idolized Ingo, though, and Ingo loved him dearly."

"The two brothers so different," I said. "But now you're with Ingo, isn't that right?"

"And if I am?"

"Your business, as you say."

"Felix is dead," she said. "We move on."

I was weary, tired of standing and longing to be back on Long Island. "One more thing," I said. "I understand Julian Communications really started to take off after the accident, after Ingo mended and came back. Acquisitions, new managements, tremendous growth. Why do you think that was?"

"Ingo and I have talked about that," she said. "He says being so near death forced him to focus, gave him a new clarity of purpose. He was bolder, had no doubts about himself or his decisions. He says the whole world was new for him, bright and lucid and certain."

"Lisa, that's goddamn beautiful, really," I said. "Does he give any credit to Arthur Brody? He was the guy who ran things while the doctors were sewing Ingo back together."

"He made Brody president. I'd say that's giving credit where it's due."

"What do you think, Lisa, about the growth of the company?" I said. "Was it Ingo or was it Brody?"

"I don't make those kinds of judgments," she said with a sense of finality, and doubled her speed on the StairMaster.

I had all the answers I was going to get this time. Now I had to make sense of them.

CHAPTER 13

Not a hundred miles from the hurry of New York City there's a village on the water where life is lived slowly and there's a single traffic light on the main road. This is Southold, which comes after Cutchogue and before Greenport as you drive due east on the North Fork of Long Island. This is where Alicia lives, and where I always head for encouragement and affection and wonderful dinners.

Southold is lively with summer people, and tourists from New York, through Labor Day. But the village thins out once the weather grows cold, as it was about to do now, in October. By winter, Southold comes almost to a standstill.

I first saw Southold three years ago.

I used to drive out for the fishing at Montauk, on tip of the South Fork, and occasionally roamed through the nearby Hamptons to study the beautiful people and eat at the good restaurants. Late one summer afternoon I was walking through Southampton when I looked through an art gallery window and saw a dark-haired woman standing on a stepladder, trying unsuccessfully to hang a large painting on the wall. The canvas was simply too big for her to handle.

She saw me watching. She clutched the painting with both hands and motioned me, with a broad movement of her head, to come inside, which I did.

"You going to help a lady?" she said. "Why are you standing there? Take that end." That delicious Italian accent.

That cheeky, I-dare-you way she had of throwing the words at you. There was no resisting.

I helped the lady. Once the painting was hanging squarely the wall, we talked, and talked some more. She closed the gallery and we went for a drink. Then stayed for dinner. Then we walked the streets for an hour and finally went to her house in Southold. From that first night there was never any question. I was for Alicia Bianchi, and she was for me. I never thought anything like it could happen to a man with all my hitches and snags. But it did.

When the pressure at Empire Security started to trouble me, and I knew it was time to cash out, it made sense to move near Alicia, to be with her all the time, not just weekends. But I had misgivings. I was leaving Empire and New York City to get away from the fast pace, yet I feared that the slow pace out here, seven days a week, would bore the hell out of me. And it did, for a time. It took me a year and a half to get into tempo with the North Fork. I settled in, and it wasn't bad. Trouble was, Teague refused to stop pulling my strings. He had this remarkable delusion that I worked for him now, and felt perfectly justified threatening my financial future, pulling me back in, giving me assignments that pissed me off and left my coronary system begging for mercy.

Alicia was my snug harbor. She was comfort and understanding. My advocate to anyone and everyone, no matter what. Yet not above telling me how she thought I should deal with the world. For my own good, she said.

At first I resisted her opinions. Getting advice from another person was something new for me at my stage of the game, and I resented it. But I came to find that this woman, a self-proclaimed Italian sorceress, after all, had an amazing talent for simplifying situations, sorting out lies and seeing right through people. I was a fair hand at those things myself, but Alicia was in a league all her own. One day I woke up to realize I didn't resent her counsel any more. I required it.

It was nearly eight by the time I arrived at her house now, after a stop-and-go trip from Manhattan on a crowded Long Island Expressway.

"Going to be another hour before we eat, because I didn't want to start before you got here," she told me. "Maybe less. We'll see. Wine in the refrigerator, and I think we drink some now, OK? Chenin blanc from Paumanok. Very nice."

I opened one of the two bottles and poured us each a glass. She was right about the Paumanok Vineyards chenin blanc. Even better than very nice. Paumanok was coming along fast among the thirty wineries now at work on the North Fork. I was not unhappy there was a back-up bottle chilling.

She said, "Lemon chicken, you remember? With rice, also. We agreed on this, OK?"

"Waiting for it all day."

"Good. Then you broil the bird. I do the lemon sauce, and the rice, too. Salad is done." She reached into the refrigerator and handed me a whole chicken.

"Not split?" I said.

"I don't like it when they're cut apart," she said. "The pieces don't match sometimes. From different chickens. One side bigger than the other. You don't want to cut it? I'll do it. Give me."

"I can handle it," I said. I split the bird in two with a large chef's knife on the butcher block top of the kitchen's island. "Just one swift, precise cut. Did you notice?"

"I'm so proud of you," she said. "How long to broil, you think? Remember, it's only good rare for steak, not for chicken." A reference to a pinkish chicken I'd served up once.

"Give me thirty minutes to cook the halves, five minutes to cut them up, another five minutes back under the broiler with the lemon. OK?"

"OK, then put them in now. I start the rice," she said. I

put the chicken in the stove's broiler pan and turned the electric oven to broil. I slid it in, not too close to the glow. Don't cook it too fast, I told myself. No more rare chicken.

Alicia diced a small onion and cooked it in butter on top of the stove. "You look tired," she said. "Bad time in New York. I can tell. You shouldn't go in there for these things."

"Didn't have a choice."

"Always you have a choice," she said, moving about barefoot on the kitchen floor. "You don't need them. You got me. Tell them all to go to hell." She added a cupful of raw rice to her pot, stirring with a wooden spoon to coat each grain with the hot butter. "You saw Teague, right? I can always tell when you get near that bastard. With all the gold all over him. Like a cheap criminal. Or a pimp, maybe." She reached into a cupboard and took a bottle of dry vermouth, poured half a cupful into the pan with the onions and rice. It hissed and sent up a cloud of steam. "Paumanok wine too good for cooking. For drinking only. Vermouth is good enough for the rice."

I sipped at the chenin blanc and told Alicia what had happened, who I'd seen, what they'd said to me. Listening to myself tell it, I was more aware than ever that there were vast gaps in the story.

Alicia stirred the rice. The alcohol in the vermouth had boiled away, and the rice had absorbed the rest of the wine. "So you were running around New York with a gun in your pocket, chasing a crazy person. Some kind of job you got." She opened a can of chicken broth and added it to the pot. She saw my quizzical look as she stirred an orange-colored spice into the mixture. "Turmeric," she said. "Turns the rice yellow. I make it very pretty for you." She put a lid on the pot and adjusted the heat. "You think he's still in New York, this Hick person? Or he's sneaking back here?"

"Don't know," I said. "I don't understand what's driving him, so I can't tell what he'll do next."

"You don't think he's mad at the company and trying to get even?"

"That's what it looks like. But no, I don't think so. I think maybe that's what somebody wants it to look like."

"Been out of jail three years, already, this person?"

"Yes."

"Then of course you're right." She started on the lemon sauce for the chicken, squeezing fresh lemon juice into a bowl. "If he was going to get even, he would have killed his enemies long ago. In Italy, he would have done it the day they let him out. Fill my glass, please."

I did. "Another mystery," I said. "I don't understand why a middling company like Julian Communications became such a hot item after Ingo returned. After all, they'd pasted him back together with duct tape. He was a mess, hardly in shape to put out the kind of effort you need to turn a big firm around. And he wasn't that great to start with. Now he says being so close to dying made him focus, gave him new drive, all that crap. Hard to believe."

She added olive oil, minced garlic and a splash of red wine vinegar to the bowl. "Could only be one thing," she said. "It wasn't him doing the decisions, the work. Somebody else. The brother was dead, right? So then there's this one who's the president. Brody is his name?"

"The brother could never have accomplished it, even if he was alive, according to Lisa, and Hector, too. Didn't have the strength, the skills, they told me." I said. "Brody? Well, he did run the company while Ingo was recovering. Ingo made him president. But the company didn't start to move till Ingo took charge again, as CEO. I just can't believe the accident made him into a different man. A killer shark now, that's what Lisa Harper calls him."

Alicia came to me and kissed me lightly, "Just for nothing," she said, and walked away. She stood quietly, thinking, staring at a cupboard. Finally she took down a bottle of dried oregano, shook some into her hand, then dropped it into the sauce. She beat everything together with a whisk. "You know what I'm thinking?" she said.

"What?"

"You're going to laugh."

"Maybe."

"But of course I absolutely don't care," she told me. "This Ingo, he was almost torn apart when the plane crashed, right?"

"Yes."

"Even now it shows all over him where the doctors put him back together. That's what you said, right?"

"Yes."

"Would you say he looks like a different man then he did before the crash?"

"I don't know. I'd say he looks like an Ingo Julian who's been through a horrible accident." I poured myself another glass of chenin blanc.

"But he has no hair now, none at all, you told me. And scars all over him," she said. "Check the chicken. Tell me when you turn it."

I opened the oven door, peeked in, then closed it. "Another minute," I said. "What are you telling me? That it's not Ingo Julian? That it's somebody else pretending to be him? Sounds like a mystery novel, or a bad movie. I can't believe it. I talked to the man."

"But did you ever meet him before the accident?" She put a skillet on a low light and poured in some pine nuts. "Pignolis. I toast them and then they go into the cooked rice. For texture. My idea," she said. "So? Did you ever see him when he was all in one piece?"

"No. Actually, I never met him until he'd recovered."

"There you are," she said. "OK, now, these two

brothers, they looked alike, do you know?"

"I don't know."

"Maybe you should find out."

"You think it's really Felix, the brother, who survived the crash.? And Ingo who died? A plot for Felix to take over the company?" I opened the oven and turned the chicken. "But Felix didn't have his brother's instincts for business."

"Who told you? This Lisa and this Hector person? Why should you believe them?" she said. "I asked you to tell me when you turned the chicken."

"You just watched me turn it."

She grinned at me. "I know, but I like when you do what I tell you. Do you resent doing what I tell you?"

"Depends what you have in mind."

"We eat this dinner, we finish all the wine. Maybe then we negotiate," she said. "I never lose at that, you know."

"I know," I said. "But right now we have to consider your theory. If Felix is running the show in place of Ingo, then that would explain about Lisa. I mean, before the crash she had something hot going with Felix. Now it looks like she's with Ingo. Unless, of course, Ingo is really Felix, and she's still with the same guy, and playing the game."

Alicia held her palms up, a gesture of triumph. "You see."

I sat on a kitchen chair and studied the wine in my glass. "Then what about Brody? He was tight with Ingo — or Felix, if you're right. Now they don't talk. How does that fit in?"

We bounced that question around while we drank more wine, and created a half dozen scenarios, none of which made sense. Then we decided we'd burned out the subject for now, and it was time to commit ourselves to our dinner.

When the chicken was nicely done, the skin charred a bit and the juices running clear, I cut it into pieces with a sharp knife and put it back in the pan. Alicia chopped some fresh parsley and added it into the sauce just before I poured it over the chicken, and put it all back to broil for a few minutes more. She grated some parmigiano reggiano cheese into the rice, added her toasted pine nuts and fluffed it up with a fork.

Soon it was all on the table. The chicken and the rice, plus a green salad from the refrigerator and some crusty bread to mop up the lemon sauce. It was delicious beyond description, and we lingered over it for an hour, draining half of the second bottle of chenin blanc as we ate.

"You saw this Lisa woman today?" Alicia said. It was ten-thirty when we finished cleaning up.

"You know I did. I told you."

"But you didn't kiss her this time. I can tell."

"She begged me for a kiss. But I said no. I told her it would be too dangerous, that you'd know in a minute, and you'd put an Italian curse on her."

"I would, too," she said. She stroked my face. "You're tired. You shouldn't drive home. All that wine, too. You stay here tonight, OK?"

"Are you telling me what to do again? You said we'd negotiate."

"All right, we negotiate. What is it you want?"

"Your undivided attention." I turned out the kitchen light and we walked to the bedroom at the back of the house.

CHAPTER 14

The first call came on my cell phone at eight forty-five, after I'd breakfasted on one of the bagels Alicia kept for me in her freezer, and some of her exceptional coffee, made from a dark roast she imported by the case from Italy. We'd both perused the Friday New York Times in contented silence for twenty minutes, passing the sections across the table. Only the sports went untouched, due to mutual lack of interest. Now Alicia was ready to drive to her gallery in Southampton, and I to my house in Greenport. This morning I was determined to apply the final touches to the shattered front window I'd repaired.

It was Hector Alzarez on the phone from New York. "I thought you should know I'm coming out there. Ingo called me at seven-thirty this morning. He and Lisa are going to Shelter Island for the weekend. Spur-of-the-moment thing, he says. He wants me to go with them." He sounded gloomy, unusual for him. "They're picking me up here in half an hour."

"Why does he want you?" I said. "I mean, people tell me you're charming, but won't you feel a little out of place at this party?"

"I'm not ecstatic about it, Ben. I'm canceling a whole day's meetings because Ingo suddenly got an idea. It's making a mess of my schedule. But listen to this. He says he has to spend some time with me about Brody. He wants to mend some fences. He thinks I can help him get talking again with Brody. Maybe now I'll be able to answer what you asked me — how they happened to wind up at each other's throats."

I was still sitting at the kitchen table as I talked into my phone, but Alicia was ready to leave for Southampton. She kissed the back of my neck and whispered, "Lock when you go."

"Why this new twist, do you think?" I said into the phone. I took Alicia's hand and gave it a squeeze. She responded with a naughty smile, then left through the back door into the garage.

Hector said, "Did you read The Wall Street Journal this morning?"

"It's not on my usual reading list."

"There's a big piece on page two, right up on top. 'Will Management Tiff Threaten Julian Communications IPO?' That's the headline. Somehow the word about Ingo and Brody got out, and now Ingo's worried. He wants the market to know the top management of the company is stable. Brody's had a lot of press over the last few years. Some analysts feel he's the real brains behind the company's growth. If they think he's in jeopardy, they're not inclined to be bullish on the stock offering."

"Why do the analysts think Ingo and Brody don't talk to each other?"

A long sigh. "They can only speculate, just like we've been doing," he said. "They think it's a power struggle — Brody flexing his muscles too much to please Ingo."

"Did the Journal mention Newalis?"

"Just in passing," Hector said. "They accept it as an accident. Not a big deal, really, because Newalis wasn't a key player. It's Ingo and Brody they're watching. And maybe Lisa, because she's the one who talks to them all the time — corporate communications."

"They looking at you, too?"

"I suppose," he said. "The Journal mentioned me in the story."

"So this is a big strategy session today. Away from the office." I got up and walked across the kitchen to make sure the electric range was off. Dumb, I realized, because Alicia had done the same thing before she left. "Be careful," I said to Hector. "Sosenko is out there, New York or here or someplace in between. See if you can't convince Ingo to let me call up tight security. Tell him if he thinks his trouble with Brody makes bad press, just imagine what would happen if the headlines were about murder."

"I'll try," he said. "But there's no way Sosenko could know we're coming out."

"He seems to have a way of knowing things," I said. "When will you be here?"

"We should be out of Manhattan through the Midtown Tunnel by a quarter to ten. If the expressway traffic isn't terrible, we should be on the ferry in Greenport by twelve-thirty, one o'clock."

"I'm going to make sure I'm around," I told him.

"That's good," he said. "You know, I wouldn't go through this except for one thing."

"Let me guess. All that money."

"You always did understand me, Ben," he said, and hung up.

The second call of the morning came just as I was opening my car door, and it was from Wally Prager. "I'm in Shinnecock, amigo," he said. "Came down to get some parts for a Merc engine I got in my shop. We don't generally do Mercs. Anyway, figured I might as well check out that shit-hole Sosenko calls home. And guess what? There's a rusty old pickup parked alongside it this morning. I don't know if he's in the shack or not. Figured finding out's a job for a hero with a gun. Does that description sound like anybody you know?"

"How long have you been watching the place?"

"How long? I watched it about twenty seconds. Then I got out of there, muy rapido. There's nowhere near the place where you can park in broad daylight and not get noticed. Course, I'm not a trained investigator like you are. Just an eager civilian who doesn't want to get clipped by a maniac."

"Then where are you?" I said.

"I am just finishing coffee with Lulu Lumpkin," he said with a cozy little laugh. "In her renowned gin mill."

"I'm going to Sosenko's," I said.

"A better plan would be for you come here on your way. You might want to hear what Lulu's got to say."

I could smell Wally's Napoli cigar as soon as I stepped through the door. It added a unique note of pungency to the assorted aromas of stale beer, fresh coffee and ripe fishermen that clung to the place. Wally himself was on a stool facing the door, leaning back, his elbows on the bar, his long legs crossed. "Lulu's brewing a fresh pot for you," he told me. "She'll be right out."

"You think Sosenko is going to wait for me while I sit here drinking coffee?" I said to him.

"I told Lulu you'd have a cup," Wally said. "She's making it specially for you."

Right on cue, Lulu came behind the bar with the coffee. "Bring your own donuts this time, sport?" she said, pouring me a cup.

"I'm off donuts, actually," I said. "Too fattening."

"You ain't so fat, really," Lulu Lumpkin said. "Anyways, a skinny man's no use on a cold night."

"That's what my lady friend says."

"Smart lady friend." She warmed up Wally's cup, then her own. "I was telling this doofus here that your pal Hick Sosenko was in last night. Very late, just before last call. First time in over a week. Jesus, I hate to see him walk in here. Soon as he came in, I looked under the bar to make sure my gun was where I could get at it."

"He give you trouble?" I said

"Nothing lethal," she said. "That was some surprise, and a relief. He had himself a shot and a beer, and didn't flash a knife or anything. But you know what?" She leaned across the bar. "He had a pocketful of money. He pulled out this big wad of cash and laid it right down on the bar here. All hundreds and fifties, as I could see. Said he had four thousand dollars. He was so proud of it. That's why he came in. To show off to me."

"You think it was really that much?" Wally asked her.

"Looked like," she said

"Did he say where he got it?" I said. I drank some of the coffee. I didn't want Lulu to think she'd made it for nothing.

"All he said, he was doing a big job for somebody," she said. "Can you imagine? Who'd pay him that kind of money to do anything?"

"First-class question," I said. "Did he say anything else?"

"Just that he liked to look at my titties."

"They are nice," said Wally, but Lulu ignored him.

"I have to get over there. Don't want him to disappear again." One final sip of coffee.

"I'm going with you," Wally said, sliding off his stool. He put some dollar bills on the bar.

"Follow me over, then," I said.

Lulu picked up the money and stuffed it into Wally's shirt pocket. "You keep your money. And I'll tell you what. If Hick Sosenko just disappears off the earth somehow, you two can drink here free for the rest of your lives."

The corroded Dodge truck was still there next to the shack, all right. But now so was the pot-bellied neighbor with the crutches, leaning against the fender, so I knew Sosenko wasn't around anywhere. The old man wouldn't be so bold if the holy terror of the neighborhood might be watching.

"You look like you're waiting for somebody," I told him, as Wally and I approached.

"I saw you nosing around before," he said to Wally. "Thought you might be back."

"You've been waiting out here that long?" Wally said.

"Taking the sun." Everything he was wearing was exactly the same as he'd worn the first time we'd seen him, only dirtier. "Still looking for my beloved neighbor, are you? Sad to tell, you missed him again."

"His truck is here. Where did he go? And when?" I asked him.

"He's out on his boat. Who knows where? Left an hour ago, maybe a little more." The old man lifted one of his crutches to point down the path that led to the water.

"Well, his truck's here, so he's got to come back," Wally said to me. "All we do is wait."

The old man said, "You might want to know this. That wooden sign he painted? He took it with him when he went to his boat. I saw him paint out the letters with white paint before he left. What did it used to say? I forgot."

"Lulu," I told the old man. I took Wally by the arm. "We can't wait here," I said. "Sosenko is out to kill somebody. And there's a car-full of candidates heading east on the Long Island Expressway right now."

CHAPTER 15

I gunned the car and kicked up gravel in Lulu's pockmarked parking lot as I swung out onto the highway. In my rearview mirror, I could see Wally following in his pickup truck.

Once again Sosenko was setting the pace, taking the initiative, making me react. Time I stopped chasing after him, I thought. Time I got ahead of him.

Peconic Bay is the water that divides the South Fork of Long Island from the North Fork.

If Sosenko motored north to Greenport, it was a twenty mile trip, give or take. Just spitballing, then, I judged he was already there, if that's where he'd headed. It would take Wally and me fifty minutes or so, driving around from one fork to the other. We'd get to Greenport after Sosenko, but before Ingo, Lisa and Hector showed up there from New York. That was one scenario.

Then I thought: would Sosenko have used his boat if he were going to Greenport? Taking his truck would have been simpler. He could park the old Dodge anywhere, much easier than looking for a place to tie up thirty feet of boat. But who knows? The bastard did crazy things.

If logic had any place at all in his plans, he'd taken his boat because he wanted to go where only a boat could take him. Like Shelter Island. That started to make the most sense. By the time I drove up to the North Fork and turned onto the main road toward

Greenport, I'd just about convinced myself that Hick Sosenko had set out for Shelter. He wouldn't go there by ferry to do something evil, because then he'd be easy to nab when he tried to take the ferry back. No, he'd need his boat to return to the mainland. Don't do a crime on Shelter Island because it's tough to make a getaway. Unless you're a powerful swimmer. Or you have a boat waiting for you.

If I was right, if he did head for Shelter, the trio from Julian Communications would be at risk as soon as they drove off the ferry there. Only a guess. Best I could do. Sosenko could be anywhere. Defying logic, he might be in Greenport right now, ready to raise hell with that rifle of his as soon as the Julian people drove in from New York. The possibilities for disaster went on and on.

Wally and I parked near the ferry terminal, a gray wooden building a few blocks from the collection of stores and restaurants, plus the aptly named Whiskey Wind saloon and an ancient movie theatre, that are Greenport's commercial area.

"Something's going to happen," I said to Wally.

"Smell that way?" he said.

"Sosenko on the move and the Julian people on the way out. Coincidence, right?" I told him the possibilities I'd considered. Then, "I need you. Another pair of eyes. You up for this?"

"Do I get hazard pay? Seems to me if I'm likely to be shot at, there should be a little something extra in it for me."

"Lobster roll. Chocolate pie," I said.

"No es basta," he attempted. "Not for this kind of work."

"What?"

"Not enough," he told me. "Means I think it's stingy."

"It is stingy," I said. "Look, the Julian people won't get here for an hour or so. We'll split up, check things out around town."

"What am I supposed to be looking for? I never saw this Sosenko guy before."

"Tall and skinny. Shoulders out to here. Pushed-in mug with ratty yellow hair. And tattoos up both arms. Snakes, I think."

"That narrows it down," Wally said.

"I'll take Front Street and check the docks. Go up to Main, and work your way north. If you find anybody looks like him, even a little bit, don't do anything dumb. Just come get me."

"Because you have the gun."

"Yes, because I have the gun," I said. "Meet back here in half an hour."

Wally took off toward Main Street, and I started working my way on Front, where the shore of the bay ran behind a row of stores, a new hotel, the movie theatre and the town's waterfront park. I heard music from the park's merry-go-round, its glass-walled enclosure open to the street. There were still visitors in town, come for the tastings at nearby wineries, and to enjoy the last of the good weather before the North Fork turned dreary.

Looking from the park, I could see the whole waterfront. There were a few commercial fishing boats in their slips, but they were much bigger than Sosenko's thirty foot Tiderunner — or whatever name he had painted on it today. That boat wasn't anywhere within sight of the ferry terminal. That's not to say it wasn't nearby, tucked away somewhere, with Sosenko on the loose around town.

I looked into every store, first on one side of the street, then the other. I'd just returned to the sidewalk after my inspection of the Arcade, an old fashioned department store with a wooden floor that squeaked when you walked on it, when a police car pulled to the curb, and the driver rolled the window down. It was Phil Rutkowski, a feisty young cop I'd met at the Whiskey Wind one cold December night when Alicia was in Italy for a Christmas visit. We'd shared a few stories and a lot of Scotch, and discovered we got on well. He'd never met a private investigator before, thought they were only in paperback books. In the spring, when the weather finally warmed up, I'd taken him fishing with Wally and me a few times.

"Hey, mister, you lost?" he said to me, a grin on that angular Polish face of his.

"Such a nice day," I said. "How come you're not up on the North Road handing out speeding tickets to the tourists?"

"Made my quota already today," he said. "You looking for somebody? I just saw Wally over on Main. He was wandering around, too."

"Yeah, thanks. I knew he was here someplace." I looked at the shotgun clamped upright to the dash of Rutkowski's cruiser. It would be comforting to have an armed cop on hand if trouble broke out, I thought. But what could I tell Rutkowski ? And if Ingo saw the police with me, he'd know I wasn't playing by the Julian rulebook. Maybe I can finesse the situation, I thought. "Park this thing," I said to Rutkowski, "and I'll buy you a coffee."

"Can't do it," he said. "Can I have the money instead?"

"Come on. Ten minutes."

"I'm on call. Hey, take care of yourself, big bad Ben." He gave a cocky wave of his hand, and drove off.

I thought: we're on our own, Wally and I. I touched my elbow to the gun in the holster under my jacket, just for reassurance. High noon in little old Greenport, New York.

I walked back to the ferry terminal and watched cars drive on and off the two open boats working the route. Six weeks earlier, in the summer, there'd been three, to handle the lines of cars, and still you'd often wait half an hour to get across. It would be no great engineering feat to build a bridge to Shelter from Greenport, and another one on the south side, connecting the island to Sag Harbor on the South Fork. But nobody wanted bridges to Shelter Island. Not the people who had homes there. And certainly not the ferry companies. Shelter Island would lose its romance if it became too easy to get there.

Soon Wally appeared. He handed me a coffee in a cardboard cup with a plastic lid, then drank some from the one he'd brought for himself. I took a swallow. "It's cold," I told him.

"Can't understand it," he said. "I kept it under my armpit all the way over here."

"See anything I should know about?"

"Didn't see a single person with snake tattoos up his arms. Funny, on a sunny day there's generally two, three," he said. "So now we wait?"

"Part of the job."

"I appreciate the lesson," Wally said.

We didn't have to wait long. At twenty minutes past noon, Ingo drove up at the wheel of a Mercedes E500 sedan, a serious automobile in which the "E" clearly stood for "Expensive." The color was a rich metallic green I'd never seen before on any car. Hector was at Ingo's side in the front and Lisa Harper in the back seat, munching an apple. Ingo pulled his car behind the half dozen others in the ferry line, and they all got out.

"We made good time," Hector said, shaking my hand. "Long Island really flies by when you're doing ninety miles an hour."

"The car has excellent performance, for a sedan. I like the feeling of stability at high speed," Ingo said. "Hector told me you'd be here. This Sosenko, he's out here someplace and you think he's going to make trouble." He looked at Wally. "And who is this?"

"He's a friend, Wally Prager. He spotted Sosenko's truck on the South Fork this morning."

Wally said nothing.

"So why do you think he's on the North Fork now?" Ingo asked me.

"He left in his boat this morning. There's a chance he went to Shelter." I pointed across the bay.

"You don't know that. He could have gone anyplace. Maybe he went to Connecticut. Maybe he went to Cuttyhunk." Again Ingo was denying the danger, quarreling with efforts to keep him and his people safe. And there I was, trying to save their lives and my future, with plenty of ways to fail, no way to quit. Ingo was pissing me off.

Hector, always the diplomat, saw my temper rising and stepped in quickly. "I asked Ben to be here," he said to Ingo. "Why chance it? Sosenko killed Newalis —"

"Are you so certain?" Ingo said

"I'm certain," I told Ingo. "And I'm nearly certain he killed him by mistake. It was you he wanted."

Lisa dropped her apple core into a trash can. "Ingo, let him help us," she said. "What's the downside? If he's wrong, nothing's been lost. But if he's right, and we need somebody — well, he does have a gun." She turned to me. "Or did you leave it in your bureau under your shorts?"

"I hadn't so much as touched my gun in years, even to clean it. Now I'm carrying it all the time. I don't do that to impress the other cowboys down at the corral." I said it to Ingo.

A ferry had finished discharging its cars, and the mate was motioning the waiting vehicles waiting to make their way onto the boat.

"All right, then, let's go. You can check things out, but then Hector takes you back to the ferry, yes? I don't want my place turned into an armed camp." Ingo got into the Mercedes and started the engine. Hector got in next to him. Wally and I climbed into the back with Lisa, and Ingo inched the car onto the boat. The mate motioned us to a spot on the starboard side. Wally and I got out to look around.

With only six cars on board, the ferry was only half full. There were two cars beside ours, a Buick sedan with an elderly couple inside, and a yellow two-door Toyata driven by a teen-age boy with too much hair, the back seat packed to the roof with what looked like dirty clothes. There was a Lexus SUV driven by a pretty mother, her little girl asleep in a child seat behind her. A middle-aged woman was at the wheel of another SUV, a Honda, the back filled with clay pots of chrysanthemum plants, all in bloom with red and purple blossoms.

The last vehicle on the boat was a Ford van-style truck covered with scrapes and dents from front to back, and painted with various white paints, none of which came close to matching the truck's original white. It looked as though there had once been signs on the truck's sides, but they'd been painted out. I couldn't see inside, because the windows on the two back doors were blocked from the inside with plywood. The driver appeared to be a tradesman of some sort, in stained chino clothes, and badly in need of a shave. He sat staring ahead stoically, his hair hanging down over his forehead, and didn't bother to look at me as I passed by. I wasn't at all sure, because of the throbbing of the ferry's idling engines, but I thought I heard movement inside the rear of the truck.

The mate was securing the sliding gate at the stern. I went to him and said, "I'm trying to find out if a friend of mine made it to Shelter this morning. I think he arrived on the north side of the island. Do you remember seeing a commercial fishing boat, about thirty feet, pretty grimy, around here this morning, maybe an hour, two hours ago?"

"I don't know. Lot of boats go through here," he said. He looked up to the captain in the ferry's wheel-house and made a signal. The engines revved and the boat slowly left the slip.

"I thought you might have noticed. It's kind of a shabby boat. White."

"Can't be sure," he said. "Maybe something like that headed into Dering Harbor on Shelter. Or was it yesterday? I'm back and forth fifteen, twenty times a day. Hard to say. Sorry." He moved away. "Got to collect the fares."

Now Hector got out of the car and stood leaning on the boat's rail at the starboard side, looking out over the water as we began our ten-minute trip to Shelter. In the car, Ingo turned around in his seat and was talking to Lisa, who remained in the back. He was probably bitching to her about me, I thought.

Wally made a quick tour of the boat, then returned to me. "That Ingo guy, he's the boss, right?"

"Right."

"Where'd he get all those scars. Looks like he fell into a meat grinder."

"Plane crash. Nearly killed him. Show some sympathy," I said. "Look, stay up front and watch the shore around the ferry terminal on Shelter. The mate says maybe he saw a boat like Sosenko's go into Dering Harbor this morning. He could have left his boat there and walked to the ferry slip. All just maybe, mind you."

"So maybe he's got himself over to the terminal and is waiting for us to dock," Wally said.

"Maybe. So look."

"And you?" he said.

"That truck over there bothers me. I thought I heard somebody moving inside when I walked around the back. There's nobody up front but the driver. Could be something's not right."

Wally went forward. Now the kid with the Toyota was standing at the rail on the port side. Ingo got out of the car and joined Hector at the starboard rail.

I went to the truck. The driver had both windows rolled all the way up, strange in this mild weather. I tapped on his window with my finger, then made a lowering motion with my hand. He gave me a glance, then went right back to staring straight ahead. He was refusing to look at me again, refusing to roll down his window. Now I was edgy. Why was he ignoring me?

I reached inside my jacket to touch my gun, as I pushed my face up close to the window. "Can I talk to you for a minute?

Would you roll down your window. It's important." My voice was loud enough to attract the attention of the couple in the Buick, who were watching me now.

The driver of the truck turned to me angrily. He glared at me for a moment, then rolled the window down slowly. "You got a problem?" he said.

"No problem. I need some help, that's all. I have a friend supposed to be on this ferry, in a truck, he said. You're the only truck here, so I thought maybe he was with you, you know, in the back. Guy named Hick Sosenko. He in there?"

"I don't know what the hell you're talking about. I got no time for this," he said, and started rolling the window up again.

"Just hold on," I said. "I heard noises in the back of your truck. What have you got back there?"

"What I got back there is none of your goddamn business. Now get the fuck away before I open this door and knock you on your fat ass."

By now I suspected the worst. I had to get a look inside that truck, so I walked back and pulled open both rear doors. I could hear the driver climbing out of the cab to come after me, so I drew my gun to give him some second thoughts about whatever he had in mind.

Even before I could make out what was inside the truck, I smelled it. A ripe barnyard stink so thick I could almost see it as it came pouring out the open doors. The source of the hideous aroma was a trio of goats, ragged creatures who'd been cooped up in the truck for much too long. The floor was covered with equal parts straw and goat-shit.

The driver appeared, ready for battle, but backed off when he saw my gun. I started to close the doors to his truck, not unhappy to seal off the smell, and the picture of the pathetic animals inside. "Mistake," I told the driver. "Sorry."

That's when it started. "Ben. Ben. Starboard side." Wally was shouting and waving his hands in the air. "Look starboard, coming up from behind! That's the boat. It's him!"

Before I could move, Sosenko's boat was about to draw alongside, running parallel to the ferry. Ingo and Hector were still at the rail. "Get down!" I shouted. Hector turned to see why I was calling, but Ingo was still looking out across the water, watching the approach of the boat. "It's Sosenko! Get down!" I screamed at them.

Hector hesitated a second, staring at me, his mouth open, finally grasping what was happening. He reached out to Ingo and pulled him back and to the side, away from the rail., a move that took Ingo out of the line of fire, but left Hector open for an instant.

An instant was all it took. Sosenko raised a rifle out of his boat's wheelhouse and fired it, a quick shot across twenty feet of water. Hector spun around, slid across the rear fender of the Mercedes and collapsed on the deck.

The second shot was slow in coming, because Sosenko had to work the rifle's bolt action, and steer his boat, too. I heard the slug hit the steel plate below the rail.

In the other vehicles, frightened people with no place to run dropped down in their seats. The mother in the SUV got out, opened the rear door, dragged her sleeping child out of the car seat, and, hugging the little girl close, dropped flat to the deck. The truck driver moved to the left side of his vehicle, wisely putting the truck between him and the shooting.

I hadn't managed to secure the back doors of the truck before the attack, and now the three goats, happy to escape from their confinement into the fresh air, pushed open the half-closed doors and jumped onto the deck, making loud bleats of liberation.

Another rifle shot, hitting nothing. Before Sosenko could work the bolt action again, I ran to the starboard rail and began firing at him. Going toe to toe with me wasn't his style, as I'd already learned. He swung out to the right, quickly putting distance between his boat and the ferry. I emptied my gun, but did no damage I could see. I could make out the painted piece of plywood nailed to the stern, masking his boat's name. He was still playing that game. And he was escaping again. There was no way to stop him.

It had all happened so fast, my angina hadn't had time to catch up. But now, with Sosenko quickly disappearing, I felt that familiar tension pulling across my chest and under my arms. I holstered my gun and dropped to one knee beside Hector, who was pumping blood onto the deck from the bullet hole below his right shoulder.

CHAPTER 16

Crouched on the deck now with her child, the mother sobbed and struggled to catch her breath. The little girl, awake and frightened, responded to her mother's fear with her own shrill screams. In the Buick, the elderly man put his arm around the shoulders of his wife, who sat with her eyes squeezed shut tight, a look of awful pain on her face. Closest to me, the woman with the SUV full of flowers sat rigid in her seat, both hands gripping the steering wheel. The three goats, protesting noisily, nosed about the deck, apparently looking for something to eat. Oblivious to them, the truck driver stood gaping at Hector.

The general counsel of Julian Communications lay on his back, his eyes open, his gaze going right through me. His head turned first one way, then the other, like a slow motion film clip. Blood began to seep from under him, as well as from the wound in front that was slowly spreading a red stain across his handsome white polo shirt. The bullet had gone through him. You didn't have to be a doctor to know he was in a bad way. He was bleeding out.

The ferry stopped, then shuddered as the captain reversed the engines, and we made for the Greenport slip we'd just left. The mate, who'd taken the stairs to the wheel-house three at a time to reach the captain, ran down again to tell us that radio calls had already gone out for an ambulance, and for the police.

Lisa was out of the Mercedes now, kneeling on the deck

with me alongside Hector, who had stopped moving. His eyes were open, I but couldn't tell if he was still alive. At the least, he was in deep shock. Lisa pressed her open palm against the entry wound, trying to keep the blood inside him. Ingo's eyes met mine for an instant, and he nodded his head at me. I was right about the danger, he was telling me.

Bet your stubborn, overbearing ass I was right. I felt like smacking him on that bald head of his, but what good would it do?

By the time the ferry bumped back into the slip, I could hear sirens approaching. Officer Phil Rutkowski arrived first, then the ambulance, then two more cop cars, one of which brought the police chief himself, a garrulous official named Nugent, from headquarters in Southold. Lisa left with the ambulance, which sped Hector away to Eastern Long Island Hospital, only several blocks away. I stared at the spot where Hector had fallen. The steel deck, warm from the October sun, was already beginning to congeal the edges of the blood spot.

Now there was a growing throng of people, policemen, local merchants, tourists and townspeople drawn by the noise and excitement, and a lone reporter from the Suffolk Times who'd heard the police call on her scanner. The Times was a the local major weekly, and if they were on the scene, you could bet that Newsday, Long Island's big daily, and the New York papers wouldn't be far behind. So much for keeping Julian Communication's situation away from the media.

I could see Wally standing at the edge of the group of onlookers, and motioned to him to leave. No reason for him to get drawn into an investigation. And if I got hung up with the police, I might need him on the outside. He slipped away and disappeared.

I knew there was no way of hiding the story any longer, no matter what was at stake for Ingo and the others. Who would believe the assault on the ferry was random madness, particularly after the Newalis drowning less than a week before? We didn't have Hector to advise us or run interference against the police now, so I made my own choice. I told Nugent a bare-bones version of the truth, that Sosenko was a crazy with a grudge against Julian Communications. I left out the parts about Sosenko shooting at me earlier, because I got the feeling Nugent didn't like the idea of having a private investigator drawing fire in his jurisdiction, and would love to nail me for obstruction, or any damn thing. So I cleaned up the story and made it sound as reasonable as I could. I thought Ingo would be pissed at me for saying anything, but to my surprise, he simply nodded his head as I talked, and added a few words of agreement. We both knew it would all be on the early evening news. What difference did it make now? We'd already bet Hector's life against eight hundred million dollars, and stood a good chance of losing both.

Again and again we repeated the story for Nugent, first standing on the ferry dock, and later sitting on the battered chairs of his office at the police station. I told the chief where Sosenko lived, and he put someone on it, but I was certain Sosenko wouldn't be stupid enough to show up there again.

In the end, Nugent gave us a rambling, endless lecture about the way we'd handled a dangerous situation, about putting innocent citizens in the line of fire, about taking on responsibilities that belonged to the police. We also got vague threats about being prosecuted, though he never said for what.

Lisa called Ingo's cell phone from the hospital. The doctors had stabilized Hector, she said, but his condition was perilous. Sosenko's bullet had torn him up badly, and he was failing. An operation to repair the damage was his only chance to survive, they'd told her, difficult surgery Eastern Long Island Hospital wasn't equipped to handle. Hector was being loaded into a MedEvac helicopter for a flight to the big medical center at Stony Brook, fifteen minutes away by air, where an operating room and a surgical team were waiting. Lisa said they'd refused to take her along in the chopper. Her voice was calm and even, exactly what you'd expect from Lisa Harper.

Ingo convinced Nugent to let us leave and get to Stony Brook. Not really knowing what to do next, but determined to make a gesture that showed he was both annoyed and in charge, the chief informed me he'd be keeping my revolver until he confirmed the validity of my carry permit, not an easy license to get in New York State. I resisted the impulse to tell him checking me out was probably something he could do on line in a minute or two. He didn't look like the kind of guy who took kindly to being told how to handle his responsibilities.

Nugent told us he'd have cops across Long Island, and Connecticut, too, looking for Sosenko. There'd soon be a mug shot of this goddamn son-of-a-bitch — his words — on the wire. He'd goddamn well be caught, Nugent told us in his all-knowing way, but until Sosenko was in custody, we'd all better be goddamn cautious.

Rutkowski appeared in his cruiser to drive us back to Greenport, the chief executive officer of Julian Communications and I sitting together in the back seat. As we raced along the north road, I turned to Ingo. "This is it. We can't screw around any more," I told him. "We need tight security coverage until this thing —"

"Do it." He never looked at me.

I called Teague on my cell phone and told him what had happened. "Get some Empire people to the Julian offices, and get some New York cops, too," I said. "Forget low profile. There are no secrets any more. Julian employees are going to hear about this and they'll be nervous. They should know they're being protected by professionals with guns."

"Why do you think Sosenko wants to hit any of the Julian people in New York?" Teague said on the phone.

"Not sure he does. Don't know if he'll head back to New York at all. Certainly couldn't be there yet. But tell your guys to stay close to Brody. He says Sosenko was stalking him."

"Let me jump on this right now. Have to pull extra people

in," he said. Then, "Oh, and Seidenberg?"

"Yes?"

"Beautiful fucking job, Seidenberg. A real pro, that's what you are."

I thought of five different things that would make me feel better if I said them to Teague, but there was Empire's biggest client sitting right next to me, so I didn't say any of them. Just hung up.

"Brody says this Sosenko was stalking him? Isn't that what you told Teague?" Ingo said, quietly.

"It's what Brody told me."

"Fascinating."

"You say that as if you don't believe it."

"I said only that it was fascinating, yes?"

Rutkowski deposited us in Greenport, where we found Ingo's Mercedes had been moved to the apron of the ferry ramp. Ingo and I got in, and Ingo drove to Eastern Long Island Hospital, where Lisa waited at the main entrance. By now even her composure was showing some cracks. It was a bad day for everybody, even the Iron Woman.

The three of us headed toward Stony Brook. In the forty-five minutes it took us to reach the medical center, not a dozen words were spoken.

We didn't even have to go inside. The MedEvac helicopter was still on the landing pad, which was perilously close to the driveway of the main hospital building. The pilot stood there talking to a doctor and smoking a cigarette.

Ingo stopped the car and we got out.

Yes, they had just come from Greenport, they told us. Yes, they had picked up a man with a gunshot wound.

Was he in the operating room now? No, he wasn't, not now. Where was he, then? Were we relatives? No, good friends.

I'm sorry to have to tell you, then, but he had a terrible wound, and he didn't make it.

Did he die in the operating room, then? No, actually, he died on the trip here, in the helicopter.

Just like that. That's how it all ended for Hector Alzarez, that thoughtful, well-mannered, elegant, beautifully dressed dude who played it smart, and came this close to becoming exceedingly rich.

CHAPTER 17

It took the better part of two hours for Lisa to answer the questions and complete the paperwork in the hospital, so we could leave. As we headed back, we listened to the radio in the car. The two all-news stations out of New York already had the story on the air, and they were churning it endlessly. WCBS had a telephone sound bite of Nugent spilling everything he knew about the shooting and predicting that the perpetrator would be run to ground in short order. "We know who he is. We know what he looks like. We'll find him," the police chief told the news anchor, and the world. WINS had their Long Island reporter on the scene, and cut away every ten minutes to his live reports, which included comments from the teen driver of the Toyota. That young man, his voice cracking with eagerness, described the shooter as a heavyset Hispanic. "That is, like, I think," he said, summing it all up.

It was the sensational kind of story that journalists pray for on slow news days. Daring one-man assault of a ferryboat on the open water. Executive of a big company shot and killed as shocked passengers watch. Crazed former employee takes revenge. Blaze of gunfire as private investigator empties revolver at fleeing murderer.

Private investigator Ben Seidenberg, that is. They gave my name, but neglected to say 'retired.'

I suggested Ingo drive back on the South Fork, taking the south ferry to Shelter Island. That way, I told him, we'd avoid the north ferry from Greenport, and the reporters who were sure to have come to town by now. He took the south route, but it didn't much matter. There were already two TV crews who'd crossed from Greenport over to Shelter, waiting at the long gravel driveway that led to Ingo's place. Fortunately, also on hand were two Empire agents, quickly dispatched from New York by Teague, to keep them away from the house. Typical Empire operatives, they were burly, stone-faced types, with a demeanor that went beyond intimidating all the way to fearsome. Not one of the TV people tried to rush the car as the two guards motioned us through.

Lisa was in emergency mode. She'd been on her cell phone in the car, giving orders to her staff in New York, pulling people out of meetings, calling in favors from friends in the media, putting a calculated spin on everything she said. Maybe the woman did sleep her way into her job, but it appeared she was more than capable of handling it once she got there. Now she was on the phone in Ingo's study, breaking the bad news to Hector's mother, a 74-year-old widow in Austin, Texas.

"Shouldn't you be doing that?" I said to Ingo. We were in the great room, looking across the bay to the lights of Greenport. It was already seven o'clock.

"This is not a good time for you to tell me what I should be doing, yes?" he said, staring me down. Then, backing off, "Lisa is very capable at these things. She knows how to read people, say what they want to hear. I'm very blunt."

"I've noticed that," I said. "Blunt, but not forthcoming."

"Oh?"

"You didn't want me around, but you knew you needed me. Even so, you refused to let me get help. You wouldn't tell me the whole story, let me inside, so I could stay ahead of the game. You kept your secrets, and now Hector is dead," I said.

Ingo turned and stepped behind a white marble bar set against the back wall. "You've had a difficult day, Seidenberg. Let me pour you a drink. You've earned it. scotch, isn't it?"

"You know everything, don't you?"

"I know everything." He filled a glass with ice from a fridge below the bar, poured a healthy measure of Glenfidich over the cubes and held the drink out to me. The willful expression on his face said if I wanted it, I'd have to come and get it.

What the hell. I went to the bar and took the glass from his outstretched hand. "You're right about one thing," I said.

"Delighted to hear it. And just what thing is that?"

"I've earned it." I swirled the ice in the glass to chill the scotch, and took a sip. "Single malt," I said.

"Do you like it?"

"Frankly, I like Dewars better. A good blend goes down easier." A framed picture on a shelf behind the bar drew my attention. It was an engaging photo of two teenage boys grinning at the camera.

"My friends who drink scotch tell me single malts are for sophisticated palates, " he said, "whiskey for the carriage trade."

"That explains it, then. I'm irrevocably committed to middle class values, myself." I gestured with my glass at the photo. "That's you, isn't it?"

"Me and my brother Felix. I was sixteen and he was fifteen."

"I see the family resemblance."

"Maybe a little," he said. "Felix was more handsome. Every girl he met fell in love with him instantly."

I pulled at my Glenfiddich, wishing it were Dewars. •Ingo watched me closely. "Aren't you having any?" I asked him.

"I don't touch alcohol," he said, in a way intended to make me feel ill at ease because I drank and he didn't. As if I cared.

"A pity," I said. "I thought if you loosened up, you might let me in on the real story."

"This Sosenko maniac? You know the story. You're the one who uncovered it."

"Why don't you tell me what happened between you and Arthur Brody."

"What does that have to do with anything? A different story entirely."

"They don't tie together?" I said. "Just a coincidence? Twist of fate, maybe?"

His face began to redden, making his scars stand out in bold relief. "It's none of your affair, Seidenberg. I suggest you remember that Julian Communications is your client, and make a strong effort not to stray into areas that don't concern you."

"But it does concern me. I've been fed a well-rehearsed line by you and Lisa, and Brody, too. A man I never knew is drowned, and a good man I admire gets shot down in front of me. I get to sidestep bullets twice now, myself, and I'm forced to irritate the hell out of a wicked angina condition. And it all happens just when Julian Communications is about to go public. Strange, isn't it? So I really don't want to hear about your eight hundred million dollar jackpot again. You owe me more than a glass of high-priced scotch. Try paying me off with some truth."

"You think we've lied to you, is that it?" It was Lisa. I turned to see her standing in the archway of the great room. She held a pad of paper, the top sheet covered with her notes, and a pen.

"Lie? No, I suspect you've told me the truth," I said to her. "Just not all of it."

"Seidenberg is about to go back on the ferry," Ingo said irritably, right to my face.

"Hector told me you asked him out here to come up with a strategy to deal with Brody, mend the fences," I said. "Tell me about that."

Ingo ignored my question. He walked past me as though I weren't there, and sank into a chair. Superb physical condition or not, he had the fatigued look of a man with too many conflicts, too much on his mind. "Tell me what's happening," he said to Lisa.

"They're trying to schedule the funeral for Tuesday or Wednesday in Austin. Will you go?" she said.

"Tell Brody to go," he said.

"I think you should."

"Brody. Go with him if you want to."

Lisa made a note. Then, "The police chief, that Nugent, says the coroner will release the body Monday morning. An undertaker in Riverhead will send it to Texas." She turned to me. "Oh, and Nugent says you can pick up your gun at the police station."

"See," I said, "even the cops trust me."

"I talked to Lowell and Manheim," she said to Ingo. "They're the crisis public relations specialists. They handled the AuditCo insider trading thing. And CIM, the currency exchange problems."

"Spin doctors," Ingo said.

"Best in New York," she said. "Tony Manheim says the story will be all over the planet by tomorrow morning. But he thinks the news can be handled, maybe even turned to our advantage. I hired him on the phone. Told him to get in his car and point it to the Long Island Expressway. He's headed out now."

"Good." Ingo turned in his chair and looked at me for a long moment. "I suppose you're waiting for me to express a measure of gratitude, yes?" he said, his voice flat and indifferent. "Thank you for your assistance to my company. Thank you for shooting at that maniac, even if you missed all six shots. Teague has two of his Neanderthals from Empire on guard now, so there's no reason for you to stay here. In fact, there's only one more service you can perform for Julian Communications. Get this Sosenko."

"Police in two states are looking for him right now." I said. "I'm just one man."

"But you don't have all the legal constraints the police have," he said. "Add to that, now you will have your gun back."

It was nearly eight when I called Alicia from the ferry to tell her why I'd missed dinner, and that I was too weary to come by tonight. She swore she would never forgive me, unless I helped her make veal marsala tomorrow night, and then stayed around for some romance. That sounded fair, so I accepted.

It wasn't until the late news on Channel 7 that anyone in the media tied the shooting to Julian Communications' initial stock offering. No one suggested that the shooter was involved in a plot bearing on the IPO, but a snotty TV business reporter with a strange toupee speculated that the markets might be wary of a company being targeted by a murderer. Not only that, he added, but there had already been reports of a management power struggle in the big communications conglomerate, making the situation complicated, indeed. "We'll watch this one with great interest," he said, with an attitude that suggested this was all happening for his amusement.

Once the IPO connection surfaced, other media picked up on it. I went out the next morning and bought all the papers. The story was squarely in the spotlight on the front pages of the

Times, the Post, the News and Newsday, too. The headline in the Post, big enough to be read from down the hall and out the door, was the most unkind. It said, "REVENGE KILLING AT SEA; Hit-and-Run Gunman Dims Company's Stock Plans." Post headlines always did have a way of cutting through to the fundamental nature of things.

The Wall Street Journal ran it, but far back, and mercifully noted that whatever troubles the company might be experiencing, its bottom line was still strong. This was the only positive note any of the media sounded all day long.

Essentially, the revenge angle was playing out just the way Ingo and the others feared it would. It looked as though their calculated program for marketing Julian Communications to Wall Street was teetering now, with a possibility that their eight hundred million dollar payoff might fall off a cliff. Unless, of course, the public relations maven Tony Manheim was as good as they hoped.

It wasn't until I'd read everybody's version of the story that I noticed the light flashing on my answering machine. A call had come in while I was out for the papers. I pushed the replay bar.

"This is for you, Mr. Seidenberg." It was a man's voice, low-pitched and halting, a distressing rattle in his throat. He sounded sick, or maybe drunk. "My name is James Giannone. I think — I think there is a huge fraud that you may — ." His voice trailed off and there was a long pause in which I could hear his labored breathing. Then he began again. "Let me say that — that you are being duped into thinking — thinking —. It's a lie. A plot, you understand. People are being murdered. I have to talk to you. I will call back at exactly one o'clock this afternoon. Did I — did I say one? Yes, one o'clock."

CHAPTER 18

It might have been a crank message, some joker getting off at my expense. Easy enough. My name was in the news, and in the Greenport phonebook. No problem finding me and ringing me up. But I didn't think that's the way it went. The call from James Giannone had sounded too pained, too desperate, to be a hoax. Anyway, I wanted it to be real because I needed a break. I was pissed with myself for letting matters pull away from me, and I couldn't get Hector off my mind.

What could I have told him to keep him alive? Don't come to the North Fork, Hector, because Sosenko may be out here. Well, then, stay in the car so he can't get a clear shot at you. Get away from the rail. Be smart and watch your ass, Hector.

Too late now. I didn't shoot the man. Sosenko pulled the trigger. But what really killed Hector Alzarez was all that money.

It was ten o'clock, three hours to wait for Giannone's promised phone call. I still hadn't had breakfast, so I walked to Jerry's Café, part rustic restaurant, part fancy grocery, on Main Street, chose a stool at the long granite counter and ordered coffee and a scone. What I really wanted was a stack of Jerry's blueberry pancakes, but thinking ahead to my dinner with Alicia that night, I thought it would be smart to pace myself today. A scone was not altogether a bad compromise, as it was studded with fat raisins, and served with Jerry's raspberry preserves. You could learn to like these.

The back wall behind the counter at Jerry's was hung with a half dozen small hooked rugs, each with words and a picture worked into the design. I'd seen them a thousand times, drinking coffee here, but only today, with my mind roaming as I searched for logic in the universe, it occurred to me that there was mistake in a decorative line of poetry that surrounded a fanciful lighthouse and seagulls. It read, "And all I ask for is a tall ship, and a star to steer her by." If I couldn't deal with life's bigger issues, I decided to pounce on a small one. I called to Jerry, who was fiddling with the espresso machine.

"There's something terribly wrong here," I told him when he stood opposite me, leaning on the counter. "Do you know there's a mistake in that rug, or whatever it is?"

"Certainly I know."

"You do?"

"You mean the part about 'all I ask for is a tall ship?' Oh yeah, it should be 'all I ask is a tall ship.' If you put in the 'for,' it doesn't scan properly. Any schoolchild would know that." He put his hand on his chest, cleared his throat and began to orate. "'I must go down to the seas again, to the lonely sea and the sky. And all I ask is a tall ship, and a star to steer her by.' Shall I go on?"

"Not necessarily," I said.

"It's been six years since I put those things up, and you're only the second person to spot the mistake" he told me.

"Really? What do I win?"

He got a pot of coffee and refilled my cup. "Congratulations."

"That's it?"

"I'll shake your hand, too, if you want."

"Surprised you'd keep that thing hung up there, knowing there's such a conspicuous mistake" I said.

"Took you a while to find it, though, didn't it?" Touché, Jerry. He set the coffee pot back on a warmer and headed for his fancy cheeses, where a customer was beckoning.

He was correct, of course. The words were right out there, not hidden away, and I'd looked at them again and again for years. Looked, but hadn't seen. But that's how it works, isn't it? Some days you just don't get it, and some days it jumps right out at you.

I had another scone, telling myself I was eating a late breakfast and an early lunch at the same time, so my second helping wasn't an indulgence. It was, in fact, a clever way to eliminate an entire meal today. The Seidenberg Diet.

It was eleven forty-five when I returned to the house. The unpleasant voice waiting on my answering machine belonged to Roger Teague, who ranted on with orders and demands until I hit the rewind button and made him stop. Let him take care of guarding the Julian people. I had my own kite to fly.

Precisely at noon my phone rang. Even before he spoke, the strenuous breathing told me it was Giannone.

"You're early, Mr. Giannone. You told me one o'clock." I said.

"Twelve o'clock, I said. And right now it's -- the time is exactly twelve o'clock noon. Precisely," he said. "And it's not -- it's not Mr. Giannone. It's Doctor."

"What?"

"It's Doctor, I said. Doctor James Giannone."

"Are you a medical doctor? A physician?"

"Just what do you -- who are you to question me?" His voice was impatient and angry. He started to cough hard, rolling, violent spasms that fed on themselves, and I waited until they finally subsided. "I am a physician. Vanderbilt University School of Medicine, Nashville, Tennessee, that's where," he went on. "I come from a family -- a family -- a distinguished line of doctors." He fell quiet.

"You said you knew about a plot. You said I was in danger. The message you left on my machine."

"What? I said they might do away with you," he told me. "And that's -- that's right. This shooting on the boat –- the man from the Julian company who died. I heard about it on my radio, over and over. And about the stock on Wall Street. It's a plot. And I know what happened back when they -- so they –- they'd be happy to kill me, too. If they could. I have to be vigilant." Silence, again.

Finally I said, "What do you know about the plot, Dr. Giannone?"

"What?"

"I said what do you know about the plot — this plot you're telling me about?"

"Oh, I know things, Mr. Seidenberg," he said. "They don't want me to talk, or –- or I could destroy everything. So that's what I want."

"What? What do you want?"

"What do you think I want?" he said. "Money, is what. Listen to me, Mr. Seidenberg. I know they pay attention to you. You tell them –- no, you absolutely insist –- that they pay me." I could hear street noises in the background. He was calling from a pay-phone.

"Who should pay you money? And why should they pay you?"

"This is –- it is not a joke, and I am not a fool." In an instant he was raging. "Just think about this. I know the secret of the Julian company. And if they don't want me to say –- to talk –- to tell about it, then they have to pay."

"What is it you know?"

Suddenly he dropped his voice to a conspiratorial whisper. "No, no. Are you insane? Not –- not on the phone. I have to see you."

"Why me? Why don't you go directly to the company?"

"Ingo Julian, you mean? Arthur Brody?" he said. "No, I can't put myself in that position. These men, they have powers, connections. They'd destroy me. No, I want to meet you, Mr. Seidenberg. They said on the radio you tried to protect the man who was — who got killed on the boat. I want to meet you to see if — you are a smart person I trust to speak for me. You have a Jewish name. You're a Jew, right?"

"Pretty much," I said. "Does that make a difference to you?"

"Oh yes, yes. You Jews are smart. You keep your word. I'm a judge of these things. I have it all completely — all figured out. You'll meet me at the train station in Ronkonkoma. You know where that is?"

"Where are you? Are you in New York?"

"I'm in Shangri-La. But I'm going to Ronkonkoma. You know Ronkonkoma?"

"I know." Ronkonkoma is two-thirds of the way out on the main body of Long Island, a busy commuter center, trains running often, with a good-sized station and vast expanses of parking lots.

"I'm taking the 1:33 from Penn Station. Come by yourself," he said. "Don't tell anyone, because — because they'll find out and follow you and the blood this time will be yours and mine. Understand?"

"All right. What time?"

"Understand?" he said again.

"Yes, I understand. What train will you be on?"

"The 1:33, I told you," he snapped back. The anger again.

"That's when your train leaves Penn Station. When does it arrive? What time do we meet in Ronkonkoma?"

"Look it up," he said. "I'll be at a bench near the ticket windows. Take the back roads. Look in your mirror. Don't let anyone follow you." There was a click. His voice and the background noises ended abruptly. Somewhere on a street in New York, Dr. James Giannone was walking away from a public phone.

I got in my car at one PM, calculating that I could make it from Greenport to the Ronkonkoma station in fifty minutes, an hour at most. The 1:33 from Penn Station wasn't due until 2:58, but I wanted some slack to get the feel of the place, discreetly and carefully, before Giannone walked off the train. Also, it would be prudent to get there before he did. I thought: about time for me to be the power guy. Any more surprises, I'd like them to be on somebody else.

I took inventory of what I knew about this man. He was unbalanced, barely coherent. He could become angry in an instant. He knew who Ingo and Brody were. He was a doctor, or said he was. He claimed to know a dark secret, wanted money to keep quiet. He was about to trust me because he thought Jews were the good guys. And he was scared.

Would I be wise to share Giannone's fears, or should I just be worried about Giannone himself? Either way, I took a certain comfort in sensing the bulge of the revolver holstered under my jacket, as I parked at the Long Island Rail Road station in Ronkonkoma.

This was basically a commuter station for the Monday-through-Friday crowd, with peak hours early and late in the day. On this Saturday afternoon at 2:20, there were only a handful of passengers waiting to go to New York, and when the 2:25 pulled out, they were gone and on their way. The station was empty, except for a ticket agent and an old man in a stained fedora hat who appeared to have fallen asleep over his newspaper. He was snoring on a bench. I had over half an hour to wait for Giannone, and I took the time to walk the platforms, the two pedestrian overpasses that crossed the tracks, and the sprawling commercial plaza that surrounded the station. The station building itself could be approached from any of a half dozen places, but because my visitor was coming from New York, he'd get off his train on the other side of the tracks, opposite the station. He'd have to use one of the overpasses to get to the station side.

I decided to wait outdoors, a distance away, where I could observe both stairways. I wanted to make certain Dr. James Giannone was alone and inside the building before I said hello.

CHAPTER 19

I had no idea what Giannone looked like. If he hadn't rung off the phone so abruptly I would have asked him to describe himself. As it was, I 'd have to rely on my instincts, try to pick out someone who looked as batty as Giannone sounded. He'd said I'd find him on a bench near the ticket office, but considering he was the same guy who'd phoned me an hour earlier than he promised — and then insisted it was my mistake — there was a good chance he'd screw me on the meeting, too.

I didn't think he was tempting me into some kind of disaster. It just didn't sound that way. But then, I hadn't thought the ferry ride would end as it did, either.

The trick was, I kept telling myself, to stay in control. Don't let Giannone get the high ground. The thing was, there were so many possibilities in this place, so many doors, so many approaches.

On the other hand, I was a seasoned security professional with a gun, and Giannone was a green civilian. That was the more comforting thought. I'd stay with that one. I decided I'd be fine so long as I didn't have to tempt my angina by running.

In any case, here I was, and this was it.

At 2:55 I started checking my watch every minute, and

listening carefully for the approach of the train. But there was no train from New York, as 2:58 came and went.

Now passengers began drifting in to wait for the 3:15 going to New York. Some stood on the westbound platform, but most went into the station building. There were several well-dressed couples, headed for Saturday night dinners and shows in the city, I suspected. Easily four hundred bucks a couple, with the train fare and all. Conspicuous consumption, I thought.

The train from New York arrived six minutes late. I watched it roll to a gentle stop on the eastbound track, but I couldn't see passengers get off because the doors opened on the other side, facing away from me, and the train was quite a distance from where I stood, anyway. I'd have to wait to see who walked down the stairs from the overpasses across the tracks.

Not many came. Most of the passengers headed for the vast parking lot on the other side. Finally people began descending from the overpasses. There was a pack of boys, teens horsing around on the stairs, whooping and shouting obscenities to prove to themselves how tough they were. They disappeared into a donut shop on the plaza. Then a young couple toting a stroller with a child, she clinging to the handle above, he below on the stairs holding up the front end. There were two women laughing together, a white-haired man with an attaché case, a tiny foreign-looking woman all in black, a girl with some kind of animal in a cage. Then several clusters of passengers, walking down the stairs and dispersing quickly into the plaza, or down the street.

Only one person hesitated as he reached the ground level. He was a stocky, unshaven man, maybe 50 years old, bundled up far more heavily than the mild October day seemed to require, in a padded winter jacket, with a long green scarf wound around his neck, and a tweed cap pulled down tightly on his head. He appeared confused, looking around uncertainly, taking a few steps in one direction, then stopping and moving off the opposite way, and stopping again. I saw his lips moving. He was talking to himself, his face an anxious grimace. Then, looking around fitfully, he set off almost at a run for the station building. Pulling open a door, he rushed inside. I could see him through the doors, brushing against waiting passengers as he hurried to a bench near the ticket window and sat, his hands thrust deep into his jacket pockets.

Clearly, he had come alone. And he was waiting at the appointed place. I unzipped my jacket to make my gun more available and walked deliberately into the station building. He stared at me as I approached and sat on the bench next to him. "Doctor Giannone?" I said.

He sat up straight, his eyes searching me up and down. He opened his mouth but said nothing.

"I'm Ben Seidenberg, the man you called." I tried to touch his arm, to calm him, but he pulled away to the end of the bench. "I'm here about Julian Communications. You asked me to come." Still no answer. After all this trouble to get me here, why was he shrinking away from me now? "Are you James Giannone?"

Now he was genuinely panicked, shaking his head in fright.

The voice came from behind me. "He doesn't speak English. He can't understand you. You should be able to figure that out, Mr. Seidenberg."

I turned to see a tall stoop-shouldered man in a gray raincoat that had a large stains on both shoulders. His cheeks were sunken into unhealthy hollows, and the whites of his eyes had that jaundiced yellow tint that made you want to back away. "He's not James Giannone. Does he look like a — look like a physician to you? I mean, use your head, Seidenberg. Me, I'm Giannone. Right here."

The man on the bench stood and sidestepped away eagerly, happy to escape from me. Giannone sat down. I could see holes in the blue suit he wore under his raincoat, and the frayed collar of his open white shirt. He gave the impression of being a worn-out man in the remnants of a worn-out wardrobe. And he smelled sour, as though he'd lain in dirty, wet places.

"You're not very good for — for, you know -- an investigator." He cast wicked looks around the station, catching the eye of one person, then another, then back to me. "You were followed, you know, even though I warned you — specifically cautioned you, more than once — not to let that happen."

"Nobody followed me," I said. "How did you get in here from the train."

"How would anybody do it? Down the stairs and in the door." He rubbed his eyes and gave a private laugh that seemed to be only for his own amusement. "I waited, you see, to come down the stairs. I avoid moving about in crowds of people. It's dangerous to let them get close. The ferrets."

"Ferrets, you said?"

"Ferrets, ferrets," he said impatiently. "You --- you don't pay attention. Look at that man over there." Giannone gestured with his head. "A ferret. He's the one that followed you."

I looked. A man in a down vest stood reading a magazine. He spotted me looking at him, and gave me a self-conscious smile.

"He'll change back," Giannone said. "But not while you're watching." He looked down at the floor. "Give me eight dollars," he said.

"What for?" I asked him.

"So I can get back to the city. Son-of-a-bitch in Penn Station wouldn't --- wouldn't give me a round trip ticket. Some ferret got to him, made him ask me --- ask me for more money."

"You mean you didn't have enough money for a round-trip ticket?" I said.

"That's not what I said, goddamn it. It was a — just as I told you." Suddenly loud and angry, he punctuated his words with chopping motions of his hands. People were staring now. The man with the magazine moved outside. "Give me eight dollars," Giannone insisted.

I removed a bill from my wallet and held it out to him. "Here's ten. Two extra, in case you want a candy bar." He took it and tucked it away without a word of thanks, or anything else.

A young man in sneakers and blue jeans entered and hugged the man I'd mistaken for Giannone. They left together, talking cheerfully in Polish. So much for my insights into identity and human characteristics.

"I'm ready now for you to tell me about the secret you know," I said. "What is your connection to Julian Communications?"

"It was years ago," he said. I waited for him to go on, but he said nothing.

"How long?" I asked him, finally.

"It was before they started, of course — before the ferrets. In Utica."

"Utica, New York?"

"Utica General, where I was a resident. Up north. Cold in the winter," he said. "That's when the helicopter brought him in." Again he stopped.

"Who? Who did they bring in?"

"Ah, Mr. Seidenberg, now that — that is precisely the point."

"Are you talking about the helicopter that brought Ingo Julian to the hospital after the plane crash? Is that what we're discussing here?"

"Don't be coy with me. You know how this story goes, don't you? You have — you have your suspicions. I can see that. Hear it in your voice. Well, I know the truth. I was there and I'm ---" He sucked in his breath suddenly and shrank back on the bench. "They're here. I told you, they — they followed you. The ferrets." He pointed around the station, jabbing toward one corner of the room, than another, with his forefinger. "There. And there. And there."

"There's nobody here but people waiting for the train," I said. "I swear to you, there are no ferrets."

"Don't tell me that, you lying shit. Do you think I'm blind? They'll chew me to pieces. I can't stay here." He started to rise, but I grabbed his coat and held him.

"I'm an investigator, and that means I have a gun," I said. "You know what I'll do if the ferrets come after you? I'll shoot them all. I'll never let them get you. So you're safe, Dr. Giannone." Just like Hector was safe, I thought

First he stiffened, then all at once he relaxed, went so limp he almost slid off the bench. I released his coat. "Your promise, then?" he said. Now he sounded beaten, pitiful. He had his ups and downs, this poor bastard.

"Absolutely. Now tell me about the hospital in Utica. Tell me about Ingo Julian"

"I want you to go to them and tell them I know their secret. Tell them I want ten thousand dollars. No --- no, not enough. A million. What's that to them?" His eyes were flashing, darting all around. "I have to go —"

I said, "You don't have to go anywhere."

"Yes, yes. To the bathroom, all right? You have to let me go now. Then I'll tell you everything." He stood up slowly. "It's all right, Mr. Seidenberg. I'm going to tell you. I need money, and I need you. And I'm only crazy some of the time."

I was afraid to let him out of my sight, this man pursued by imaginary ferrets. He knew something I needed to know, and now that I was face to face with him, I couldn't run the risk of having him disappear on me. "I could use some of that, too," I said. "I'll go with you." I walked at his side toward the sign that said rest rooms.

Now the 3:15 to New York had moved into position at the platform, and the doors were open. The station building emptied out as passengers left to board the train. Through a station window I could see the conductor leaning out to signal the engineer. As Giannone and I were about to enter the men's room inside, the train doors closed, and I heard that sharp hiss trains make when the brakes are released.

The sound spooked Giannone. Maybe his ferrets had returned, or maybe some other kind of insanity had suddenly possessed him. He made a frightened moan, and bounded away from me. With surprising speed he was out the station door, and up the few stairs to the platform. I started after him, moving as swiftly as I dared, faster than a jog but slower than a run. And not fast enough to catch Giannone. I called to him, but he never looked back.

He clawed at the rubber strips where the sliding doors came together, got his fingers inside and managed to pull the two panels several inches apart. He put his shoulder against the edge of one and pushed with his palms against the other, forcing a bigger opening, and quickly slipped inside the car. The doors shut, and the train pulled out of the Ronkonkoma station.

Son of a bitch.

CHAPTER 20

Alicia's day had been much better than mine. As soon as I walked into her kitchen, she started singing to me in Italian, a ballad, she explained, about the virtues of love with an older man. She was vamping me shamelessly. "This is a night you remember forever," she said, stroking my cheek and boring right into me with those dark eyes. "This dinner will be in the history books as one of the perfect things."

"Perfect veal saltimbocca," I said, trying to get into the spirit of the thing, even though the latest of my string of fiascos was sitting heavily on my shoulders.

"Yes, that. But more. Even better." Alicia smiled her playful smile, not to be confused with her naughty smile, which was slower, more calculated, less spontaneous. "You remember, of course, my salad of the sea, which was for your birthday last year."

"It was remarkable. With the shrimp and calamari and crabmeat."

"And lobster, don't forget. Fresh lobster meat," she said. "I stop today in Braun's fish market, everything the best. We have this salad tonight, before the veal."

"Lobster and crabmeat and all that. You must be a rich woman." I kissed her lightly, brushing her lips with mine.

"I am," she said. "And you should kiss a rich woman better than that."

"Sorry, I'm a little preoccupied. Can I try again?"

"I give you one more chance. And if you fail me this time, there will be no salad of the sea."

I tried again. It wasn't my best, but it was all right, because she said, "OK for now. Maybe with this dinner you will improve."

"Is this an occasion? Something I don't know about?" I said.

She opened the refrigerator and started removing packages, laying them out according to some mysterious logic on the butcher block island. "Seafood here, veal there," she said, more to herself than to me. Then, "Yes, an occasion. Three paintings I sold today. A big floral by Moreno, you know, the Spaniard from Brooklyn who writes all over the back of the canvas. Twenty-six hundred, which is a good price for a Moreno. And two small landscapes by the Austrian, that Waldman. A man and his wife bought them as a pair. Thirty-four hundred for both. Paid cash and put them in the back seat of their Cadillac. A good day for money. The town was full of tourists, and the sun was out. People spend when the sun shines." She gave my arm a little punch. "So what do I care about the price of lobster meat?" She took a bottle of white wine from the refrigerator and handed it to me. "Gewurtztraminer. From Lenz Winery. Has a nice bite to it. See what you think."

She watched me as I opened the wine and poured out two drinks. We lifted our glasses in silent toasts to each other, and drank. She said, "For a man who is enjoying good wine and going to have an incredible dinner with a beautiful rich woman, you don't show a great deal of enthusiasm. Tell me what your trouble is, so I can help."

"My trouble is I'm losing my edge," I told her.

"What does this mean, edge?"

I touched a package in white paper, on the butcher block. "This the veal? How can I help?"

"You remember how, I know this. Because you are very good at making this dish. Yes, that is the veal" She pushed a smaller package toward me. "And this is the prosciutto. Fine prosciutto, from Parma. You start the veal dish, and I do the seafood. And while we work you tell me everything and we drink this bottle. Good idea, you think?"

"I think, yes." I opened the packages, placed a slice of prosciutto on each veal scallop and put the assembled pieces between sheets of plastic wrap.

"Gorgeous veal," Alicia said. "Look how light the color, almost white." She washed half a dozen small squid under running water, then separated the tentacles from the bodies. She filled two small pots with water, put some lemon juice and salt into each, and set the tentacles into one pot, the bodies into the other. She put both on the stove to cook.

"Why don't you boil them together?" I asked.

"Because the color from the tentacles will get on the bodies. Calamari bodies should be beautiful white. Everybody knows this," she told me. "Now you flatten the veal. We cook the veal after we finish the salad." She opened a package of huge shrimp and began to shell and devein them. "Now you tell me about this edge that has been lost."

I couldn't get the words out right away. It's not easy to say these things, even to the most understanding woman I've ever known. Alicia waited quietly, working with the shrimp. "I've been letting things happen," I allowed, finally, "things that shouldn't happen. A killer ridicules me right on the streets of New York. Hector Alzarez gets shot to death in front of me. And today, I let my best lead get away from me. I had him, as close to me as you are now, and he just ran away from me and disappeared." I took a wooden mallet from a drawer beneath the kitchen island and began to pound the prosciutto into the veal, flattening the scallops through the plastic wrap.

"Not so hard with the hammer," Alicia said. "You break the meat."

"Sorry," I said.

"These things you do are life and death," Alicia said. "Who else even attempts such things? Who could do them better than you?"

"I could," I said. "Fifteen years ago. Even five years ago. I'm not what I was. I don't have the edge any more. The bad guys are getting ahead of me. I'm not thinking smart and I can't run fast. Actually, I can't run at all."

"But it's not over yet." Now she took the two pots of calamari off the stove, put the shrimp on to boil. "Sometimes you don't win right away, no. But in the end, yes."

"I shouldn't have to be dealing with this," I said. "The thing is, I got out of this business. They keep dragging me back in. I don't want to be in. I want to be out."

"Yes, you should be out. I keep telling you. But right now, today, you are in. That's the fact of it." She held out her wine glass and I refilled it. "You don't give in now, not in the middle," she said, and turned back to the stove.

The veal was properly flattened now, and I took the scallops from between the sheets of plastic wrap. I ran out of things to respond to Alicia, and the whole world got uncomfortably quiet. I went into the living room and put a CD on the stereo, to fill up the empty spaces. I thought Errol Garner's "Concert by the Sea" would lighten the mood, but the happy drive of Garner's jazz piano was at such odds with how I felt, it didn't do the trick. Not for me, anyway. But I let it play.

When I came back to the kitchen, Alicia had chilled the calamari and shrimp in icy water, and was assembling her seafood salad. She cut the squid bodies into rings and bathed them, together with the tentacles and chunks of shrimp, in a bowl of vinaigrette sauce, then with a slotted spoon divided the pieces between two serving plates. She did the same with lump crabmeat, and finally with lobster meat. She put a big lemon wedge and a sprig of parsley on each plate. Nothing more. It couldn't have been simpler, but all you had to do was look at it and you knew it would inspire awe in anyone lucky enough to get some.

"We eat the salad of the sea now," she said, sitting at the kitchen table. "The veal will take a few minutes, only."

I refilled Alicia's glass and my own, and sat -- guiltily, because I hadn't ventured to speak for so long. I began on my seafood.

After a moment, Alicia said, "So? How is it?"

"I can't find the right word," I said. "Sublime doesn't do it justice. Remarkable is an understatement. I think this may just be the best thing to eat in the entire solar system."

"It pleases you. Good." She raised her glass in a salute to me. That was a signature gesture of hers, to toast at every opportunity. Then, quietly, "You are a success. You built a business, and served clients well. It's true you are not a young man any more, and for that I am grateful. Young men don't know anything. You have the wisdom and the thoughtfulness of middle age. You know a great deal. And running? Why should you run, anyway? Fools run."

"You know, it's women like you who turn ordinary men into kings," I said.

"You are no ordinary man."

"Look, you've said to me that I should tell Teague to go to hell, just walk away, and whatever happens, happens," I said. "Of course, what will happen is, he'll find a way to stop paying me. You said you don't care, that the gallery makes more than we need."

"Yes. I said it and I meant it."

"I haven't decided, you understand. Just wanted to make sure you meant it."

"I did then, but I don't now."

"Oh?"

"It amazes you," she said. "So let me tell you why I say this. I know in my heart you mustn't walk away from this thing with the big company now. You think you made mistakes, and maybe you did, but you haven't lost, because it's not finished. But if you leave now, it will be on your mind forever that you left because you failed. The money from the gallery won't be because of love. It will be because of failing. You understand? If you lose your edge, as you say, you don't give up. You find it again." She leaned back in her chair, and with a wave of her hand, she said, "When this is all over, then we talk about how you tell Teague to go to hell."

For a long moment, I could only look at her and smile. Finally I said, "I feel better already," I said. "Did I tell you this seafood is marvelous?"

"You said you couldn't find a word to describe it."

"I found one."

We finished our seafood down to the last shreds of crabmeat, and Alicia cleared the dishes. "Now the veal," she said.

She heated some oil in a big sauté pan, dredged the veal scallops in flour and browned them quickly on both sides. Removing the scallops to a serving platter, she turned the heat all the way up on the sauté pan and added broth and Marsala wine, plus a generous chunk of butter. "A lot of butter, I know," she said, with a shamefaced wince. "But just this once, OK?" She stirred the mixture as it bubbled, and seasoned it with salt and pepper when it had thickened slightly.

She poured the sauce over the veal. You could have taken a picture of it for one of those high-priced cookbooks.

We attacked the veal, mopping up the sauce with chunks of crusty bread.

"This is also a marvelous dish," Alicia said. "I think we are attracted to each other because we do so well together in the kitchen." She smiled her naughty smile. "Now you are supposed to say we're good in the bedroom, too."

"Now you're doing your lines, and mine, too," I said.

"Look, this man who ran away from you today, can you find him again? He had to come from someplace."

"He says he's a doctor. Worked at a hospital in Utica. I was thinking I'd make a call, start there."

"Good," she said. "I know I have said too much already. But now you will forgive me if I tell you just one more thought. OK?"

"Say what you think."

"It seems to me you fight this battle all by yourself. These people in the Julian company, they aren't on your side. Teague isn't on your side, either. It's only you against everybody else."

"You're on my side."

"Always. But I can't run very well, either. And I don't have a gun. But Wally, he's a younger man, and smart. And he's your friend. I think you must ask him to help you."

"He has helped me," I said.

"Then he must help you more. Just my thinking, that's all."

"Should we clean up the dishes?"

"One more thing, first."

"You said the last thing was the last thing."

"I lied. Now I want to see if a good meal has improved your kissing."

She said it had.

CHAPTER 21

Roger Teague used to say to me, "Why do you have such a morbid devotion to the truth?" He couldn't understand why I wasn't as dedicated to lying as he was. In Teague's view of the world, lying was the stock-in-trade of investigators and security professionals, and he took absolute joy in deceiving people, often for the most obscure reasons, or no reason at all. He did it, I always thought, just to prove he was above the truth. He believed whatever he was doing somehow justified any lie he cared to tell.

So it wasn't so much on moral grounds that it troubled me to lie. Compared to all the really nasty sins there are in the world, lying is often minor stuff. No, lying bothered me — a little, though not enough to stop me when I had to — because in my mind it tended to put me into the same low-life league as Teague. I would rather be compared to Vlad the Impaler.

Beside, the truth has, as they say, a ring to it. People recognize it when they hear it. Bullshit tends to smell, even from a distance. In my experience, people tend to believe me when I tell them the truth. Maybe it's the sincerity in my voice. Or maybe it's my homely face.

In any case, I felt telling the truth was likely to be my best shot at learning the whereabouts of Dr. James Giannone. That is, if I had any shot at all. If he really had been at Utica General Hospital as he claimed, that institution might take a dim view of releasing information about him, especially over the phone. Hospitals are sticky about matters of confidentiality. My strategy was to give them the real story, and impress them with my concern.

I told it as clearly as I could, stressing that Giannone was about to stumble into a dangerous situation. But the personnel director was not inclined to be patient. "What does this have to do with the hospital?" she kept asking with a raspy voice, once, twice, three times. I reviewed it for her again, while she continued to dispute, and in the end she responded with a long surge of liquid throat-clearing. As I listened to the spatter, I could picture an overweight lady at a messy desk, drinking coffee and hoping to sneak outside soon for a cigarette. "There's no James Giannone here now," she said, when she finally recovered.

"I know he's not there. I thought you might have a forwarding address for him, someplace where I could contact him and tell him he's at risk."

"Well, wait a minute," she said. I heard her walking away, clearing her throat all the while, and then the sound of a file drawer opening and closing from across the room. "He left here three years ago," she allowed, when she returned. "That was before I came here. Can't tell you more than that."

"Didn't he leave a forwarding address?"

"We don't give out information about our people." She said it as if she'd suddenly remembered a hospital rule. I was beginning to get the feeling she was sitting there with Giannone's file open in front of her, looking at information that made her uneasy.

"James Giannone is in danger. I must find him."

"You should send us a letter," she said, without conviction.

"I understand your wanting to keep information confidential," I told her. "I wouldn't want you to get into any trouble. Maybe there's somebody else who could approve this. There's a lot at stake here for Dr. Giannone."

"Dr. Waldrup is the only one," she said. "Chief of staff. I

report to him."

"Fine. Can I speak to him?"

"He's not here this morning," she said, tidying up her throat again, with great determination. "He'll be in his office at noon."

"I'll call."

"No, let me ask him to call you. I'll explain it to him."

Don't push any harder or I'll spook her, I told myself. There are no more options. "That's very kind of you. I'll wait for his call." And I gave her my number, fearing a callback would never happen.

But it did. By the sound of him, Dr. Waldrup was the big daddy of hospital chiefs of staff, with an Alabama drawl that made me wonder what he was doing in upstate New York. And there he was returning my message at 12:15, as a decent gentleman would, and anybody else might or might not.

"You want to know about Jim Giannone," he said. "What are you, the *police?*" Emphasis on the first syllable.

"Dr. Waldrup, did you hear about the killer on Long Island who ambushed a ferry boat right out on the water and shot a man to death. It was on the news."

"Read about it in the paper. Hell of a story."

"I'm Ben Seidenberg, an investigator. I was on that ferry."

"You the private detective? You the one who shot at the fella in the other boat?"

"Yes."

"And missed."

"Yes, I did," I admitted. "Look, the killing on the ferry wasn't just some random thing. I'm convinced it was part of a complicated plot. And James Giannone is about to blunder right into the middle of it. He doesn't know it, but if he gets mixed up in this, it could cost him his life. I have to find him and keep him away."

"This doesn't make sense to me. How did Giannone get involved in this, anyway?"

"All I know is that it probably had something to do with a patient in your hospital years ago. That same person was on the ferry. He was with the man who got shot," I told Waldrup. "Giannone thinks he knows something valuable, and he's looking for a payoff. I can't be certain what he thinks he knows. But I am sure James Giannone is unstable, and an easy mark for people who don't mind killing."

"You've met Giannone, then?"

"Once, yesterday," I said. "He was totally unbalanced. He said there were ferrets chasing him. He slipped away from me, and I don't know where to find him. And now I'm afraid he's headed for a disaster. You're my last hope. Please help me find him."

"How do I know you are who you say you are? Maybe you're the one wants to make trouble for him."

"Tell you what, Dr. Waldrup. I'm calling from my home in Greenport, New York. I'll hang up. Then you call information and get the number for Ben Seidenberg. You ring that number, and I'll answer. Is that fair?"

"All right, then. I believe you. I sure wouldn't want anything to happen to Jim. He's been through enough. They'll never let him be a doctor, you know." He took a long pause, and I could feel the climate shift from positive to negative. "But you understand we don't turn over information, just like that. I mean, no matter what the background, what the circumstances — never mind what Jim's been through." He was talking in code. There was something behind Giannone's departure from the hospital that he didn't want to spill. But it was in there someplace.

"What are you telling me, Dr. Waldrup? Are you going to help Dr. Giannone?"

"You have to understand that I have certain constraints," he said. "Not exactly sure what the hospital's exposure might be here, but we're inclined to be kinda conservative in these matters. Besides, Jim's been on the move. I doubt he's still at the address we have for him." Now the climate started to thaw again. "I do want to help him, of course. I think we owe the boy that. Tell you what. He has a sister, you know."

"Didn't know that," I said. Waldrup was going to give me something.

"If Jim's sister knows where he is, she may choose to tell you. That would be her decision, of course. We have a New York address and phone number for her. It's three years old, but she may still be there. I'll try to call her and see if she wants to talk to you, and call you back after I reach her. I'll do that much for you, Mr. Seidenberg. "

Her name was Jane O'Connell, and she lived in Queens in one of those beehive apartment buildings lined up, mile after mile, along Roosevelt Boulevard. The place was clean and presentable, but everything looked old and worn and in need of replacement. The elevator was scratched and dented everywhere, and the hallway that led to her apartment on the sixteenth floor had a badly tattered carpet, and smelled like Chinese take-out.

Jane O'Connell was forty or so, a timid, soft-spoken woman who sat absolutely still with her hands folded in her lap. I had no way of knowing what she was thinking, but her eyes told me she was one of those innocents who trust people, probably not always wisely. I told her what I knew — the call I got from her brother, the unsettling meeting in the train station, the phone conversation with Waldrup. My point to her was that if her brother had information damaging to Julian Communications, and tried to approach them directly, he'd be putting himself at risk. Especially because he seemed to be — I put it as delicately as I knew how — unsteady. "I can insulate him from any action they might take," I told her. "I'll protect him."

"I still don't understand. Why would anyone want to harm Jimmy?" She was confused and fearful. Her brow wrinkled as she peered at me.

"I'm not altogether sure," I said. "All I know is that

something big is being played out. There's a great deal of money at stake, and two people have already been killed because of it. One of them was a friend of mine, a man I liked a great deal. If your brother jumps into this, he'll be complicating a situation that's already dangerous. Somebody's going to want him out of the way. I have to find out what Jim knows and what he wants, and I'll keep him them away from him."

"What about you? If you get involved, won't they try to, well, to get you out of the way, too?"

"I'm involved already. I don't want to be, but I am," I said. "Anyhow, I'm not an easy person to get out of the way." I settled back in my chair. "Tell me about your brother, Miss O'Connell. Or is it Mrs.?" I could never bring myself to say miz. Miz is not a word.

"It's Mrs. I'm a widow. My husband Al was a fireman. He was killed when a roof collapsed. A fire in a supermarket. In the Bronx."

"When?" I asked.

"Thirteen years ago. Fourteen, in February. Valentines Day, it was."

"I'm sorry," I told her.

"They said it was arson, but they never found out who did it. Al and I, we'd only been married five weeks. Still had a little of our tans left from our honeymoon in Jamaica." There was a faraway look about her now. She was playing it all in her head, thirteen years after the fact. "Jimmy, he helped me through it. Little brother always there for me. He's a sweet boy, really. Impulsive, reckless sometimes. But decent, you know."

"What happened to him in Utica? Why did he leave the hospital?"

"They took away his residency," she said. "They said he'd stolen drugs from the hospital pharmacy. They said he was an addict, that he was high when an old woman under his care died. He should have been able to save her, they said, but he didn't know what he was doing."

"Was it true?"

"The old woman dying because of him? I don't know. She was well into her eighties, and terribly sick. The family couldn't prove it, and they didn't take it to court. But the drugs thing, the addiction, those he couldn't deny. The pressure, the long hours, they got to him. He was always the nervous type, on edge. I guess he looked for an escape, turned to drugs." She sat there rubbing her hands together, slowly, for no reason I could see.

"Where did he go when he left Utica? Another hospital?"

"No. Couldn't," she said. "The hospital in Utica reported Jimmy to the state medical people, and they told him he can't be a doctor anymore. Can you imagine? After college, medical school, internship and a year of residency. He was lost, desperate. Finally he got a job at a medical lab in Chicago, but it didn't last, because he couldn't give up the drugs. He had nowhere to go, so he came to me. Slept on the sofa. He had no money, and —" Her soft voice began to crack. " — and he was having periods when he talked to people who weren't there, saw things that weren't there. Animals."

"Ferrets?"

"I think so," she said. "Sometimes he was all right. Just sometimes. He stayed here in the apartment, mostly. Only went out to buy drugs. I don't know how he found them around here, but he did. Out on the streets somewhere."

"You said he had no money."

"He'd take my money."

"Steal from you, you mean?"

"Yes, steal." She said it with a flicker of guilt, as though she had done it, not her brother. "There was some cash I kept in my bedroom, you know, for emergencies. A few hundred dollars. He found it when I was out at work. When that was gone, he'd take what I had in my purse when I was asleep. Once he got hold of my checkbook, forged some checks and cashed them. We had a bitter fight about it. I don't have that kind of money. Just Al's pension from the city, and what I make running the office for an orthodontist in Manhattan. It's not that much, even together. It didn't take long before I was in debt. Wasn't sure I could keep paying the rent.

"One day I came home from work and Jimmy was gone. He left a note. Said he couldn't go on letting himself ruin my life. Said he'd have to make his way on his own. Oh God, I was so worried. Where would he live? Who would take care of him? I was sure something terrible would happen to him. But what could I do? I had no idea where he went.

"Weeks went by, and no word from him. Then one night he called. He was at a church shelter in Manhattan, he said. He was trying to straighten himself out. He sounded better. Almost — " She stopped to search for a word.

"Lucid?" I volunteered.

"Yes, lucid," she said. "I told him I'd come in and see him, but he said no, he wasn't staying there. He had a job, sort of. A warehouse in a building near the old docks, you know, on the West Side. He said they gave him a space there, a room to live, in exchange for watching the place at night. And a little money, too, off the books. So that's where he is."

"Have you been there?" I asked.

"No. Every time I say I'll come see him, he tells me no, he wants to be straightened out first. He won't let me come. But I don't think he's getting better. Because he isn't so — lucid — any more. I know he's spending the money they give him on drugs. He calls sometimes, but he says strange things. I cry when he hangs up. It's so awfully sad."

"Mrs. O'Connell, let me see if I can help. Tell me where he is. I'll get to him and do my best to keep him safe." I leaned forward and took her hand. "I promise you."

Jane O'Connell looked at me for a long moment. Then she wrote down an address on a small pad, tore off the page and handed it to me.

CHAPTER 22

The building looked out over the West Side Highway and across the Hudson River, for an unobstructed view of the least attractive waterfront features of Weehawken, New Jersey. And that only if you could find a clean window to look through. At ground level, fronting the street, was a murky and sinister hamburger joint, a tiny shoe repair shop and a no-name store that apparently sold used office furniture. Upstairs were full-story loft spaces, accessible by riding an open elevator that trembled its way up at a pace so slow it made me begin to wish I'd brought a bite to eat.

The slip of paper Giannone's sister had given me said I could find him at Lucky Imports, Ltd., which turned out to be a distributor of made-in-Asia novelties, on the sixth floor. It was a vast space almost entirely filled with boxes stacked on wooden pallets, and so dimly lit that the far end seemed to bleed off into blackness. Maybe it would appear less forbidding, I dared to hope, when my eyes got used to the gloom.

Two men were moving pallets here and there, while a third, who seemed to be in charge, was keeping score with a pencil, pad and clipboard. None of them appeared Asian, even vaguely.

"I'm looking for Jim Giannone." I said it to the

clipboard guy. I believe in going right to the top.

"Why?" he asked me, without looking up.

"His sister told me to stop by," I told him. "Jim will want to see me."

Clipboard guy shrugged. "He's sleeping, probably. Down at the end, the brown door."

I made my way through a long aisle between walls of stacked boxes. The brown door was open an inch or two. I knocked, but there was no answer.

I pushed the door open slowly, and saw that clipboard guy was wrong. Giannone wasn't sleeping at all. He was in his briefs and a tee shirt, sitting on a cot, his back against the brick wall. Even in the dim light, I could see there was sweat streaming out of him. His breathing was shallow and labored, and he swayed from side to side. The room smelled of sickness and despair. It was clear that James Giannone was suffering, the result, I felt certain, of his need for drugs. He stared at me.

"Remember me?" I said.

"You're — Seidenberg." His voice was a whisper. "You — you're —you're the one who knows Ingo Julian."

"Yes, I know him. You asked me to meet you in Ronkonkoma, at the railroad station. Do you remember that?"

He wiped his face first on one arm, then the other. "Not much," he said. "I went there. But then I came back. I was crazy that day. When was it — yesterday? Day before?"

"Are you crazy now?"

"Sick."

"Do you see any ferrets?"

Giannone didn't answer. His shoulders began to jerk forward as though he had a tic, slowly and then faster. He winced with the effort as he pulled himself off the cot and made his way into a tiny bathroom in the corner of the room. He got down on his knees in front of the toilet, with his feet sticking out the door. His dry heaves at the bowl were so excruciating, and went on for so long, I could feel the poor bastard's pain in my own gut. Finally the heaving stopped, and he stayed there motionless for several minutes, with his head hanging in the bowl, before he could pull himself to his feet and lurch back to the cot.

"You all right?"

"Better now. I'll get by."

"Cold turkey?" I said

"Trying." His voice was so faint, I could barely hear him. This wasn't the wild-eyed maniac who gave me the slip in Ronkonkoma. Today he was a pathetic addict, sick and defeated, going through withdrawal, trying to save his own life. But reasonably rational.

"This has to be the hard way, don't you think?" I said. "Why don't you get some help, get into a program?"

"Did that — three, four times. Not for me. Never stayed. I'm just — just too righteous to get down and — and grovel with those pathetic losers."

"Because you're better than they are?"

"Yes, I am," he said. "I can only do this myself. Nobody watching me. I got in. I'll get out. Or die, maybe. Either way, this will be over. But I — but I need — uh —"

"What?"

"Money. I don't have any. Nothing. How can I get back on my feet if I can't even afford a haircut?"

"And you want money from Julian Communications."

"Yes."

"Because you know something."

"Yes. You tell them about — about the secret I know."

"So what do you know that's worth — how much do you want?"

"I don't know. Let's say — let's say twenty-five thousand dollars. Then I could get a place, some decent clothes. And I owe money to my sister. I stole from her. Jesus,

I put her money in my arm."

"I know. That's how I found you. Through your sister."

He rubbed his eyes with his fists. "Twenty-five thousand, then. All right?"

"Whatever you say. What's the big secret you know?"

Giannone forced himself to his feet, took a pair of trousers hanging over a chair, and hopping on one foot, pulled them on. "The owner comes in around this time. He thinks I'm crazy, but he knows I'll be here. He just wants a — a warm body here at night, because people have broken into this building. I don't let him see me when — when the ferrets — when they —. He doesn't know about — about my problem. He's so — incredibly dumb." He put on a shirt and stepped into a battered pair of loafers. "Just in case he looks in, you understand."

"I'm waiting for you to tell me what you know."

"All right." He sighed as he sat on the cot. "You think you know Ingo Julian, but you don't."

"Oh? Why is that?"

"Because — because the man is dead. Been dead for six years."

"Are you going to tell me that the person running the company today is his brother Felix? That it was Ingo who was burned up in that plane crash in the mountains, and Felix who survived? I've heard that before. It's nonsense, a story somebody dreamed up."

"The story is true," Giannone said. "I overheard the whole plot. I'm the — the only one who knows what really happened. Beside Ingo — Felix Julian, that is — and Arthur Brody."

"Brody? How Brody?"

Giannone leaned forward, his elbows on his knees. He was still sweating heavily, and his shirt had already begun to soak through. "This is what I know, what I heard. I'm — I was

— a resident at the hospital. They brought a man in by helicopter. They said it was Felix Julian. They said there was another man on the plane, his brother Ingo, who burned up in the fire. That's what — what I was told when I went on shift at six in the evening. Twelve hour shift. Twelve on, twelve off.

"The man they'd flown in had second degree burns over a third of his body, multiple fractures on one leg, fractured arm, fractured ribs, severe thoracic trauma. The medic on the helicopter had cut most of his clothes — burned clothes— cut them off. He was nearly naked when they brought him in, they said. He was on the operating table for — for a long time, and it looked as though he might not survive. When they finally got him into the intensive care unit, he was covered with bandages."

Giannone sat absolutely still, his eyes staring straight ahead, as if observing a scene from the past that only he could see. He was in a sort of reverie.

"I was on shift when Brody arrived from New York in the middle of that night. He asked me about Felix's condition, and I told him the man had a decent chance to survive, but that he was facing more surgeries to repair the damage to his face and his body. His burns and other injuries were so — so extensive, he'd never be the same man again. Brody was so concerned, and he was completely — he was desperate to see the man. I told him he could. The ICU was nearly dark at that hour, and Brody stood by the bed. Felix had his eyes shut. Never moved. I saw Brody leaning close. He was very intense. That's when I went off shift."

Brody, intense? The same serene executive who had handed me an envelope stuffed with money and calmly suggested I do away with Sosenko? "What do you mean, intense?" I asked Giannone.

Annoyed at the question, he broke away from his reverie. "I mean anxious, very apprehensive about Felix. Look, you want to hear this, or not?"

"Go on."

"When I came back the next night, I checked the ICU and saw that Brody was still there, all that time, sitting in a chair by the bed. Felix was still unconscious. Later, Felix — he opened his eyes for a while, but he didn't move at all. He was heavily medicated, of course. For — for the pain. Finally Brody left. Said he'd get a room at a hotel. But he was back again in a few hours, just sitting there, watching the man in the bed. It wasn't until the next night that Felix finally — finally was able to turn his head a little. I saw Brody talking to him, but Felix couldn't answer. He just — just stared up through the bandages. He might have heard Brody. I don't know.

"Later that night, coming back to check, I was outside the curtain at Felix's bed. Brody didn't see me. I couldn't hear everything, just — just pieces — bits of what Brody was telling Felix. But I did hear him say, 'Now we don't have to sell the company. You'll be a better Ingo than your brother ever was. I'll show you how to make the smart moves.'"

Giannone seemed to be running out of breath. "I never thought about it then. Meant nothing to me. Company politics — I don't live in that world. Beside, I had my own troubles at the hospital. But years later I read something about Ingo Julian, chairman of Julian Communications. And I laughed because I knew Ingo was dead. I knew it had to be Felix playing the part of his brother."

"Did you ever ask yourself why Felix would do that? Why should he bother?"

"Were you listening to me?" he said, with the same sudden anger I'd seen in him at the railroad station, when the ferrets were nipping at him. "Without Ingo, they'd have had to sell the company. That's what Brody said. Pay attention, Seidenberg. Brody was — he had this scheme. He used Felix, to hold onto the company."

"And you got all that from what you heard Brody say?"

"Yes! The patient in the bed was Felix!" Now he was shouting at me.

"Maybe," I said. "Or maybe the guy in the bed was Ingo all the time."

"Ingo was dead in the crash."

"I don't believe it," I said. "It sounds like a bad movie."

"It's what happened. I was there."

"Didn't anybody check? Didn't anybody question all this?"

"Why?" he said. "Nobody said — nobody was disputing it."

I sat there shaking my head. I didn't believe anybody could pull off such an outrageous con, and make it stick, year after year. So many people knew Ingo. Nobody could fool them all. "I have to ask you something," I said. "I know why you had to leave the hospital, all that. Were you on drugs six years ago, when Brody was there?"

"You think this whole thing was a hallucination?" he snapped.

"You do see ferrets," I said.

"I know what's real. I can tell the difference."

"All right, it was real," I said. "Just one more thing. You knew about this from the beginning. How come it took you six years to say something?"

He stood and walked unsteadily into the bathroom. I heard the water run in the sink. He came out wiping his face and neck with a towel. "What did I care?" he said. "It was none of my business." Then, heavy with sarcasm, "And beside, doctors aren't supposed to talk about patients."

"And now?" I asked.

"Now Julian Communications is all over the news. Now Felix and Brody are going to make — what is it, hundreds of millions — with their scam. And now I need the money. Anyway, I'm not a doctor any more, now am I?"

CHAPTER 23

By the time I liberated my car from the garage, crossed town to the east side and made my way through the Midtown Tunnel, it was past four in the afternoon. The sluggish procession of homeward-bound commuters had already begun, and there was no choice but to join the endless line of cars on the Long Island Expressway.

With the crawl of traffic testing my patience, I had more time than I needed to ponder Giannone's story. I was satisfied that he was who he said he was, a doctor, now defrocked, who'd been at Utica General Hospital when a badly injured Felix — or somebody — was brought in. But had Giannone actually heard Brody propose a grand scheme to the patient in the bed, or was the whole episode just an imagined fantasy that seemed real to a rogue doctor tripping on drugs? Maybe he'd simply misinterpreted what he'd heard. Or maybe it was something Giannone's addled mind misconstrued now, years after the fact. After all, this was a guy subject to spells of irrational anger, a pathetic addict who saw little animals where there were none.

For all of that, should I still believe him? He'd been lucid today, and almost reasonable. And why should he lie? He'd have no hope of a payoff from Julian Communications if he were making it up. He couldn't bamboozle Brody and Ingo.

They'd both been there six years ago. They knew the truth.

If Giannone was right, how did it involve what was playing out at Julian Communications? What if the man I knew as Ingo was really Felix, and Brody was the brains behind all his moves? It would pay them to stick together, a winning combination, especially now, with Wall Street waiting for the Julian stock offering. Not only that, if word got out about Felix impersonating a dead brother, the whole stock deal could collapse. So why the falling out? Smart guys would know better. Maybe that's why Ingo — or whoever — wanted to kiss and make up with Brody.

The ringing of the cell phone in my jacket pocket put my thoughts on hold while I fumbled to answer it. Wally's lazy drawl sounded good to me, familiar and comfortable after my labored talk with Giannone. "Where are you at, amigo?"

"Driving east on the LIE, talking on my cell phone, which is against the law. I'm in the traffic with the worker bees. Just passed exit 36," I told him. "What's up?"

"Thought you might have a casual interest in this," he said. "Our buddy Sosenko is nosing around out here again. Cops are after him, but he's staying ahead of them. I saw his boat pulling away from the gas pumps over at Tyson's marina. Still had that piece of white plywood nailed on the stern, but I could tell that was the boat."

"Which way was he heading?"

"East, when I saw him. But he could have gone anywhere once he made it around the east end of Shelter."

"You don't suppose Ingo Julian and Lisa Harper are still on Shelter, do you?"

"I do suppose," Wally said. "They're in residence."

"How do you know?"

"I saw them through my binoculars. I think it was them. Swimming in front of the Julian place. Back and forth. Swimming in October, for chrissakes. Got to be loco, no?"

"Through your binoculars? What are you, some kind of secret agent?"

"I take this stuff seriously, compadre. I'm just trying to ace this assignment so you'll make me a private eye. You know, with a badge and all."

"Too much stress for you," I said. "Make you old before your time."

"Look what it did to you," he said.

I wasn't going to win this exchange. "But Sosenko didn't put in on Shelter, did he, at Dering Harbor?" I said.

"Why is it so hard to understand me when I talk? Try and watch my lips over the phone. I told you no. He went right past Dering Harbor. But Dering isn't the only landing on the island. Or he could just wait for dark and then come back," Wally said. "You want me to go over there, look around? "

"Not necessary right now. Teague's got two strongarm types guarding the Julian place," I told him. "Anyway, I'm going there myself. Time I had another talk with Ingo."

"I'm here to serve," Wally said. "Call any time, day or night." I could hear him waiting for me to end it, so I did, the best way I knew how.

"Goodbye."

The Empire night-man at the front gate of Ingo's place had blue eyes, close-cut blond hair, a chest the size of a bale of hay, and might have been a Nazi storm trooper, somehow misplaced in time. I had some hesitation telling him my name was Seidenberg, but evidently Teague had blessed me, because herr guard did everything but snap to attention and click his heels when I showed him my ID and asked to go inside.

Lisa was in the great room, intent on a laptop computer balanced, appropriately enough, on her lap. Clad in jeans, a sweatshirt and tennis shoes, she sat cross-legged on a couch, transcribing data from the computer screen onto a pad lying beside her. Seeing her again, it occurred to me that she always looked athletic, even in repose. There was a certain coiled-spring aspect about her. I was convinced she might suddenly leap up and run around the room, just for the exercise.

"Surprised you're still here," I said. "Thought you and Ingo would be back in New York, guiding the destinies of Julian Communications."

"We're guiding them from here," she said. "Your Mr. Teague persuaded Ingo to stay out here a day or two longer. Said security for us was less complicated here. Promised he'd have the problem solved by then."

Yeah, solved, I thought. "Where's Ingo?"

"I'm not certain. He was on the phone most of the day, and then he seemed to be getting antsy. I think he sneaked out for a run before the sun sets completely."

"A run? Without a guard with him? Why would he try to defeat the security?" I said. "That's dumb."

She set the computer down and turned it off. "You're probably right, Seidenberg. I think you should tell him. Tell Ingo he's dumb."

"I wouldn't presume to tell Ingo anything. But I do have something to ask him," I said.

"Oh? Why don't you ask me? I know what Ingo knows."

I sat on the couch beside her. "I'm sure you do. All right, I'm going to tell you a story I heard, and I want you to tell me if it's true." I never mentioned Giannone's name, but I went carefully through the scenario he'd revealed to me.

Lisa never took her eyes off of me, but said nothing. Finally, "Are you telling me you buy this fairy tale? Do you actually think Ingo is Felix?"

"It might explain a lot," I said. "Brody pulling the strings, making all the key decisions for the company. The power behind the throne. After years of it, Felix coming to resent him. An argument. A falling out. I can see that happening."

"Except that it never did happen. Anyone who ever knew Felix will tell you he couldn't possibly be the man who's chief executive officer of the company today."

"You knew Felix."

"Well. Very well."

"And Ingo?"

"I know Ingo. Very well, also. Better than anyone."

"Tell me exactly why you're so sure he isn't Felix," I said. "What was Felix like? You two were together, weren't you?"

"Oh come now, Seidenberg. I was with Felix. Now I'm with Ingo." She undid her cross-legged position and planted her feet on the floor with a thump, punctuating what she said. "Do you really think I can't tell the difference?"

"What are we talking about here? Pants on or pants off? Style? Technique?"

"You are tactless," she said.

"We're way past tact," I told her. "What do you know about Felix?"

"I told you that story. You know about his business — the mail-order flower thing down in Orlando. How it failed, so he came back to work in the company with Ingo."

"You told me what had happened, but you didn't tell me much about Felix," I said.

"All right. Listen, then, and tell me if I'm describing the man you call Ingo." She stood, thrust her hands deep into the pockets of her jeans, and began pacing about the perimeter of the room. "Felix was younger, always in awe of his big brother. Ingo was the bold one, the aggressive one, the one who took a few thousand dollars and built a huge business. He offered Felix a piece of the company, but Felix wouldn't take it. He felt he had to prove himself, do something on his own, just like his brother. Well, he tried, and you know what happened. He did everything wrong, let everybody take advantage of him — employees, suppliers, everybody. He was too nice, too easy, to be a boss. He trusted everybody. Even that woman in Orlando who roped him in, got him to marry her."

"What was her name?" I asked.

"What does it matter? Lisa said.

"Could you let me decide what matters?" I said. "I'm getting more than a little tired of people holding back on me. Just for one minute, I'd like to have a look at the whole picture."

"Now you're making me feel guilty," she said, in a way that told me she didn't, at all. "All right. Let me think. It was Mary Jean. You know these southern girls. They all have two names — Betty Jo, Sally Mae. Anyway, she was a Mary Jean. Mary Jean Christensen. They were only married seven months, and she took him for four hundred thousand. Ingo paid it.

"Anyway, the point is that Ingo and Felix couldn't have been more different. Ingo's a smart, shrewd, forceful man who knows what he wants and where he's going. He was always that way, and he became even more determined after the accident. He drives tough deals, and sure, he's made his share of enemies. He is not universally loved. Show me a successful leader at his level who is.

"Felix was a decent guy. But in the game he tried to play, you don't get any points for that. He was soft."

"Soft and decent. Is that why you loved him?" I said.

"I suppose it was."

"If that's the kind of guy who appeals to you, isn't it strange that you're with Ingo now? Being that the two brothers were so different."

Lisa stopped her pacing and faced me, her fists now on her hips. "You know what, Seidenberg? I've had enough of being forthright and open. My choices are my choices, and I don't have to explain them. You think I care what you believe? I really don't. You're not the first one to think I traded my ass for a vice presidency.

"Now let me tell you what I think. I think it's time for you to go home. If you came in here believing Ingo is really Felix, you've been set straight by someone who knows the truth. I can't think why your source would want you to believe such a preposterous thing. He — or is it a she? — has some agenda I can't begin to understand. Ingo is Felix? It's simply not possible. And goodnight."

Ingo had heard what she said. He'd evidently been standing just outside the archway leading into the room, and now he strode in with that peculiar rolling gait of his. Though there was a slight October chill in the evening air outside, his face glistened with perspiration. From his run, I assumed. "You think I am Felix?" he said to me. "That's almost blasphemy. My brother died six years ago, yes?"

"I think that point's been made," I said, nodding toward Lisa.

"Still," he said, "you have no cause to investigate my brother. I find it distressing, because his memory is sacred to me. I must tell you, Seidenberg, that your speculations are not strengthening Empire Security's relationship with me. Am I being clear?"

I don't respond to pointless questions, so I let it slide by. I said, "I'm here to tell you that the man who shot Hector has been seen out here today. The Empire people can't protect you if you insist on giving them the slip."

"Point taken," Ingo said. "Is there anything else?"

"We're trying to keep you alive."

"I know that. Don't think I'm not grateful," he said. "But understand that I resent absurd stories about Felix. In any case, this situation today is not about my brother. Not in any way. Goodnight, Seidenberg."

I nodded at him and forced a smile, pointedly insincere. I looked to Lisa, but she was already back on the couch, playing with her computer again and refusing to meet my eyes.

No sense telling them about Giannone's payoff request. They'd already dismissed his story as a lie

I walked back to the ferry, sharply aware that the truth was still being twisted. But I was getting close. All I had to do was hear Ingo say 'blasphemy' and 'sacred' in the same breath as his brother's name, and I knew I'd struck a nerve. As the boat moved out into the bay toward the lights of Greenport on the other side, I suspected Ingo's brother was key to this puzzle. And I had a good idea who might have the answers I wanted.

CHAPTER 24

There was an early morning plane to Orlando out of MacArthur Airport, an easy hour's ride by car along the eastern half of the Long Island Expressway. By eight-thirty I was on my way to Florida, up above the clouds, drinking airline coffee from a plastic cup, and eating a Danish which was scandalously small and far too sweet. But what the hell. I always thought it was something of a minor miracle, anyway, that you were able to sit and eat as you flew through the air.

As I looked down on the white billows below, I wondered just how much of a bimbo Mary Jean Christensen really was. To hear Lisa Harper tell it, she was a cornpone femme fatale who snagged Felix the innocent, chewed him up and then took him for a mound of his brother's money. My conversation with the southern lady in question on the phone last night, however, didn't reveal that degree of wickedness. Ms. Christensen, in fact, sounded like the very soul of consideration one expects of women in polite company, especially below the Mason-Dixon line. Given the unhappy way in which she'd parted company with the Julian family, I was surprised that she agreed so quickly to talk to me. I told her I was trying to clear up questions about Felix's death, and she seemed eager to help, though she reminded me she'd been divorced from Felix for a two years before he died, so there probably wasn't much she could contribute. But all nice, very nice. I've known some bimbos in my day, and none of them ever sounded like Mary Jean Christensen.

Last night I'd thought a chat on the phone would give me the information I needed, but what I heard was such a contradiction to what I expected, I felt I had to see this lady for myself.

Straight answers were in short supply in this whole matter. I'd found there were two stories about everything. A good story. And the real story.

It was pouring rain when we landed in Orlando, and by the time I got behind the wheel of a rental car, my blazer was damp all over, and the crease in my pants had melted away. It was clear that when I arrived at Mary Jean Christensen's doorstep, I'd be forced to compensate for my bedraggled appearance with extra charm and charisma, both of which I had in abundance, according to a certain Italian lady who knew the real stuff when she saw it.

After a false start which took me to the wrong side of town, I finally made my way to Mary Jean Christensen's address, a neat ranch house in a sub-division of neat ranch houses. There was a Spanish tile roof, which seemed to be de rigueur in this neighborhood, a handsome brick driveway, and three orange trees, loaded with fruit, in the front yard. It all looked so clean and sweet, it might have been a set for an old TV sitcom.

She must have been watching for me, because the front door opened as I rushed up the front pathway through the downpour. "You come right in this house," she said, taking my hand and pulling me inside, out of the rain. "We've had nothing but sunshine and more sunshine for three weeks, do you believe that? Now, just because you've come, we get this, this cloudburst. Oh, you poor man. I am so, so sorry. Let me get you a towel." She started toward a hallway, then stopped, turned, and smiled. "You are Mr. Ben Seidenberg, aren't you?"

"Yes, I am," I admitted.

"Oh good," she said.

She left, then quickly reappeared with a towel, which I used to wipe my face and head. She took my coat and hung it over a doorknob to dry, then led me into the living room and motioned me into a chair. "So, now, Mr. Seidenberg, you've come all the way from, where is it? Long Island, to talk to me. This must be important."

"It's important to me. And please call me Ben."

"Ben, then. What can I tell you, Ben, that will be worth this long trip? You were rather guarded on the phone last night."

Mary Jean Christensen was a elegant, raven-haired woman in her mid-thirties who moved gracefully and looked you right in the eye. She had a way of leaning forward when she spoke that gave you the impression she meant what she said, and meant it for you alone. She had a compelling presence, and I could see why Felix, or any man, for that matter, would be attracted to her. "I need to know what Felix was like, what you learned about him when you were married" I told her.

"Well now, Ben, I could have talked to you about that on the phone," she said. "Why don't you tell me why you flew here today, really."

"I suppose I wanted to see for myself what kind of woman Felix married. I'm trying to get a sense of the man, what he liked, what choices he made, how he acted."

"Why do you care?" she said.

I looked at her without replying. She watched me back in silence, and the wait began to get awkward. She expected an answer. Here I was, invited into her home, wanting her to tell me things she just might find painful. I had to level with her.

So I did. I told her the whole story — the murders,

Sosenko, Giannone's belief that Ingo was dead and Felix was alive. I watched her begin shaking her head slowly as I talked. "Don't you believe this?" I asked her.

"Oh I believe it," she said. "It's just that I'm in awe at how perverse and bothersome the Julian family can be. No, I don't doubt anything you tell me about them, and about their company. They are disruptive. They make people unhappy."

"Did Felix make you unhappy?"

"Oh yes, he did."

"I never knew Felix," I said, "but I was told he was easygoing, too easygoing. People took advantage of him. He tried too hard to be a good guy. He wasn't tough enough, and that's why the business he tried to start down here failed."

"Who told you that?"

"The woman he took up with when he got back to New York."

"Lisa Harper, you mean?"

"You know her?"

"I know of her," said Mary Jean Christensen. "I heard about her. The office assistant who somehow got to be a big executive. Well, if that's what she told you about the man, maybe she and I aren't talking about the same Felix. Maybe that fellow you told me about was right. Maybe there was a switch somewhere along the line."

"What do you mean? You telling me he wasn't the dear man she says he was?"

She held her left hand up in front of her face. I saw at once that her ring finger was badly misshapen, twisted sideways at the first knuckle, and again at the second. The little finger, too, was splayed away from the others, sticking out at an eccentric angle. They were ugly deformities. "A gift from Felix Julian," she said.

"He did that? Can you — will you tell me about it?"

"Oh I'll tell you," she said. "The business was losing

money every month, and he liked to take it out on me. One morning I got up and found him pacing around our apartment, muttering to himself. He'd been awake all night, worrying about bad sales and employees who detested him, and thinking up reasons why I kept him from being successful. It was a mistake to marry me, he said. He grabbed me and tried to pull the diamond ring he'd given me off my finger. It wouldn't come, so he twisted my finger, first one way and then the other, till the finger broke. I was screaming in pain, begging him to stop, pulling away, But he still had hold of my little finger, and he yanked it back and broke it, too. He never did get the ring. They had to cut if off at the hospital."

"Was he always violent, or was this the first time?" I said.

"This wasn't the first time," she said, "but it was the last. He had hit me a dozen times by then, and humiliated me every day. A marriage that turned into a nightmare. When I first met him, he was completely different. He was fun, he was charming, and nothing was too good for me. But after we were married, and the business started to go bad, the whole thing changed, turned dark. Felix took charge of everything, where we went, what we did, what we ate, even. No discussion. Just do it his way. That's how he ran his company, too. He wouldn't listen to anybody about anything."

"Was he drinking? I said.

"Felix never touched alcohol. It wasn't drink that made him the way he was. I guess way down deep, where you couldn't always see it, he was mean."

"You left him, after the ring incident?" I asked her.

"At the hospital, they realized my broken fingers couldn't have been an accident, so they called in the police. The police wanted to charge Felix with assault."

"Did you press the charge?"

"No, I didn't," she said. "That same day, Ingo showed

up. Flew down right away to get his brother out of trouble. He told me he'd give me a quarter of a million dollars if I insisted the broken fingers weren't Felix's fault. Then I could have a quiet divorce. I was so crazy with pain, and so angry. I was lying there in bed with my hand bandaged, and I wanted to hit him, but I couldn't. So I spit at him. I actually did. Ingo never flinched. He asked me, what did I want, then? I told him a half million dollars." She looked at her damaged hand. "In the end, we settled at four hundred thousand. Every man has his price, and that goes for women, too. I would never have let myself be bought if Felix hadn't been so cruel. It just seemed to me that I earned that money."

"I think you did," I said.

"So now I have this house and a bank account," she said. "And a left hand I try to hide."

"What do you do? Do you have a job?"

"Yes. I am the maitre d' at the best restaurant in Orlando," she said, smiling. "I do for myself, and very nicely, thank you."

"Let me ask you, do you think maybe this Giannone person is right, that Felix is alive, and that he's been playing the part of Ingo since the airplane crash? I mean, you were married to Felix. Do you believe it's possible?"

"I haven't seen Felix since that day he broke my fingers, so I'm not sure. Yes, he looked a little bit like Ingo. I mean, you could tell they were brothers. But they certainly weren't identical in appearance. And they were different in so many other ways. Ingo had discipline, intelligence, talent. Felix seemed always to be on his way to a defeat. He saw it coming, I thought, but he believed it was because of circumstances, other people — anybody's fault but his own. He was constantly scrambling to find somebody or something to blame for his own failure. Could he take over for Ingo? Hardly. I can't believe he could manage Julian Communications, not for a month, not for a day." She looked out the front window at the orange trees in the yard. The rain had stopped.

Then she added, "Unless he just sat there at the big desk, and let somebody else make all the decisions, I suppose."

I saw a tee-shirt once that said 'Life is too short to drink bad wine,' But at thirty thousand feet, with the only wine available in little screw-top bottles from the flight attendant at five dollars a drink, I contented myself with the notion that bad wine was better than no wine at all.

In the air back to Long Island, I looked into my glass of too-young merlot and tried to assess what I'd learned for a day spent traveling and three hundred sixty-three bucks round-trip airfare plus another fifty-five for a cheap rental car. Now I knew Felix Julian was hardly the happy-go-lucky sweetheart Lisa Harper had made him out to be. How had she put up with him when it got to be her turn? I suspected she'd put up with anything, if she figured the payoff was a vice presidency.

The truth was, Felix was a frustrated loser with violent tendencies, a man desperate to emulate his brother's success. But was he really part of a bold scheme by Arthur Brody to take over a dead brother's company, prestige and fortune?

With the lights of New York City passing below, for the first time I began to realize that the switch of identities had never happened, that Felix Julian was indeed dead and buried.

CHAPTER 25

It was nearly nine the next morning when I made it to Jerry's's for coffee and a raisin scone. I'd wiped the raspberry jam off my fingers and was dusting the crumbs from my stomach when Wally pushed open the door, strode quickly across the wooden floor to my table and stood there, rocking from side to side and rubbing his hands together, expressions of eagerness unusual for him. "Nobody at the house. Figured you'd be here," he said.

"Want coffee?" I said.

"No time, compadre," he said. "Your pal Sosenko is at Lulu's, right this very minute. She gave me a quick call when he went into the crapper."

"How long ago?"

"No more than ten minutes. He was waiting at the door with the early morning rummies when she opened up. Scared the monumental shit out of her, she says. Turned out he came in to brag, impress her, crow about his big deal to the love of his life."

"What deal?" I said.

"Something in New York, she says. Flashing around a fistful of hundred dollar bills he got from somebody to do something in the city."

"When? When does he go to New York?"

"Don't know. Pretty soon, seems like," Wally said. "Whatever it is he's going to do, it's today. That's what Lulu says."

"But he's still at the bar?"

"Was, ten minutes ago. Having a couple of eye-openers." Wally made an impatient get-up motion to me with both hands. "We can be at Shinnecock in half an hour, if we go like hell."

"Going to call Lulu first," I said, taking the cell phone from my pocket, "see if Sosenko's still there."

I got the number from information, and Lulu answered on the first ring. "This is Ben Seidenberg, Wally Prager's friend," I told her. "You remember me."

"Oh sure," I heard her say.

"Sosenko's there, right?" I said. I got the sense that he was close and listening to her end of the conversation.

"Yeah, you said it," Lulu said.

"So you can't say too much, right?"

"Right," she said.

"Is he going to stay there? Just say yes or no."

"No."

"Is he getting ready to leave, do you think?"

"Yeah, I think so."

"Right now?"

"Sure, absolutely," she said.

"For New York?"

"Yeah, you bet."

"Be cool, Lulu. We're going to get this guy. Just say goodbye," I said,

"Goodbye," said Lulu Lumpkin.

"He's leaving now," I told Wally. "He'll be gone by the time we get to the south side."

"What now?"

"We get to the Expressway before he does and pick him

up. We'll snag him at exit 70." I stood up and dropped some dollar bills on the table. "Got to go back to the house, get my gun," I said. We left in Wally's bright red pickup, the one that read 'Southold Marina, Sales, Service, Dockage' on the doors. After a speedy stop for my .38, we took off for the North Road, the long way to our destination, but quick because it avoided nearly every stoplight and most of the in-town traffic.

You could tell from the reek of stale cigar smoke that this was Wally's truck. "It smells like a pool room in here," I told him, rolling down my window.

"I don't smell anything," he said. Wally was hunched over the steering wheel, grinning with excitement like a kid, as he punched the accelerator and flew the truck down the road.

"Never saw you so turned on before," I said. "Enjoying this?"

"Loving it, amigo. How many chances do I get to be a hero? Come on, in Southold?" Wally said. "I mean, right now I'm this far away from the real thing. This is the closest we've been to grabbing a real-life, honest-to-Christ killer. How many guys get to do that, ever?"

"Maybe you ought to think about it," I told him. "Just because we're close doesn't mean they're going to interview you on the eleven o'clock news. Au contraire. You just might get a bullet up your skinny ass."

"Be worth it," Wally said, pushing the pickup still faster. "Time I went for the glory."

"Maybe it is," I said. "Alicia thinks I should be quicker to ask you for help, because you're my friend."

"Alicia is right," he said. "And not just for friendship, either."

"For what, then?"

"Look at it this way. You are getting a little bit long in the tooth. You're kind of going to flab, too. And there's the way you wheeze. These are problemos muy grandes for a person in your line, I should think." Wally looked over at me, which made me uncomfortable, because the pickup was pushing eighty and beginning to edge onto the shoulder of the road. I pointed straight ahead, and he got the idea, returning his attention, and the truck, to the blacktop. Still he went on, "And on the other hand, there's me. Young and strong,"

"You're not so young," I said.

"Forty-two is younger than you are, pappy. And I'm muscle, mostly, with snappy reflexes, too. Plus I'm brave. Not fearless, you understand, or foolhardy, but respectably brave. Way I see it, I've got everything."

"Except the gun," I said.

"Yes, except the gun."

"The gun is a big thing."

Wally shrugged, in a way that told me he didn't care, and wasn't ready to back off, gun or no. "You know, I'm thinking," he said, "maybe Sosenko stayed on the south, took the Sunrise Highway."

"Maybe, but he won't stay on it. Too much traffic in the morning. Too many lights. He'll cut north to the expressway."

"Is it your investigator instinct saying we should watch the expressway?" Wally asked. "Like, a little voice inside your head?"

"Do you have your own voice telling you to do something else?" I said.

"I don't get voices."

"Then how about we listen to my voice. Get us on the expressway, and find a place to stop just behind the on-ramp at exit 70."

"All right. But only because you got the gun."

We barreled ahead, skidding through the curves as the road narrowed, then we cut over to the expressway and got on at exit 71.

"So, what you think he's on his way to do in the city?"

Wally said. "Your little voice letting us in on that?"

"You need help figuring that out, you have no future in the investigation business," I said.

"He's on his way to murder somebody," Wally ventured. "That wad of hundred dollar bills he's flashing around, that could be the payoff for a killing. Only Sosenko just can't keep himself from showboating. Got to let Lulu know what a big man he is. Got to be hot shit."

"That's the easy part," I said. "Now the big question is: who's he after? And why?"

"You just going to ask that," Wally said, "or you going to answer it, too?"

"He's not after Ingo or Lisa. They're both still on Shelter," I said. "Maybe he wants Arthur Brody. He's stalked Brody before. One thing I think is becoming clear. Sosenko isn't into this thing out of revenge. Not his own revenge, anyway. No, he's for hire."

"Why would anybody pick a loco like him to hire?" Wally said. "You want somebody killed, you find yourself a pro who gets the job done and disappears, not some idiot who sings about Lulu Lumpkin's tits, and keeps hanging around till he gets caught."

"Interesting point," I said. "You may have a career in the security industry after all. Leave your resume at the front desk."

"No, really," he said. "If you were looking for a hit man, would you get involved with Sosenko? He's a maniac. He's bound to fuck up."

"Still," I said, "he's killed two people, and he's still on the loose. Anyway, could be somebody chose him because he has an obvious motive. Julian Communications put his ass in jail, so it's logical for him to be knocking off Julian executives. That's what it looks like, what everybody thinks."

"What if he gets caught and he says, 'Wasn't my idea.

Somebody hired me to do this'?"

"What if, in the process of getting caught, he gets dead, and can't say anything?" I said. "Or if he's still alive, maybe he doesn't even know who hired him."

"So who did hire him to do these murders? And why would they pay him more money at this stage of the game?"

"Don't know yet. My little voice has stopped whispering to me," I said. "We'll find out when we get Sosenko."

"Right. And what's the plan for that, by the way?"

We passed the exit 70 off-ramp, which meant the on-ramp that would bring Sosenko onto the Expressway was a half mile ahead. "Slow down," I said. "Get off onto the shoulder up ahead and stop. This is where we wait. Keep the engine running."

"And the plan?" asked Wally, as he pulled off the highway..

"You're the one wants to be a hero. What do you think we should do?"

"If he's not already on the Sunrise Highway, you mean? OK, I think if this guy does show up here, we take off after him. I make like I'm going to pass him, and when we get side by side, you open your window and shoot out his left front tire. He has to stop, and that's when we pull over and get him. What do you think?"

"Excellent," I said. "You ready for this?"

"Absolutely."

I took the gun out of my holster and held it in my lap. "Don't take your eyes off that ramp," I said.

CHAPTER 26

Now there were dark clouds along the horizon to the north, bringing the threat of an autumn storm as they rolled slowly southward. But no rain yet.

We waited on the shoulder of the road with the engine running, scrutinizing each vehicle as it descended the ramp. The long line of morning commuters had thinned out, and the traffic was spotty now, one or two cars at a time slipping onto the three westbound lanes.

Wally was more than ready to go, sitting there pumping the accelerator to race the engine as every new vehicle appeared. "Hold your water," I said to him. "Save something for the chase."

"I'm trying to have an adventure here," he said. "Know what your trouble is? You forgot how to enjoy this stuff. Get into the spirit of the moment."

"Just another high-speed chase down the Long Island Expressway, guns blazing," I told him. "Done it a dozen times."

"Not with me at the wheel you didn't, amigo. It's a more satisfying experience when I'm driving."

"I'll be the judge of that."

A commercial van descended the ramp and weaved onto the expressway. Across the two rear doors the signage read, 'A Blind Man Is Driving This Truck' in bold blue lettering. "Look at that," said Wally, laughing and pointing. He was pumped up, flying, almost frenzied.

"That's Harrison's truck, from Easthampton. They sell Venetian blinds," I said.

"Christ, I know that," he said. "Everybody knows that. Had that sign on their trucks for twenty years."

"So what are you laughing about?"

"Do you mind if I laugh? Do you? I'm psyching myself up because I'm about to go into harm's way. I'm proving that I laugh at danger." He had turned toward me to make certain I got a good look at how brave he was. He was laughing in my face, actually.

"There's something you should know," I put in, as he continued to hoot.

He seemed amused that I would intrude on his little show of pluck. "And that is?"

I pointed at the rusty Dodge pickup that had blasted down the ramp and was quickly swinging into the fast lane, crossing perilously close to the rear of a car in the center. "It's adventure time," I said.

"Is that Sosenko?" Wally said.

"Hideous guy. Dirty yellow hair. Disgusting tattoos up both arms. Old piece-of-shit truck. Just might be him. Why don't we take a vote?"

Wally put the truck into gear and stomped on the accelerator, spinning the wheels against the shoulder of the road, as the vehicle fishtailed out into the traffic. Sosenko was already two hundred yards ahead of us, and going faster than anything else on the highway. "Why didn't you say something?" Wally said, holding the steering wheel in a two-handed death grip. "Now we have to catch him. Son-of-a-bitch must be doing eighty in that old wreck."

"I did say something," I told Wally. "That's why we're chasing him now. Just don't lose him."

Wally moved past an immense moving van into the fast

lane and pushed the accelerator to the floor. The engine howled in one key, and the tires sang on the concrete in another. Now we wove in and out of the fast lane, scaring the hell out of drivers who blocked our path. The speedometer inched past eighty. "We're closing," he said, above the noise. I watched the distance to the old Dodge shrink, wondering if Sosenko had any idea he was being chased. Hell, why should he? He was just tooling along, his pocket full of money, planning his next murder, never realizing that two simpleminded heroes were about to jump all over him.

When we were just fifty yards behind him, both trucks in the outside lane, Wally hollered, "I think I just discovered a flaw in our plan."

"You mean because we can't get on his left side so I can shoot out his tire through my window? That flaw?"

"Yeah, that one. He's not going to move out of the fast lane. What do we do? Get up behind him and you take out a tire from the back?"

"Low-grade idea," I said. "Can't see enough tire from back here for a decent shot. No, pull up close on his right."

"Then what? You're on the wrong side. How you going to shoot?"

"I'm not," I told him. "You are."

"I'm the driver."

"I'm promoting you to shooter."

"Muchas gracias. Who drives while I shoot?"

"I'll watch the road and hold the steering wheel from here. You keep your foot on the gas and take the shot. One's all you need."

"Wait a minute. You're the one with the gun license. I'm not even supposed to touch a pistol."

"Heroes sometimes have to do these things," I said. "Anyway, what's Sosenko going to do, report you to the police? Swing into the middle lane and open your window." He did. The wind roared in and sucked Wally's cigar ashes out of the open ash tray, swirling them around the cab. We drew closer to Sosenko. I held the .38 out to Wally. "Here. Cock it before you fire."

"You think you're dealing with a child here?" he said, taking the gun. "I know how these things work."

It dawned on some kid in an open green convertible that a curious thing was happening on the Long Island Expressway this morning, and he decided to join our chase, pulling close to get a better look. "Stupid shit. All we needed," Wally said. He pointed the gun at the kid and made a fierce face, all teeth and blazing eyes. The convertible took off for the slow lane and disappeared.

I put both my hands on the wheel. "I'm watching the road now. I'm steering. Give it a little more gas. When we get alongside, take out his front tire. Easy shot."

"Easy shot," he repeated, without conviction. We pulled close to Sosenko's rust-pocked truck and Wally stuck my .38 out the window, sighting down the barrel.

"Shoot," I said. But in the two seconds it took Wally to line up the shot. Sosenko looked over and saw him. Our quarry hit the brakes and the old Dodge slowed instantly, dropping back away from us, out of Wally's range as we flew ahead.

Wally tossed the .38, still cocked, onto the seat between us, and clutched the steering wheel again. I took the gun and set the hammer down gently, grateful he hadn't plugged me with my own weapon. But I didn't have time to give him my lecture on firearm safety. Sosenko had decided we weren't chasing him any more. Now he was chasing us.

He swung behind us, and began moving up. In my side-view mirror I could I could see him leering at us, his truck not fifteen feet from our rear bumper. "He wants to hit us," I said. Wally twisted the steering wheel and we lurched to the left, jumping into the fast lane. Sosenko followed from one lane to another then back again, as Wally struggled to maneuver away from him. We were in the newer truck, faster, too, I was sure. But we couldn't outrun Sosenko because there were cars ahead of us, in our way.

Sosenko rammed into our rear bumper, a terrifying jolt at the speeds we were traveling. The impact made us waver, first to one side then the other. "Shoot the son-of-a-bitch," Wally shouted, as he wrestled with the steering wheel.

But there was no time to shoot anybody. As Wally fought to get us onto a straight path down the highway, Sosenko backed off and made another run at us. The hit was a bone-cruncher this time, and dangerously off center, smacking us on the right, at the very end of the rear bumper, pushing the back of the our vehicle to the right and sending us spinning out to the left. Our tires screamed, sending up clouds of blue smoke, as we slid around completely twice, and finished our maneuver at a dead stop, engine still running, on the grass of the median. Cars were slowing to gape at us as they passed

We sat there struggling for breath, watching the old Dodge race down the expressway, getting farther ahead of us every second. "Wasn't a bad plan, really," Wally said. "Could have used some fine tuning, was all." He wrinkled his nose at the smell of the burnt rubber.

I could feel the angina tightening me up, and I rubbed my chest to make it go away. Didn't work. Never did. "Sosenko is not an easy man to catch," I said.

"I noticed that," said Wally.

"You still up for this?" I asked him.

"You couldn't possibly stop me, compadre," he said, gunning the engine and pulling back onto the expressway. There were metallic clattering noises coming from the rear of the truck. "Doesn't sound too good for my truck back there, does it?"

"I'll pay for the damage," I told him.

"Yes you will." Wally floored the accelerator. We were into it again, except now Sosenko was a half mile in front of us, weaving his way ahead. "I see him. He's up there," Wally said, moving his head from side to side, trying somehow to get a better look down the road. "I'll catch him."

"That would be good," I said.

It was darker now. The clouds had moved directly overhead, casting a grim shadow over the road and draining the fall colors from the landscape around us. Then the rain came, suddenly, and with an immediate downpour, a torrent that soaked everything as though a gigantic bucket of water had been heaved at us. Wally turned the windshield wipers on high, but even that wasn't enough to provide a clear view of the highway as the rain beat down. All around us, cars were forced to lower their speed, and we had no choice but to do the same.

In frustration, Wally hammered the steering wheel with his fists. "How we going to catch him now?"

"He's had to slow down, too," I said. "Do what you can. It's a long way to the city."

"Some kind of chase this is," Wally said. "Everybody walking."

I took my cell phone from my jacket. "I have to give Brody a heads-up," I said.

"One of the suits at Julian?" Wally said. "Why? You think he's the one Sosenko's looking to whack?"

"Whack? Did you actually say whack?"

"Yes, whack." He glanced over at me. "What? They say it in the movies all the time." Then, "You making fun of me?"

"I wouldn't," I said. "It's such a cheap shot. But yeah, I think Sosenko may be looking to whack Brody." I called Julian Communications on the cell phone, but when I got Brody's office, they told me he was in a meeting. I said to tell him I was on my way, and not to leave his office. "Got to get Sosenko before he gets to Brody," I told Wally as I tucked the cell phone back into my jacket.

"Why is Sosenko after this Brody?" Wally asked. He was straining forward over the wheel, trying to get a better look at the road through the downpour.

"It's a murder for hire. Sosenko flashing all that money around."

"So who's hired him?"

"Best guess?" I said. "I think Ingo Julian. I think Sosenko was on Shelter Island last night, and Ingo met him somewhere. I mean, look how it all sorted out. We know Sosenko was in the area, prowling around out there. Empire Security has two muscle-guys stationed on Shelter just to protect Lisa Harper and Ingo from Sosenko. So what does Ingo do? He slips away from the security guys and disappears for awhile. Alright, I know he's supposed to be fearless, but he's not stupid. I think he knows he doesn't have anything to fear from Sosenko. Sosenko is his man now, bought and paid for."

"I don't get it," Wally said. "Wasn't Sosenko after Ingo Julian when he shot up the Shelter Island Ferry? And didn't he drown that other guy, that Newalis, by mistake? Thought the guy was Julian out there in the water? Isn't that what you told me?"

"And I was right, too, I think. My take on it is Sosenko had been hired to kill Ingo, and screwed it up, not once but twice. Ingo got tired of being the target, and bought off Sosenko, paid him to turn against the guy who'd hired him in the first place." I gave Wally my most charming smile. "To whack him."

"Wait a minute," Wally said. "How does Ingo buy off a guy who's trying to kill him? How does he contact Sosenko, put an ad in the paper?"

"Don't know yet," I said.

"Here's another one for you," Wally said. "Why did Brody want to see Julian muerto, anyway?"

"I'm still working on that, too," I said. "But I think it goes back a long way, back to the plane crash. Something happened between Ingo and Brody right after the accident. It drew them together. They were inseparable for years. Then they had a falling out. Nobody seems to know why. Or they're not saying, anyway."

"Why do you think?"

"Not sure," I said. "But is it a coincidence it happened just when the company is about to go public? Could be eight hundred million dollars in play here."

"It's a money thing, is what you're saying?"

"Isn't it always?"

The traffic was thicker as we grew closer to New York. The rain continued, and the clouds grew even blacker. It was as if nighttime was approaching, even though it wasn't yet noon. It was impossible to move ahead of the other cars. Just stay in line and try to break away somewhere ahead. I took the smallest measure of comfort in the possibility that Sosenko was up there having the same problems we were. I could only hope if we weren't gaining on him, at least we weren't slipping farther behind, either. Couldn't bear letting him trounce me yet again.

"I think I see him," Wally said. "Isn't that him? Look behind the white truck."

"Where?"

"There. There," he said, pointing ahead with a sweep of his hand that could indicate any of a dozen vehicles. "It is."

I looked, but to me it was all a dark gray, liquid blur, appearing briefly behind the wiper blades, only to be washed away again by the rain. "I can't see," I said. "How can you be sure?"

"Because I'm young and strong and have the sharp eyes of a hawk," Wally said. "It's him. How many rotting trucks like that you think there are on this highway?"

"Stay with him," I said. "Can you get closer? We'll be into the tunnel in a minute."

Wally tried to inch up, pushing across aggressively into other lanes, as we approached the entrance to the Queens-Midtown Tunnel. His perseverance didn't go down well with other drivers. Most refused to give way, and at least two flipped him the ultimate reflection of disrespect: the middle finger salute New Yorkers love so dearly. But Wally wouldn't be denied. Doggedly, he insinuated us into one lane, then another, moving up one car length at a time.

Now I saw Sosenko's truck, perhaps eight cars ahead, one lane to our right. And through the rain I could barely make out the openings of the tunnel less than a half mile away.

The red tail lights of the cars in front of us began to flash as drivers applied their brakes. The traffic was coming to a halt.

Wally was forced to stop. I could see Sosenko stopped, too, only a hundred feet ahead. "Shit, that's him right up there," Wally said. "Maybe we go grab him up while he's stuck in traffic."

"Let's do it," I said. Holding the gun low, I opened my door and stepped out into the downpour. Wally got out the other side, leaving the motor on. We ran through the water toward the rusty truck, but before we'd covered half the distance, the traffic started up toward the tunnel entrance, and Sosenko was on the move again.

We had no choice but to turn and hurry back to Wally's truck. We were both soaked, and horns behind us were blaring, as we climbed back in and took off into the tunnel. "Don't the good guys ever get a break?" Wally said, wiping his face with the back of his hand.

The short delay had cost us more distance between us and Sosenko. He was up there ahead somewhere in this long tunnel under the East River, but we'd lost sight of him. And when we finally emerged onto Thirty-Fifth Street in Manhattan, Hick Sosenko and his decaying truck were nowhere to be seen.

CHAPTER 27

The rain had ended while we were making our way through the tunnel, and now the air was washed clean for the moment, even at this tunnel exit customarily fouled with a haze of exhaust. I opened my window, hoping some fresh air might somehow steady my heartbeat and dilate my arteries. It was yet another angina therapy that never worked, but at least gave me the sense that I wasn't just sitting there waiting while my heart decided whether to carry on or sputter to a halt.

"What now, muchacho?" Wally said as he drove onto Thirty-Fifth Street. "Any idea where he went?"

"Happens I do." Long pause, breathing deeply, willing my blood pressure to drop, trying to stabilize, refusing to clutch at my chest even though I wanted to. "Turn right on Third Avenue. He's gone uptown."

"Good," Wally said. "Then he's somewhere between Thirty-Fifth and the Canadian border."

"Just to Forty-Ninth, at Park," I said. "Brody told me once that Sosenko had stalked him. I don't think that ever happened. But Sosenko knows his way to Julian Communications. I saw him there. Chased him around the building, down Park, all over."

"Chased? You? Wish I'd seen it," Wally said. He turned onto Third Avenue and headed north. "So what are you telling me, it was Brody hired Sosenko in the beginning? To whack Ingo Julian?"

"Makes sense to me." Forcing a grin I hoped was enigmatic, plus a chuckle for emphasis.

"What's funny?" he said.

"It amuses me when you say whack."

"Sosenko's on his way to the Julian company, you think? Would he try to assassinate Brody in the guy's office, just like that? He knows we're right behind him."

"Sosenko did a one-man assault on a ferry, for chrissakes, murdered Hector Alzarez while a whole boat-load of people watched him. Beyond ballsy, right? Don't forget, after he'd drowned Newalis at Ingo's place, he actually turned his boat around and came back to watch. Couldn't stay away, quirky bastard."

"Tough guy, right?" Wally said. "Do something just to prove he can get away with it."

"I'm just saying, the basic rules don't apply to Hick Sosenko. Taking chances doesn't bother him. He was born without a risk gene."

"But Empire's got an armed guard there, no? At the Julian offices?"

"That's no guarantee," I said. "Remember the ferry. We were both there, and I had a gun. Hector still got popped right in front of us. Somebody really wants you dead, it's hard to keep you alive."

"I'll write that down," Wally said. "For when I take my exam."

"Turn here. Park in one of the garages down the block. And look for his truck. He has to put it someplace. Maybe we'll get lucky. My little voice of intuition is speaking to me again."

He took a left and we moved slowly down Forty-Ninth, looking into the parking garages. We saw no rusty truck. Wally sighed. "Sometimes your little voice is full of mierda."

"Happens sometime," I told him. "Pull in and park. Let's get to Brody's office."

When we stepped off the elevator onto the thirty-sixth floor, there was a reassuring sense that everything was as it should be. The sounds of carefully modulated voices, and telephones chosen for their non-threatening ring, were hushed by an acre of deep carpeting that soaked up noises before they might offend. The air smelled subtly of freshly laundered clothing and expensive cologne. The young woman behind the marble reception desk was so downright gorgeous and immaculately groomed, you felt blessed if she so much as smiled at you. It was an environment designed to project flawless taste, civilized people, and a considerable investment of money.

It wasn't wasted on Wally. "Look at this fucking place," he said, just loud enough to make me wish for an instant that I'd come alone. "I'm going to re-do my office at the marina just like this. What do you think if would take for that blonde to come to work for me?"

"A miracle," I said.

The Empire plainclothes guy was there, a bald, stocky man in his fifties who looked as though he'd handled his share of hostile people. He stood quietly where he could see the bank of elevators and the door to the stairwell. There were no other ways to get onto the thirty-sixth floor. Or off. I told him who we were and what we were doing there. He nodded, but his look told me he knew already. Then we went to see Arthur Brody in that vast, spare office of his.

Brody stood when we entered, walking around his desk to us. "May I have the pleasure of meeting your friend?" he said, his voice polite but wary. He looked at me but held his hand out to Wally.

"I'm assisting Ben on this case," Wally said before I

could stop him. He shook Brody's hand. "My name is Prager. Wally."

"Prager Wally?" said Brody.

"Wally Prager, actually," I put in before Wally could confuse the issue any further. "He's a close friend who's helping. In an unofficial way. The situation is getting sticky, and I thought backup would be wise."

"If you say so." Brody's suit today was banker's gray, with the merest suggestion of pinstriping. White spread-collar shirt with discrete gold links adorning the French cuffs. Solid blue tie. And the inevitable plain-toed black shoes buffed to an impossible shine. Perfect.

"Sosenko is in New York," I said. "We chased him on the Long Island Expressway."

"You lost him, then?" Brody said.

"In the Midtown Tunnel. But we think he's nearby. And we believe he's come to get you."

"Kill me, you mean?"

"Yes, what we mean," Wally announced, to my surprise. He was determined to be a player in this. Well, what the hell. I nodded my head in agreement with him.

"There's an Empire guard outside, and it's doubtful Sosenko will try to get past him," I said. "That would make his job harder than it has to be. But he's around somewhere, and he's going to try to find a way to get to you."

"Then stop him, Seidenberg," Brody said with absolute calm. "Defeat him. I believe we have an agreement, you and I."

"I wouldn't rely on any agreement just yet. I haven't spent the money you gave me. You might want it back," I said.

"I gave it to you. It's yours." Brody clasped his hands behind his back and paced to the window, looking out across the cityscape and the Hudson River. Dark clouds were moving across the sky. Maybe it would rain again. We watched in silence. Finally Brody turned to us. "Why would I want it back?"

"Because I know what you've done, and I think you won't be happy about that," I said.

"And what have you discovered about me that is so disturbing?" Brody smiled benignly. He walked to the chair behind his desk, sat down, took a fresh pencil and began making notes on the yellow pad in front of him.

"Mr. Brody likes to take notes on what goes on in his office," I explained to Wally, who looked mystified. "Helps him focus." Then to Brody: "I have a theory that explains a great deal. You and Ingo Julian. Sosenko's two murders. Ingo and his brother Felix. Dr. James Giannone."

"Forgive me for interrupting you," Brody said, still writing, "but I'm trying to follow this. Who is Dr. James Giannone?"

I took a seat across from Brody. Wally moved to stand behind my chair, tall and steadfast, the picture of fidelity. What a guy.

"Giannone is the wild card in this game," I said to Brody. "He was a resident at the hospital in Utica when you arrived there after the plane crash."

Brody looked up from his note-pad. "If you say so. What does this have to do with me?"

"More than you know," I said. "Help me out on this, will you. Do you remember how you heard Ingo's plane had crashed?"

"That was a long time ago," Brody said.

"You don't forget things like that. You got a phone call, right?"

"Ingo's secretary got the call from the hospital in Utica, as I remember. She came in and told me."

"And what did she say to you?"

"What do you mean?"

"I mean, didn't she say, 'Ingo's been killed, and Felix is

in critical condition?' Because there was a mix-up at first. At the hospital, they thought their patient was Felix, and that Ingo had been burned up in the plane. And when they called, that's what they reported. They didn't know then that it was really Ingo who'd survived."

Brody was making notes again. "I recall something like that," he said. "It was a mistake that was soon corrected."

"Not so soon. Not until days later, right?"

"Is there a point to all this?"

"Certainly," I said. "Here's the story. You arrive and they take you to Ingo's bedside. You and everybody else thinks it's Felix there, all bandaged up. You wait days for him to regain consciousness. When he does, he can't speak, but he can understand you, and you lay it all out for him. You tell him he's inheriting control of the company, and this is his opportunity to turn it into a money machine that'll make him enormously rich. And finally get him some respect, because right now everybody — including him — knows he's a loser. You'll show him how to be a shrewd manager, and avoid all the dumb mistakes made by poor dead Ingo, who was just too shortsighted to recognize the company's potential. All Felix has to do is make you president of Julian Communications."

"I'm putting down two words under my notes on all this," Brody said, not looking up. "Absolute nonsense." He wrote boldly, and turned the pad around on his desk so I could read the words. "You haven't the least notion of what I said to Ingo."

"But I do," I told him. "I heard it from Giannone. Here's the rest of the story. See, Giannone thinks, just as you do, that the man in the hospital bed is Felix. He hears you telling that man about taking over the company. He doesn't think much about it then, because he has his own troubles. The hospital is onto him for his drug habit, and is just about to kiss him goodbye. In fact, Giannone is gone from the hospital before the Ingo-Felix mistake gets straightened out."

"I'm trying to understand this," Brody said. "Is there anything here that's not the flimsiest conjecture?"

"I'm getting to the good part," I told him. "It's years later, Giannone is a down-and-out junkie. He sees Ingo's name in the news, and he thinks 'This can't be Ingo Julian. Ingo Julian is dead. His brother must have taken his place.' He gets it all wrong, a fantasy in the fried brain of a drug addict. But now Giannone needs money, and he figures he has something to sell. He wants to be paid off, or he'll tell the world about the fraud at Julian Communications. Only he's afraid to show up himself, so he tells me the story and asks me to take it to Ingo."

Brody leaned forward, his elbows propped on the desk. "And this story, this is what you really believe?"

"I really do," I said.

"Have you asked yourself why Ingo didn't just get rid of me if I'd made such a blunder?"

"He needed you," I said. "There he was, barely alive, unable even to reach down and scratch his balls. He was facing a long road back, and you were the only one in sight who could run the company for him. While he was lying there, he had plenty of time to think about what you'd said when you thought he was Felix. You know, about Ingo being a half-assed manager. He did some soul-searching, maybe, and decided you were a little bit right."

"What a curious story," Brody said, writing again. "Then what?"

"Then the truth came out. You learned Felix was dead, and the man in the bed was Ingo. But he went along with your scheme, anyway. What choice did he have? He made you his right-hand man, let you call the shots, whisper in his ear, just as you wanted to do when you thought he was Felix. He let you put him on the track to an IPO. A man can be very forgiving when he's looking ahead to that kind of payoff."

"You know Ingo Julian. He's an autocratic bastard — a description of him I've articulated to his face, by the way," Brody said. "Do you think for a moment he's going to let me or anybody control him the way you suggest?"

"No, I don't. Not any more, he won't," I said. "But back then, he looked past your insults, and made a deal with you, made you the president of the company. And in the end the deal turned out to be everything you'd promised. He has a hot company, and the IPO is about to make him hundreds of millions of United States dollars. The thing is, once that happens, will he still need you?"

"They told me you were smart, Seidenberg. But I'm starting to question it." Brody tore a page of notes from his pad and slipped it into a desk drawer. "Even if everything you say were true — and none of it is — do you really think Ingo Julian would kill the goose that's laid a golden egg for him? Whatever personal differences Ingo and I have had, he's always been sharply aware of how valuable I am to the company. Certainly Ingo will still need me. Because there's a lot more money to be made. Ingo knows continued growth will drive the stock up after the offering. And growth is my great strength. Read what they say about me in the financial pages"

"I have. So has Ingo," I said. "I have to think he doesn't like reading that you're the brains of the company, not him. As you say, he's an autocratic bastard. And just maybe he's learned enough over the past years to run the company skillfully on his own. Tell me, when did he give you the news you that you were on your way out? It must have been a very satisfying moment for him after resenting you for so long. "

Brody stared at us for a moment, then said, "I'd really like to hear more of this because it's so bizarre. But I have a lunch."

"Where?" I said.

"Where? To the Yale Club. I have lunch there with

Lawson Carey, my old college friend. Every Wednesday."

"At the same time?" I asked him.

"What is this about?" Brody said.

"Do you go to the Yale Club every Wednesday always at the same time? And do other people know you do it?"

"Twelve-thirty every Wednesday, when Lawson and I are both in town. Yes, I suppose other people here know it. It's no secret." His annoyance with me was beginning to break through the Brody reserve. He stood and started for the door. "Forgive me. I try never to be late."

"I told you Sosenko is in New York," I said.

He stopped. "Yes, you did say that. I don't intend to spend my life hiding from Sosenko."

"Any reasonable man would be concerned. Sosenko's killed two people already, and you told me he'd been stalking you."

"I'll be late," he said.

"Are you unreasonably brave," I said, "or is there something else?"

"Meaning what?"

"Try this. You believe Sosenko won't touch you because you're not the target. Never were. You're the one behind it all. You paid him to kill Ingo before the stock offering, before Ingo could get rid of you. Sosenko was an interesting choice, because he had his own reason to hate the company. But he screwed up again and again. He drowned Newalis by mistake. And later, when you called him from New York to tell him Ingo would be on the Shelter Island Ferry, he shot Hector Alzarez by mistake. You regretted getting involved with someone as erratic as Sosenko, didn't you? So you gave me a lot of money and suggested I kill him for you. Did he ever know you were the one who hired him to kill Ingo, or did you manage to stay anonymous?

"I can't believe what I'm hearing. Do you really think

I'd involve myself in a scheme like that?" he said.

"Sure I do," I told him. "But what I think isn't the issue. I don't suppose I can prove it, anyway. My job is to serve the best interests of Julian Communications. And I have to admit it's getting harder to know what those interests are. Keeping company officers alive, I imagine. So I should tell you that Sosenko is in New York to assassinate you."

"You're certain, are you?" Brody said.

"The thing is, he doesn't work for you anymore. Ingo got tired of being the target. He bought Sosenko off last night on some dark shore of Shelter Island. Not only has Hick Sosenko failed you. Now he's coming after you. And you can bet he's been told exactly when you're leaving here for lunch, and where you're going."

"You're in a dangerous position," said Wally, joining in the spirit of the thing.

If Brody was at all shaken by my news, or by Wally's announcement of the obvious, he gave no indication. "Lunch," he said, and walked out the door.

"We're coming with you," I said.

"Suit yourselves." Brody walked smartly toward the elevators.

Wally leaned toward me as we followed him and spoke quietly behind his hand. "He's trying to make like a hero, but I think he'd be crapping in his pants now if we weren't right behind him."

Brody never looked at us as we all made our way to Vanderbilt Avenue, and over to the celebrated Yale Club, a distance of three blocks. I went inside with Brody and prowled around the lobby. Not surprisingly, I turned up no one with matted yellow hair and tattooed snakes up his arms, only old boys of Yale with flawless haircuts and dark suits, on their way to lunch. The uniformed concierge assured me that no one matching Sosenko's description had been seen on these hallowed premises. Ever,

Brody went upstairs to the dining room, presumably to meet a certain Lawson Carey. I joined Wally back outside on Vanderbilt Avenue, across the street from the club.

"Sosenko's not in there," I reported. "But you can bet he's nearby. No coincidence. Ingo slips away into the dark last night, Sosenko comes to New York this morning."

"And your guy Brody going to the same Wednesday lunch he does every week," Wally said, finished my thought. Then, hunching his shoulders and rolling his eyes, he added, "With all those Yalies."

"You got something against Yalies?" I said.

"When I was at City College, we thought they were kind of la-de-da. You know what I mean?"

"They seem to have turned out all right. They wear nice clothes." I looked up and down the Vanderbilt Avenue, which was heavy with lunchtime traffic, both automobiles and pedestrians. "Sosenko could try to get it done when Brody leaves the club, then just duck into Grand Central Station and disappear. Let's work both ends of this block."

Standing at each end, Wally and I did our best to check out the people who walked between us, plus the passing taxis. After an hour, no Sosenko. How long before Brody would come walking out the door of the club with his pal Lawson? Were they leisurely lunch types who lingered over coffee, or the one-hour-and-back-to-work variety?

Then, above the traffic noise, I heard Wally call to me. I looked in time to see him wave me toward him, then turn and take off toward the Vanderbilt Avenue entrance to Grand Central Station, his long, skinny legs flying and his arms pumping as he pursued a hard-running Hick Sosenko, killer for hire, disappeared into Grand Central carrying the big, black portfolio that hid, I was quite certain, the same rifle that he had used to shoot at me, and to end the life of Hector Alzarez

CHAPTER 28

I broke into a run before I fully appreciated what I was doing to my circulatory system. This was not a smart move. I hadn't gone ten paces before I felt my chest tighten and my breath stick in my throat. No choice, I had to stop, wait. Then take off again with an ungainly quick-walk. Best I could manage.

Ahead of me I saw Wally sprint into the taxi drive-through and head for the Vanderbilt Avenue entrance to the station. He was getting farther ahead of me with every stride, running flat out in pursuit of Sosenko, while I walked as fast my heart would authorize. At this rate, by the time I made it through the station, Sosenko and Wally would be crossing into New Jersey.

I pushed on, desperate that there was still a way I could get close enough to do some good, and longing for the days when I could still manage a run. I remember thinking to myself: Wally is chasing a man who has a gun, and you're the one who got your friend into this, you pathetic fat-ass.

I saw the cab heading for me as I crossed into the drive-through, but I pressed on, gambling that the driver would show some respect for my middle age and general portliness, and surrender the right of way. In the end he did, but not until he'd stopped inches from me, honking his horn to show he had the moral high ground. No time to tangle with a cabbie now. I stepped up onto the curb and hurried across the walkway to pull open a door to the station.

Inside, I stopped at the top of the big stairway that descended into the grand concourse, a space the size of a football field, covered by an enormous ceiling that reached to the stars. There were people everywhere I looked, criss-crossing the floor, on stairways, on escalators, standing in ticket lines, heading for their trains, heading for the exits, everywhere. There were a dozen ways into and out of the teeming concourse, and I knew Wally might be chasing Sosenko through any one of them. I stood there looking from one side to the other, trying to take it all in at once, knowing that whichever way they were headed, the distance between them and me was growing even faster than before. But I didn't see either of them.

I couldn't just stand there. With no idea which way I should go, I started down the stairs anyway. They had to be in here someplace. I was still on the staircase when the blur of Wally caught my eye. He was the only runner among hundreds of walkers, heading under an archway that led toward the far end of the building toward the Lexington Avenue exit. I set off after him, hearing the labored noise of my own breath hissing in my ears, and feeling my heart jumping against my shirt.

By the time I struggled to the archway, Wally was gone. Had Sosenko led the chase toward the Lexington Avenue exit and out onto the street? His truck was probably parked in one of the nearby garages, after all. Or wasn't he thinking about his truck just now?

Then I heard the screams. They were coming from the food market, a long, brightly lit passage that ran inside the station all the way to Lexington Avenue. It was lined on both sides, I knew, with vendors of gourmet foods — seafood, meats, exotic produce, cheeses, baked goods— toothsome viands at fancy prices.

Now, as the screams continued, people began spilling out of the marketplace, fleeing back into the concourse. Holding my hands out in front of me, I bucked the flow of frantic customers, and vendors in white aprons, and made my way just inside the market. A struggle was exploding halfway down the passage.

"Where's a cop? Get a cop," I heard someone say.

I felt a pull at my sleeve, and turned to see a tiny, seventy-something woman looking up at me. "Are you going in there?" she said, "Would you get my tuna steak. It's in a bag on the counter, there, where those two idiots are fighting, with a gun, yet. I'll be right outside."

"Can't," I said, pulling away from her and heading toward the brawl ahead.

"Twenty-two dollars a pound, it cost," the woman called after me. "What am I going to serve. I got company coming. Have a heart." When it became clear I wasn't going to rescue her fish, she added, "I'll remember your face forever, you big piece of shit."

Now the market had emptied, except for me and two men locked in a struggle. Display tables were overturned, and the seafood market's refrigerator case was smashed, shards of glass sparkling on the fish fillets inside. Wrapped wedges of cheese from the cheese monger littered the floor, along with picture-perfect pineapples and grapefruit from the greengrocer across the passage. I saw what could have been grandma's bag of tuna steak on the floor, too. Someone had stepped on it.

Wally must have been getting too close. Faced with my friend's speed and tenacity, Sosenko's only option was to stop and make a stand — pull the rifle out of his portfolio case and put an end to his pursuer. But Wally was on top of him before he could work the bolt and fire. Now both of them had hold of the gun, shoving and stumbling, smashing into displays of food. Sosenko was growling like an animal.

I reached under my jacket and pulled my gun out of its holster.

A cop came through the door at the Lexington Avenue end of the market, and started toward us. "The one with the tattoos is a killer," I shouted at him. I saw the cop go for his gun.

It's amazing how much can happen in less than five seconds. Sosenko pulled the butt end of the rifle down, then brought it up sharply against Wally's face. Stunned, Wally released his hold on the gun and fell heavily against a shelf piled with vegetables, then slid to the floor, blood running down his chin..

Sosenko racked the bolt and made ready to fire at Wally. The cop had his pistol in his hand, but was still twenty yards away.

I screamed something at Sosenko, and raised my .38. Recognizing that I was the most immediate threat, he swung the rifle around from Wally to me.

I fired only once, catching him squarely in the chest. The rifle dropped out of his hands. He fell instantly to his knees, then toppled onto his side.

I set my gun down on the floor, so the cop wouldn't get the wrong idea. I knelt next to Sosenko and looked into that primordial face of his. He didn't die all at once. His eyes were open and he was working his lips. He was getting ready to spit at me, the only fight he had left in him.

But he crossed over before he could let the spittle fly.

CHAPTER 29

I waited until I was on the ferry, watching Greenport grow smaller off the stern as we made our way to Shelter Island, before I called Roger Teague on my cell phone. I wanted him to know I'd been up all night. I wanted him to know I had to face a hearing in New York, but after talking with me until four in the morning, the cops appeared willing to accept the Sosenko shooting as self defense, and let me loose for the time being. I especially wanted him to know I was on my way to deal with Ingo Julian, a confrontation Teague would fear, but had no way to stop. The idea of a face-off between me and Ingo was certain to drive him wild, and he'd earned some aggravation.

Teague did not disappoint. "What the hell you going to Shelter for?" he said on the phone, much louder than was necessary. "This thing is over."

"Not quite," I told him. "I feel a real need to share some ideas with Ingo."

"*Share? Ideas?*" It sounded filthy the way he said it. "About what?"

"This whole business is not what you think it is," I told him. "We've been jerked around royally by Ingo and by Brody, too. They used us. Me, you, Empire."

"So they used us. That's what they pay us for, to use

us." Then, "How did they use us?"

I boiled the story down into two precisely worded minutes, ignoring Teague several times as he tried to interrupt me. When I finished, I could hear his heavy breathing mixed with a few unintelligible syllables as he gathered his wits to respond.

What came out, finally, was, "Some wild-ass story, Seidenberg. But can you prove it? Can anybody prove it? And so what, anyway?"

"No solid proof," I said. "But I know it doesn't matter to you. Great moralist that you are, you don't care if it's true or not."

"What does it matter what I believe," he said. "It's what they think that counts. Julian Communications pays the bills we send them. We just do our job."

"Seems to me *I* do our job," I corrected him.

"An ex-con with a grudge against Julian Communications tries to get even, kills two of their suits. Tragic, right? We find the guy and take him out. Job finished. Why piss off Ingo Julian now with some story you can't prove, anyway?"

"Don't forget Brody," I said. "I already pissed Brody off."

"Oh, Jesus."

"He won't complain. I did prevent him from being murdered outside the Yale Club yesterday. That ought to be worth something. And so far as Ingo is concerned, I doubt that he would dare dump Empire, no matter what I say to him this morning. He'll know we're onto the game of killer-take-all he and Brody have been playing. I'm sure he'd rather we keep it to ourselves, even if we can't prove it."

"We need Julian Communications. We don't need you fucking up the relationship. Just what are you trying to accomplish?" he said.

In my mind's eye I could see the anger distorting Teague's face as he spoke, that way he had of looking like an over-inflated balloon ready to pop. I could go on and give him all my good reasons for having it out with Ingo, but I was saving that speech for Ingo himself. Anyway, I knew the surest way to infuriate Roger Teague now that I had lured him into the truth of this bizarre story would be to shut him off. Which I did, just as the boat bumped its way into the ferry slip. "We're at Shelter. Got to go," I said into the phone, then rang off before he could respond.

Ingo and Lisa Harper were in their Park Avenue business attire and about to head for the car when I arrived at the house on Shelter Island. Ingo's custom-made suit did little to compensate for the warped posture and odd gait that dominated his appearance. He seemed a well-dressed, oversize gnome, covered with scars and discolorations. What had he looked like, I wondered, before the accident?

"We're about to leave for New York," he said. "But I'm pleased to see you. Come sit a moment, yes?" He led the way into the great room and we took seats. "I heard what happened yesterday at Grand Central. It's a relief to know we don't have to worry about that Sosenko animal any more. You're a courageous man, Seidenberg. Good job. We won't forget it."

"I should hope not," I said.

Lisa leaned forward on the sofa with her elbows on her knees, as a man would do. "Yes, good job. I think I told you once I wondered if you were as good as Hector told us you were. It seems you are."

"I'm sure that was meant to flatter me," I said to her. "But actually, I'm much better than you think."

Her smile was part amused, part puzzled. "Don't be modest, Seidenberg."

"And how good are you, then?" Ingo said.

"Good enough to know when I'm being manipulated.

Good enough to understand, finally, that you never told me the truth behind this business with Sosenko." It seemed a good time to pause and let it sink in, let them come to realize they hadn't pulled it off. Not quite.

They both looked at me in silence, trying, I thought, not to betray any doubt or vulnerability. Not that I cared. I stood and made my way to the white marble bar, which glowed in the morning sun streaming through the sliding glass doors to the balcony. "Would it trouble you if I made myself a drink?"

"At nine thirty in the morning?" said Ingo.

"Not morning for me. As I haven't been to sleep, it's still very, very late at night. I'm sure you understand my need for a potent adult beverage," I said. "Been under a lot of stress. Need to loosen up."

"Help yourself, by all means," he told me.

Moving deliberately, I sought out a decent scotch blend behind the bar. Not finding any, I took the Glenfiddich and poured myself a gentleman's portion, as opposed to a child's portion, inspected my drink in the rays of the sun, and had a healthy swallow.

"Let me save you this awkward little drama, Seidenberg," Ingo said, after watching me savor his high-priced whiskey. "To begin with, I'm relieved you no longer think I'm really Felix."

"No, you are indeed Ingo Julian. Felix went to his reward a long time ago. My error. But you must admit I wasn't all that far from the truth."

"You mean this fantasy of yours about Arthur Brody mistaking me for my brother in the hospital, and proposing a devil's bargain? Brody told me about it."

"You actually spoke to Brody? You two have kissed and made up, then?"

"That's an overstatement, I think. Let's say we have finally agreed to set our differences aside in the best interests of the company."

"What are those differences you're setting aside, Ingo? No one ever knew for sure." I paced across the room and looked down at Lisa, who sat there on the couch. "Except you, maybe." She made no response.

"A personal thing," Ingo said. "Nothing to do with you."

"Yes, personal," I said. "Was it because you told him you'd had enough of him, that you were dumping him after the IPO? You'd let him get rich on the stock, but he wasn't going to be the celebrated president of Julian Communications any more. Problem was, the power meant even more to him than the money. He liked that corner office. He'd sooner have you killed than let you fire him."

"No such thing ever happened." Ingo's raspy voice was composed and unemotional. He was very good at this.

"Are you telling me that Brody wasn't behind Sosenko's attempts on your life?" I said. "That Sosenko just happened to know when you usually went swimming, the day he drowned Newalis by mistake? Just happened to know when you'd be on the ferry, the day Hector took the bullet meant for you? Tell me, please, how he could possibly have known you and Lisa were driving out with Hector if he didn't get the word from New York."

"This Sosenko appears to have been a crafty and resourceful person," Ingo said. "He had his methods, I'm sure."

"And I suppose you didn't get to Sosenko and buy him off, turn him against Brody? Of course, who could blame you for fighting back? I'm sure it's tiresome when someone keeps trying to assassinate you. But of course, that's just another fantasy of mine."

"It would seem," he said.

"Now the killer you and Brody both paid is conveniently dead. What a break. A perfect time for you two to strike a new bargain, make a new show of solidarity and save the stock offering. What's the deal, Ingo? You let Brody stay president and he stops trying to have you killed?"

"Arthur Brody is immensely valuable to my company. There's never been any plan for him to leave," Ingo said.

Lisa fidgeted uneasily, looking up at me as I stood beside her. "Think what you want, Seidenberg," she said. "What I can't understand is why you're marching around here with a drink in your hand and telling us your absurd story. In addition to alienating your biggest client, what do you hope to accomplish? Why did you come here again?"

I had some more of the Glenfiddich. "First, I promised Giannone I'd give you his message. He wants twenty-five thousand dollars to go away."

"And not tell anyone his nonsense about what he says happened in the hospital?" Ingo said.

"That's right."

"Don't do it, Ingo," Lisa said. "No one's going to listen to the babbling of a drug addict. And if you give him money now, he'll be back for more."

"I could be wrong," I said, "but I think this is a one-time thing. Giannone just wants to straighten himself out. Give him the money, and I believe you'll never hear from him again. Don't give him the money, and it's likely he'll embarrass you, even if no one believes him."

"It's a bad idea to —" Lisa began, to Ingo, but he held up his hand and silenced her.

"All right, twenty-five thousand for this Giannone, then." Ingo said. "I don't suppose there's anything else?"

"There is," I told him. "My friend's brand new pickup truck got badly smashed on the Long Island Expressway while we were chasing Sosenko. As we were in the process of putting our lives on the line for Julian Communications — "

"We'll pay for a new truck," Ingo said. "Anything

else?"

"Only one thing," I said.

"Say it, then. We have to leave for the city." She rose to her feet, smoothing her skirt.

I wished I were as loose as I'd hoped, with the scotch and all, but the truth was, I was at such a keen edge the drink didn't matter at all. Didn't even taste it going down. "You wouldn't let me in on what was really going on. While I was getting shot at, I was also being lied to and manipulated by experts — Ingo Julian, Arthur Brody and Lisa Harper. Face it, because of you, Hector got slaughtered in the crossfire. And you nearly got my friend shot while we were chasing your killer through Grand Central Station. The sad part is, you really don't care, any of you. The stock deal will go forward and you'll all get even richer than you are already. But I want you to know that in the end, I found you out." I set my glass down on a side table. "I know what you did."

"Are you finished, Seidenberg, yes?" Ingo said. I did not respond. He went on, "No matter what you may believe, Kenny Newalis and Hector Alzarez were murdered by a man who thought he had a reason to seek revenge against our company. Working for us, you found that man and put a stop to him. I'm truly sorry if that sounds too simple for you, but clearly that's what happened. Why confuse the issue? Julian Communications will always be grateful to you and to Empire Security. Our debt of gratitude will be even more valuable to you as our company grows, and Empire becomes more important to us." He stood, and steered Lisa through the archway that led to the front door. Then, with what appeared to be an afterthought, he stopped, and turned to look at me. "Of course there's the matter of the fifty thousand special fee Arthur paid you. And another fifty yet to come. No reason for Teague to know about it."

"You want it back?" I said.

"Of course not," Ingo said. "Given what was at stake, I told Arthur you were cheap at the price. And now this matter is completed." He opened the door. They both walked through it without looking back.

CHAPTER 30

The Elysium was one of ten boats working the incoming tide at Plum Gut, but none of us were doing any good, that I could tell. I hadn't seen a fish being boated since we got there.

We'd motored through the Gut into Long Island Sound and drifted back into the bay a half dozen times, Wally and I dropping chrome jigs to the bottom and reeling them up fast, trying to entice bluefish to chase the shiny lures. Alicia was at the helm, doing a skilful job of keeping the boat right at the edge of the rip where the blues like to snap up the baitfish and squid. Right place, right time, gorgeous calm day. In a perfect world, the big October blues would be walloping anything that moved, but either they weren't hungry or they weren't there.

My experience at the Gut was, if you couldn't get a strike in the first half hour, chances were you wouldn't get one all day long. I was ready to move on. "Let's head out and try Pigeon Rip," I said. "When they're not here, they're at Pigeon Rip."

"You know that for a fact, right?" Wally's voice was muted and constrained, because he barely opened his mouth as he talked. The rifle butt Sosenko had smacked him with had left his jaw an unhealthy shade of purple, and the inside of his mouth painfully scored by his own teeth. I didn't even like to think about it, but Wally never complained.

"Guaranteed bluefish at Pigeon Rip," I told him. Then to Alicia, "Go around the buoy, then steer zero-three — "

"Zero-three-zero. Yes, I know. Don't insult me with your directions. I know all the secrets of the sea." She pulled at the wheel and steered us north out into the Sound.

Pigeon Rip is a bluefish hot spot three miles from Plum Gut, roughly halfway to New London, Connecticut. Surrounded by water two hundred fifty feet deep, the bottom at the rip rises like an underwater mountain to a depth below the surface of a hundred feet or so, shallow with respect to the rest of the Sound, but still enough water to wear you out when you're pulling a fighting twelve-pound bluefish off the bottom and up the whole way to the boat.

As I'd promised, the fish were waiting for us, and while Alicia maneuvered Elysium back and forth across the rip, Wally and I had our way with the blues below. They attacked in a fury with every drift, bending our poles over sharply as they struck the lures, then battled for their lives. Shouting encouragement to each other, Wally and I strained against our poles again and again, and soon had eight fat blues thumping away inside the Elysium's fish-box.

"Enough," Alicia said. "Who's going to eat all these fish? Leave some for the poor people. Anyway, I'm hungry for lunch. What a lunch I got. Wait till you see." She motored Elysium out of the path of the two other boats working the rip and headed back toward Plum Gut. In a few minutes she killed the engines and let the boat drift to a standstill in the calm water off Plum Island. She ducked down into the cutty cabin and reappeared with the cooler box, then opened it to reveal, first, a plate of fresh white figs, halved, with each piece wrapped in prosciutto. "Melon with prosciutto is for tourists. Fresh figs with prosciutto is for royalty," she told us. "Dried figs you get everywhere, but fresh figs are completely impossible to find."

"Where did you find these, then?" Wally asked her, wincing with the discomfort of talking.

"I went to the ends of the earth, and I begged for them, "

NICE PLACE FOR A MURDER

Alicia said. "To please two such brave men as you, it was just my small gesture." She uncorked a bottle of red wine and poured three generous portions into plastic glasses. "A cabernet from the Macari winery, over on the North Road. Pressing from the older vines. Makes a difference. Taste."

The lifted our glasses in an unspoken toast and drank, eating the figs until they were gone. Then Alicia unwrapped sandwiches of roasted red peppers, slabs of feta cheese and capers, on French baguettes, perfumed with fruity olive oil and fresh herbs. Wally ate his with some difficulty, moving his jaws in slow motion, but seemed to savor it, anyway. The combination of tastes was just slightly superior to remarkable. The three of us sat in the sunshine, washing down the last of Alicia's brilliant lunch with the remains of the cabernet. The boat rocked almost imperceptibly in the slight breeze that was beginning to come up from the south.

"So, Wally," Alicia said, "you have bought a new pickup truck, then? For the one smashed on the expressway?"

"Actually, no," Wally said. "Did the next best thing, though. I took the old one to the auto body shop in Mattituck. They said it'll be as good as new."

"How much?" I said.

"To the body shop?" said Wally. "Forty-eight hundred."

"So subtract that from the twenty thousand Ingo handed over to buy you a new truck, and that gives you —"

"Fifteen thousand two hundred dollars is what it gives me," Wally said. "I figure that part's my fee for pain and suffering. Little enough. You don't have trouble with that, do you, amigo? Hell, you got a hundred large, altogether, and you didn't have to get slugged with a rifle butt to earn it."

"I get paid for delivering the goods, not for taking a pounding," I said. "Anyway, you'd been a little quicker, Sosenko wouldn't have tagged you."

Alicia leaned toward me and screwed her fist, none too gently, into my arm. "You shut up, you. Without Wally you don't get that Sosenko, and just maybe Sosenko gets you instead." She brushed her fingers lightly against Wally's bruised jaw, squinting at him to show she shared his pain. "You are a beautiful man, Wally Prager. Courageous, and handsome, too. I love you forever."

Wally smiled a crooked smile, distorted by his tender jaw. "I think I could get to like this investigator stuff. You get adventure. You get money. You get a sexy Italian lady telling you she loves you. I may sell the marina."

"I wouldn't," I said. "These twenty thousand dollar payoffs don't come along every day."

"And what about that drug addict, the one who used to be a doctor?" Alicia said to me. "They give you money for him, too? What does he do with it."

"Giannone? I figured if he lived in that warehouse with all that cash on him, somebody'd kill him for it before too long, so I gave it to his sister, " I said. "He owed her a good piece of it, anyway. And I thought she'll dole out a few bucks to him when he needs it for clothes, food. Maybe he won't be able to pump it all into his arm."

"So sad," Alicia said. "A doctor. You think he can recover, ever?"

"He wants to," I told her. "But he's pretty far gone. He sees little animals. I don't know. Anybody's guess."

"This is such a strange story, all this business," she said. "Those two men from the company — what are the names?"

"You mean Ingo and Brody?" I said.

"Yes, them. They actually try to kill each other. Now they forgive everything because of all the money. Like it never happened. Unbelievable. In Italy, one of them would be dead a long time ago."

"They going ahead with the stock thing, then?" Wally said.

"I think they'll wait now, for a quarter, maybe two," I said. "Show the world that Julian Communications continues to be a moneymaker, no matter about Sosenko and the killings.

"And the bottom line is, people get killed, and those guys get rich," Wally said.

"You did what they asked you," Alicia said, looking from me to Wally and back again. "You got the killer."

"I suppose you might say that." I shielded my eyes from the bright sun and stared across the Sound. Gulls soared far out over the water, and the Connecticut shoreline was sharp and clear in the autumn air.

THE END

I hope you had a good time reading this mystery. I thought you might like to have the recipe for Alicia and Ben's Lemon Chicken, so here it is. It's a favorite at our house.

Bruce Jay Bloom

Alicia and Ben's Lemon Chicken

3-pound broiling chicken, split in half
1 cup fresh lemon juice
1/2 cup extra virgin olive oil
2 tsp red wine vinegar
1 tsp minced garlic
1/2 tsp dried oregano
1/8 cup chopped parsley
Salt and pepper

Broil the chicken halves until the skin is golden and just starting to char, and the juices run clear when you pierce the thigh where it joins the breast. While the chicken is cooking, prepare the lemon sauce: whisk together the lemon juice, olive oil, vinegar, garlic, oregano and chopped parsley, plus salt and pepper to taste. Using a very sharp knife, cut each cooked chicken half into pieces (with each breast cut into thirds). Place the chicken pieces on a baking sheet that has sides, and pour the sauce over the chicken. Put the chicken and sauce under the broiler for four or five minutes. Serve the chicken with the sauce, and plenty of crusty bread so your guests can mop up the sauce.

About the Author

Bruce Jay Bloom is no stranger to the North Fork of Long Island, the setting for this mystery. He's lived there many years, and — like Ben Seidenberg in his book — prowls the waters of Long Island Sound looking for big fish to catch. For 18 years he was president and creative director of his own advertising agency, which he sold to become a full-time mystery writer. Earlier, as a young graduate of Cornell, he was an Air Force officer, then a promotion specialist in television. Bloom is a painter and printmaker, and says he's an "advanced amateur."

He lives on Long Island with his wife Sara, who is also a writer. They have two daughters, Mimi and Jenny.

Proof

24171023R00130

Made in the USA
Charleston, SC
14 November 2013